David Stuart Davies is a member of the Crime Writers' Association and edits their monthly magazine, *Red Herrings*.

David lives with his wife Kathryn in Yorkshire. You can find out more information about David and his work at www.davidstuartdavies.com

REQUIEM FOR A DUMMY

London 1943. Successful ventriloquist Raymond Carter begins receiving death threats over the telephone. These calls are especially unnerving as the threats are made in the voice of his dummy, Charlie Dokes. Disturbed, Carter calls on the services of private detective Johnny Hawke to get to the bottom of this bizarre case. However, when a member of the cast from Carter's radio show is brutally murdered, the ventriloquist becomes a suspect and the investigation begins to take a dark and surreal path. This places not only Johnny in danger, but also those who are close to him.

DAVID STUART DAVIES

REQUIEM FOR A DUMMY

A JOHNNY ONE EYE NOVEL

Complete and Unabridged

ULVERSCROFT
Leicester

First published in Great Britain in 2009 by
Robert Hale Limited
London

First Large Print Edition
published 2010
by arrangement with
Robert Hale Limited
London

British Library CIP Data

Davies, David Stuart, *1946 –*
   Requiem for a dummy.
   1. Private investigators- -England- -London- -Fiction.
   2. Ventriloquists- -Crimes against- -Fiction.
   3. London (England)- -History- -Bombardment,
   1940 – 1945- -Fiction. 4. Detective and mystery
   stories. 5. Large type books.
   I. Title
   823.9′2–dc22

   ISBN 978–1–44480–402–7

Published by
F. A. Thorpe (Publishing)
Anstey, Leicestershire

Set by Words & Graphics Ltd.
Anstey, Leicestershire
Printed and bound in Great Britain by
T. J. International Ltd., Padstow, Cornwall

To the Heaton Roaders
(you know who you are)
Cheers!

Acknowledgements

I would like to thank Ray Alan, the doyen of British ventriloquists, for his advice and anecdotes regarding the wonderful and often crazy world of ventriloquism.

As always, my love and gratitude are delivered in large measures to my wife Kathryn for her perceptive and constructive criticisms.

PROLOGUE

1919

The shadows closed in on her, their hard edges softening and blending with the growing darkness. She lay for a long while on the bed, allowing the gin and the sorrow to seep into her soul. Somewhere in another room there were sounds of voices raised in merriment and a gramophone was playing ragtime music. Happy people enjoying themselves — an ironic counterpoint to her own situation. As she contemplated her sad lot, a thin, dry, twisted smile crept on to her tear-stained face. She knew at heart that she had a tendency to over-dramatize situations very much in the manner of her favourite silver screen heroines, Gloria Swanson and Theda Bara, but that was partly because extreme situations and more particularly tragedy had been with her for most of her life, especially after meeting Frank. At the thought of his name, the fragile smile crumbled and faded. With sluggish movements, she pulled herself upright on the bed and reached out once again for the gin bottle. She held it close

1

to her face. It was nearly empty but she could squeeze another double measure from the residue.

As she gulped down the tepid alcohol, she knew that it would be the last she ever tasted. She just didn't want to go on. Not even for Freddie's sake. He'd be better off without her anyway. What chance in life would the poor blighter have tied to a mother like her? Suddenly it all became clear to her; the answer to all her woes. Strangely, as she drained the last of the gin, she seemed to sober up. The room did not appear so fuzzy anymore, nor her limbs as leaden. Perhaps it was because now her mind was more focused. Focused on her last act. Her sudden resolve had brought her a strange clarity of thought and energy. She took a deep breath and swung her legs off the bed and attempted to stand up. For a moment her body swayed uneasily, but she blinked hard, forcing her mind to take control of her limbs. She took another deep breath and things stabilized once more.

She knew what she had to do and she wasn't frightened. Now that it was inevitable — or so it seemed to her — it could be approached in a practical fashion and methodical manner.

She could do it. She would do it.

Moving slowly across the room, she made her way to the dressing-table and extracted a pair of nail scissors from her handbag. As she did so, she caught a glimpse of the snapshot she kept in there of Frank. She pulled it out and gazed at it. The face with the taut features, square chin and unruly wavy hair cascading on to the brow stared back at her, coldly defiantly, refusing to smile. Despite everything, she still loved him. How could she not? She had given her heart to him. The bastard.

Carrying the scissors and photograph with her, she crossed to the little sink by the window. Suddenly there was a further burst of hysterical laughter from the adjoining room and the gramophone started up once again with another loud jazz tune. She placed the photograph between the two taps and then ran a basinful of hot water.

Slipping her left wrist into the steaming liquid, she pierced the flesh with the sharp edge of the scissors and then dragged the blades along the flesh below her palm, along her wrist, scoring a thin red line. The blood squeezed its way through the fine rupture in the flesh and was soon creating bright crimson tendrils in the water, which floated gently to the surface. To some extent the alcohol and the warmth of the water dulled the pain a little but she still found herself gritting her teeth. She waited a few moments while her heartbeat steadied and then she repeated the process with her right wrist. This proved to be a more difficult manoeuvre to execute and the resultant cut was less precise than the first. In frustration, she scored the flesh viciously, creating a savage, ragged wound. She emitted a small yelp of pain and staggered backwards towards the bed.

The jazz music seemed to pound into her head and her wrists throbbed violently. She threw herself on the counterpane and prayed for the darkness to come soon.

On the sink the photograph had slipped into the water. The trails of blood embraced the little piece of cardboard, wrapping their scarlet fingers around the face of the man in the picture.

1941

'C'mon, Tommy, let's get out of this dump. It's starting to get on my nerves.'

Raymond Carter leaned over and picked up the ventriloquist's doll, automatically inserting his hand through the flap at the back, allowing him to make the eyes and mouth work, the lips parting noisily in a fierce rictal grin. Tommy's face suddenly came alive, the gobstopper eyes swivelling left and right as though in furious excitement.

'We didn't do so well tonight, did we, boss?' he said, in the eerie half-schoolboy, half-harpy voice that Carter had created for him.

'You could say that,' Carter said, carrying his dummy over to the large suitcase on the makeshift camp-bed in the corner of the dingy dressing room. Gently removing his hand from Tommy's innards, he placed the doll carefully face upwards in the case.

'I would say that . . . because you did,' responded the now inanimate dummy.

''Night, 'night, Tommy,' said Carter, grinning at his own conceit.

''Night 'night,' came the muffled reply, as Carter closed the case.

With a sigh, he slipped on his jacket and drained what was left of the flat Guinness in the glass on the dressing room table. Tommy had been right, he mused. They hadn't done so well tonight. In fact they had walked off to half-hearted applause, peppered with a few cat calls. Soldiers, no doubt, drunk on leave. There were no Jerries around so they took a few pot shots at Ray Carter and partner instead. To be fair, it wasn't the audience's fault. He couldn't blame them. The act was stale. He was still peddling the same old material that he'd been using long before the war. It was tired and past it — like him.

'If you want my opinion,' said a voice from the suitcase.

'I don't want your opinion,' snapped Carter.

'Well then, don't give it to me to give to you.'

'Shut up!' There was a real spark of anger in his voice now.

'It's in your hands,' came the defiant response.

Carter kicked the case and this time it remained silent.

He gazed at himself in the smeary dressing room mirror, his face still bearing some traces of stage make-up. He looked tired, he thought. He looked like a no-hoper. A dead beat. Carter tried to manufacture a shrug in response to this self-analysis but he failed.

There was a knock on the door. Carter groaned. This was no doubt the manager warning him to improve his act or he'd be out of the show. The burly bastard had intimated something of the sort earlier in the week. With another sigh, Carter opened the door. It wasn't the manager; it was a tall, young man dressed in a sharp overcoat with a trilby hat perched on the back of his head.

6

A pair of large tortoishell glasses was balanced precariously on the end of his nose. With an agile finger he pushed them back to the bridge.

'Hi there,' he said, smiling a pleasant smile. His voice had a mid-Atlantic ring.

'Hi there,' Carter responded in kind, but there was a sarcastic edge to his voice. He wasn't in the mood for visitors, whatever they wanted.

'Caught your show tonight.'

Carter nodded non-committally. He didn't know quite what to expect.

'You are a mighty fine vent man.'

'Thank you.'

'But, if I may be frank — actually my name's Al — but if I may be frank for a moment, your material . . . how should I put it? — it stinks.'

Carter groaned inwardly. Oh no, he thought, not one of those. 'Thank you for your comments. I'll bear them in mind. Goodnight and goodbye,' he said swiftly and moved to close the door, but the young man stood his ground.

'Hey now, please, don't cut up rough. I'm here to help you. Seriously. My card.' The young man handed over an ivory calling card with a flourish like a magician completing a trick. It read:

Al Warren
Comedy Writer
Mermaid III
Chiswick Reach
London

'I do quite a bit of stuff for the BBC,' said the young man, surreptitiously slipping his way further into the room, causing Carter to retreat. 'I'm the main writer on *Forces Fanfare*; maybe you've heard it.'

Carter had. It was one of the top variety shows on the radio. He nodded. 'What exactly do you want with me, Mr Warren?'

'Al. Call me Al. Everyone does. I want to help you. I want to write for you. I think you are a great vent — well, I said that already — but what you need is a new angle and some fresh material and I think I can provide that for you. Let me tell you, Mr Carter, you have the potential to go places. And I mean big time, like your own radio show. You no doubt know how successful Edgar Bergen is in the States with his little fellow, Charlie McCarthy. I reckon you could be that successful here in Britain. Let me buy you a drink and we can discuss this further. What d'you say?'

8

1

LONDON 1943

Sometimes I dream that I have my full sight back again — two bright, clear blue eyes which stare out at the world with a balanced panoramic vision. I stare with the eagerness of an alcoholic in a brewery. I can see everything without turning my head. There is no blasted eye-patch to shade one corner of the window on my world. I walk into a room of strangers and no one does a double take, wondering what that black mark is on my face.

In the best dream I am shaving. I look at myself in the mirror, chin fluffy white with lather like a hoodlum Father Christmas. I smile, gazing at my eyes, both my eyes, as they both gaze back at me. They shine with humour. I am happy because I'm normal. There is no facial blight, no raw flesh to conceal from the world — just a smooth unsullied countenance. As I smile, both eyes sparkle and ripple with pleasure.

Then I wake up.

In the gloomy half-light, with my damaged

half-sight, my fingers automatically seek out the rough crater where my left eye used to be and I groan. For a fleeting moment I have been seduced by the dream. It had all been so real.

Don't you remember, I tell myself sharply, you are Johnny Hawke, Johnny One Eye, the Cyclops detective?

I don't let these moments linger. It would be dangerous to do so; I could easily spiral into a state of permanent despair if I let such dreams haunt me for long. And I'm not going to let that happen. With an energetic shrug I slough off the feelings of self-pity and thoughts of what might have been. Yes, so I lost an eye and thus failed to get in the army to fight for king and country, but at least I am alive and functioning — after a fashion — as a responsible patriot. Well, that's what I tell myself. And it seems to work. A hot cup of strong Camp coffee and a cigarette and all thoughts of my dreams are usually banished — until the next time. I've trained myself in the procedure.

On this particular morning in the November of 1943, I allowed myself the luxury of a second cigarette before I set about attending to my ablutions. Part of my procrastination was designed to delay the dash down the cold corridor to the even colder bathroom for a wash and shave. Scraping a dullish razor over a chin dotted with goose pimples, while shivering, naked to the waist is a very easy way to cut one's throat.

I pulled back the blackout curtains and gazed out over the higgledy-piggledy rooftops of London. A dull slate-grey sky loured over the city and fronds of frost decorated the roofs. Below me, although I could not see them from my vantage point, I knew that the streets would be bustling with Londoners on their way to work or returning from some night shift. We were now into the fourth year of the war and in this surreal situation the population of Britain had created new routines for themselves, a revised sense of ordinariness from the bleak and uncertain times in which we lived. To some extent it was, as I am sure patriotic historians will claim in years to come, part of the British indomitable spirit; but it was also the need to create some form of familiarity and routine out of the chaos that surrounds us. If we behave normally then perhaps normality will be resumed.

I carried these thoughts with me down the corridor and into the ice box of the bathroom. It struck me as I dragged the reluctant razor over my stubble that in recent months I, too, have created some kind of normality out of my life, a sort of routine out of the crazy patchwork quilt of my existence. Since Peter, the young lad I had befriended, had returned from Devon to live in London he had become part of my life on a regular basis. I suppose I was his unofficial dad. He lived in the care of two delightful spinster ladies but, investigations permitting, I saw him most weekends usually in the company of Nurse Susan McAndrew who was another of his unofficial guardians. To see us out together, each holding one of Peter's hands, we looked like a family. But of course we weren't. There was no romance between Susan and me. I don't really know why. She was a pretty woman, in her mid thirties, a few years older than I am, with a pleasant personality and a comely shape. But there was no romantic chemistry between us. I am sure she felt the same. We got on well together and we both were very fond of Peter but, although we had never discussed it, we knew there was no spark there to ignite any passion.

However, Susan and I had taken it upon ourselves to assure the authorities that we would be responsible for Peter's welfare. We both cared deeply for the lad. As Peter had run away from his foster home in Devon to come back to London to be with me, they were content to let us share the burden of care.

Weekends now meant trips to the cinema, walks by the river, visits to the zoo and other such activities which entertained a twelve-year-old boy. He was a great one for comics was Peter and I don't think he was ever happier than when he was sitting in Benny's café with a lemonade, hunched over a pile of comics, caught in the magic of their cartoon world.

I grinned back at myself in the shaving mirror at the thought.

★　★　★

Although I fancied a breakfast fry up at Benny's café, I had to steel myself against it this morning. Financially, I had been going through a bad patch and coins were a little on the scarce side. I knew if I explained this to Benny, he'd give me a free breakfast but I really didn't want to lean on old friends like that and, besides, I'd never hear the end of it. He'd rib me till the cows came home about saving me from starvation through the kindness of his heart or something like that. So, dressed and ready for work, I settled for another coffee and another cigarette. They would help concentrate the mind; although to be honest I didn't know why I needed to concentrate my mind. I had no case on hand. No devilish puzzle to challenge my intellect. Not even a bad debt to chase up. I had zilch.

Still, I told myself, as I lit the cigarette, the last but one in my packet, I've been here before, clinging by my fingernails to the rock face of penury and then someone or something had always turned up in the nick of time to save me from the debtors' prison. Fate had so often proffered me a helping hand to drag me back up on to the ledge. Then the thought struck me that maybe this was going to be the one time that the fateful hand failed to make an appearance.

Just as this gloomy thought was making its unpleasant presence felt, a shadow appeared against the door of my office and the doorbell rang. With a taut grin, I called out, 'Come in.'

The door opened and instinctively my grin broadened. I reckoned that the hand of fate had yanked me up once more. Here, surely, was a client and from his appearance a well-heeled one, too.

2

Raymond Carter gave a little chuckle and tossed the script on to the floor. He glanced over at the dummy on the chair opposite him.

'It's another good one, Charlie,' he said, the smile still hovering about his lips.

'It should be for the money you're paying him,' said the dummy, although none of its facial features, including the mouth, actually moved. The voice was almost identical to the one that Carter had used for Tommy, but that doll had long been consigned to the dustbin. Carter now had a sparkling new partner with a new name, Charlie Dokes, and a new personality to go with it, sharper and more cruel than Tommy. If Tommy had been a naughty schoolboy, Charlie was a sneering, sarcastic arrogant adolescent with a penchant for barbed put-downs and insults. But Charlie had become very popular and successful. And this was reflected in the decor and trappings of Carter's newly acquired elegant mews cottage in Kensington. From playing third-rate music hall bills two years ago, he had risen to starring, with Charlie of course, in his own radio show, headlining in a revue at the Palladium theatre and now there was even talk of a Charlie Dokes movie.

'I don't begrudge Al the money. It's his brain and talent which have helped me get where I am today,' Carter said, still addressing his dummy.

'Yeah', came the reply, 'where you are today: standing on the stage and talking to yourself.'

'That's one of the old ones. I don't do those any more.'

Charlie said nothing. He just gazed at Carter with his fixed glacial stare.

Carter rose from his chair and crossed to the doll and picked it up. 'I think you need a new jacket, old boy. You're starting to look a little shabby. We're having our picture taken next week for the *Radio Times*. I want you to look smart.'

The doll remained silent and so, instinctively, Carter slipped his hand inside and took hold of the controls. The eyes rotated in their sockets and the mouth clapped open noisily.

'Oooh, *Radio Times*. That's *très* posh,' it said.

'Certainly is, but I don't have to remind you that 'Okey Dokes' is the top entertainment show on the radio.'

'Chum, you don't have to remind *me* of anything.' Charlie winked an eye.

Suddenly the door opened and a tall, lean man with wavy hair entered. Like Charlie he was fairly new on the scene, too. Larry Milligan was Raymond Carter's manager. He was dressed in a smart double-breasted suit with a garish tie that flopped out of the jacket like a large vibrant multicoloured tongue. Despite his youth, Milligan had a tough, careworn face and looked older than his years. Still only in his mid-twenties, Milligan had been in the business nearly ten years. As a lad he had always had a yearning to be involved in show business, but, quickly realizing that he possessed no skill as a performer himself, he soon developed a talent for managing acts. While he was only seventeen, he was already looking after two small jazz groups, one of which, Tom Haley's Smooth Sounds, caught the attention of a record producer and had a minor success with a couple of discs. That had been the start for Milligan. His stable of artistes grew and within five years he was handling some of the top names in the business.

'You talking to that bit of wood again?' Milligan said without humour.

'Why shouldn't he?' snapped Charlie. 'He talks to you, doesn't he?'

'Yeah, yeah, very funny. It's a good job Al writes the scripts and not you.'

'I see you're in a good mood this morning,' observed Carter easily, setting the dummy down and returning to his chair.

'Is it still only morning? I thought it must be at least midnight. I've just had one of those days, this morning. I've been trying to negotiate a contract with the two bloody scatterbrains known as the Prior Sisters. They are a nightmare. When one says one thing; the other says the opposite. How they ever sing in harmony, God only knows.'

'I think money might have something to do with it.'

Milligan gave a sigh of exasperation. 'Yes, you could be right. I can tell you I could do with a drink, but I promised myself that I would lay off the juice until the sun goes down. So let's go, shall we? Let's be early for the rehearsal for a change.'

Carter grinned and picked up the script. 'That's fine by me. Have you read this?'

Milligan nodded. 'Skimmed it. It seems OK.'

'OK would not be good enough for Ray Carter and Charlie Dokes. This is the best.'

Milligan narrowed his eyes and placed an arm on Carter's shoulder. 'I know,' he said softly.

The two men looked at each other for a few moments, exchanging unspoken thoughts.

Milligan was a very sharp operator. Although he hadn't been in the business for many years, he had managed to collect around him a group of talented and successful artistes that provided him with a very comfortable living. However, he had learned very quickly never to get too close to his charges. Show business was a fickle master and while one day your client could be top of the heap, it was the way of the world that he would eventually slide down towards the bottom as someone new, younger and better came along to take his place. No one stayed at the centre of the spotlight for ever. Once they had slipped into the shadows it was time to cut them adrift. At present Raymond Carter was his top banana, but Milligan knew his novelty value had a limited life span. It was his job to make sure that while the performers came and went, he survived.

Milligan suddenly patted both sides of his jacket. 'Drat. I'm out of cigarettes. You know I can't sit through the rehearsal without fags to keep me going.'

'I can let you have some of mine.'

Milligan pulled a face. 'I hate those. No, no. Look, you get the car out, and I'll just pop down the road and buy a pack. Be back in five minutes. OK?'

Carter nodded. 'Sure.'

Some minutes later, as Carter was ready to leave, the telephone rang.

'I'll get that,' said Charlie.

'I'd like to see you try,' grinned Carter, as he lifted the receiver.

'Hello, Raymond Carter here.'

'Hello, Raymond.' The voice was thin and high and recited the words in a sing-song manner.

For some reason which he could not at first explain, the greeting chilled Carter and he tensed, his brow furrowing with concern. 'Who is this?' His tone was abrupt and urgent.

'Surely you recognize the voice of an old friend.' Carter did recognize the voice. It was his voice, or to be more precise, it was the voice he used when he was being Charlie. Someone was impersonating him.

'Is this some kind of joke?'

The voice chuckled. 'It is far from being a joke, old boy. Actually it's more in the nature of a warning.'

'I've heard enough — '

'I wouldn't put the phone down if I were you. That would be very foolish.'

Carter was unnerved now. 'What do you want?'

'Did you hear the one about the fellow who

20

carried a calendar around with him? His days were numbered — and, my dear Raymond, so are yours. Just wanted you to know that. Goodbye for now.'

There was a faint Charlie Dokes' chuckle and then a sharp click followed by a fierce buzzing noise. Slowly Raymond replaced the receiver.

★ ★ ★

'You OK?' asked Milligan as he got inside the car. He sensed there was something wrong. Suddenly Carter was awkward and sullen. The easy, jovial demeanour had evaporated and with his brow contracted into a permanent frown he seemed edgy and strained.

'I just had . . . the strangest of phone calls.'

'Who from?'

'I don't know,' replied Carter, slowly shaking his head. 'A disgruntled listener, I expect.' He flashed a false half smile. He wasn't going to admit it to Milligan or, perhaps, even himself, but the incident had really rattled him. Silly though it had been, he couldn't shake off the notion that there was something quite sinister behind the bizarre call.

'What did they say?' Milligan was keen to

learn all about this telephone conversation which had turned his usually easy-going, relaxed client into a tense and nervy soul.

Carter shook his head. 'He said nothing of significance . . . said he hated the show. Stuff like that. The funny thing was, he used Charlie's voice.'

Instinctively Milligan glanced at the dummy on the back seat. 'Sounds like it was someone on the loose from the nut house.'

Carter attempted another grin. 'I reckon you're right. Let's forget about the damn call, shall we? We have a show to rehearse,' he said, switching on the engine.

'Indeed. We can't please all the people all of the time . . . eh?'

'Why not?' observed Charlie in the back of the car.

By the time Carter and Milligan reached the rehearsal studio in Broadcasting House, the rest of the cast had assembled. There was Gilbert Manville, a short, stocky, bald-headed man in a crumpled tweed suit, who did most of the character voices, including Mr Molesworth, Charlie's tutor; and Evelyn Munro, a pretty young girl in a fetching flowered dress, who played Raymond's secretary in the show as well as having a solo singing spot. There was the announcer Percy

Goodall, plump and dapper in a grey suit with dark hair slicked back with Brylcreem so that it looked like a patent leather toupee; he was the target for many of Charlie's putdowns. Looking uncomfortable, like a sleek fish out of water, was this week's special guest, the film star Harry Mason. And there was Arthur Keating, an unmade bed of a man with a large raspberry for a nose, the result of many years imbibing the grain. Much to Carter's annoyance, Keating had been given a comic monologue each week as The Hot Chestnut Man which had been a hit with the listeners and he'd garnered quite a following. However his drinking made Keating unreliable. He'd failed to turn up for a few rehearsals, fluffed some lines on air and had missed one broadcast altogether, having lost track of time in a pub somewhere. To Carter, this irritating mix of increasing popularity and unpredictability had made him determined to get Keating off the show and he didn't hide his animosity towards the man.

The group was completed by producer Edward Simmons, dressed in a brown corduroy suit with a floppy bow tie which fluttered like some damaged butterfly when he spoke. He was one of the BBC's *wunderkind*. He was only in his middle twenties, although to Carter he looked much younger, as though he hadn't started shaving yet. However, despite his boyish, naïve appearance, Simmons had risen quickly through the ranks because of his perceptive flair and ruthless determination. Carter respected the producer but was also wary of him. After the usual rounds of greetings and introductions, Simmons took the troupe through some cuts and changes in the script. Now they were ready to rehearse.

'Where's wonder boy?' asked Simmons, as he headed for the control booth. 'It's not like Al to miss a run through.'

'I'm here,' cried Al Warren, slipping in through the door as though on cue at the mention of his name. 'Sorry I'm late. Traffic. So many detours because of the demolition work. You'd think there was a war on. Hey, Eddie, I hope you left in that gag about Mae West.'

'You must be joking,' responded Simmons. 'That was the general idea.'

Simmons mimed a throat cutting gesture to indicate that the gag had been cut. 'We do want to be on the air next week. If I'd have left that little sparkler in, it would have meant fireworks for all of us. The BBC wallahs are very hot on bad taste. Remember, Al, smutty isn't always witty.'

Al rolled his eyes, but then grinned broadly.

'And what did Charlie think of the *risqué* riposte?' asked Gilbert Manville.

Carter, who had just lifted Charlie Dokes from his travelling case, deftly swung the dummy round and rested him on his knee. Taking Charlie's arm, he held the doll's hand up to its face. 'Oh, gosh, Mr Manville, I was so embarrassed. An innocent fellow like me shouldn't be reading such stuff.'

There was a ripple of laughter and then, as though they had been well drilled by practice, the cast assembled in their set places ready for a dry rehearsal, one without music or effects, while Edward Simmons retired to the control room. Out on a limb, the film actor Harry Mason had to be shepherded into place by Evelyn Munro.

'OK you lot. Let's give it a whirl.' Simmons' tinny voice emanated from a small speaker in the studio.

Percy Goodall stepped up to the microphone and began:

ANNOUNCER: Once more it's time to meet up with that little fellow with the big mouth.

CHARLIE: That's me, folks, Charlie Dokes, the woodpecker's friend.

ANNOUNCER: Along with his keeper, Raymond Carter.

25

RAYMOND: Hello there, Okey Dokers.

ANNOUNCER: And the assembled throng that is Gilbert Manville.

GILBERT: (in several voices) Good evening. Hello. Hi there. How do you do and What ho.

ANNOUNCER: Also joining in the fun is Evelyn Munro.

EVELYN: Sometimes Charlie drives me to distraction.

CHARLIE: And I don't even have a motor car.

ANNOUNCER: And of course, there's Arthur Keating, The Hot Chestnut Man.

There was a pause while Keating rustled his script, apparently already having lost his place.

'For God's sake, man!' snapped Raymond Carter.

'Yes, yes,' muttered Keating, still turning over his script.

Simmons's voice came over the tannoy: 'OK, Percy, give Arthur his cue again. And Arthur, please keep your eye on the ball, eh?'

'Yes, yes,' repeated Keating, having found his place.

ANNOUNCER: And of course, there's Arthur Keating, The Hot Chestnut Man.

ARTHUR: Buy me chestnuts. They're real tasty. I've got some real hot ones for you tonight.

ANNOUNCER: This week's special guest is the star of Renown Pictures *Danger at Midnight*, Harry Mason.

HARRY: How on earth did I get into this mess?

ANNOUNCER: They're all here to bring you: 'Okey Dokes'.

And so the rehearsal continued more or less smoothly. Harry Mason fluffed his lines a few times and Gilbert Manville had difficulty with one of his accents but to Larry Milligan, who was sitting back in a corner of the studio watching the proceedings while he puffed away on a chain of cigarettes, it all seemed to go smoothly as it usually did. Even Arthur Keating glided through it without further mishap and was very funny. Milligan knew that any minor slips would be ironed out when the crew were before a real live audience and they upped their game. It was only towards the very end of the rehearsal that something strange seemed to happen.

Carter was thanking Harry Mason for guesting on the show, while Charlie was making snide comments and trying to get the actor to find a part for him in one of Mason's movies:

CHARLIE: I want to play someone who's a handsome hunk and looks good.
HARRY: Don't you mean a handsome chunk who's made of wood?

Carter turned over the last page and froze. He emitted a gasp and dropped the script. Everyone around the microphone had been gazing at their own scripts but now they turned towards their star in surprise.

'What's the matter?' asked the bewildered producer over the tannoy.

For the second time in a few hours, Larry Milligan saw his client's face drain of colour and a thin sheen of sweat cover his brow.

However, Carter managed to recover his composure quite quickly. 'I'm sorry,' he said sharply, snatching his script from the floor. 'It's nothing. Don't mind me. I'm not myself today.'

'Now that's a major improvement,' said Charlie, and rolled his eyes.

'OK, let's go back a page and start with Harry's line at the top,' said Simmons.

After that disturbance, the rehearsal concluded without any further delays.

Edward Simmons emerged from the

control room, beaming 'Great, everyone. We've got a very good show here. Good work, Al.'

Al Warren gave a salute and smiled.

'Right. Have some lunch you lot. Nothing too liquid mind. Band call at three-thirty. We record at six.'

The cast nodded and murmured their farewells for the moment and dispersed.

'You want to catch a light lunch at Mario's?' asked Larry Milligan, as Carter began packing Charlie away in his case again.

'I think I'll give it a miss if you don't mind, Larry. I've a bit of business in town I need to attend to. I'll see you at the theatre at three-thirty. OK?'

'Sure.' Milligan pulled on his overcoat and sauntered to the door, but before opening it, he turned round to face Carter.

'Are you all right, Raymond?'

'Why, yes. Of course I am.'

'What happened when you dropped your script? You looked as though you'd seen a ghost.'

'Did I? It was nothing. Nothing.'

There was an edge to his voice now and Milligan knew his client was lying.

'That 'nothing' seems to have spooked you somewhat.'

Carter forced an uneasy smile. 'It was

nothing. Believe me.'

'OK,' drawled Milligan easily, deciding to drop the subject. 'Well, as I'm not performing later today, I reckon I'll wend my way towards a few large whiskies. See you later.'

Carter was now left alone in the room. Taking a deep breath, he picked up his script and turned to the last page. There it was. He hadn't imagined it. Scrawled in red ink at the bottom of the page were the words: 'Not long now'.

* * *

Carter still wore a concerned frown when he left the recording studio some five minutes later. In one sense he was determined not to let these strange occurrences — the phone call and the scrawled message — impinge on his life and particularly the early afternoon relaxation he had planned for himself, but what the brain decides is often negated by the instinctive emotions and so the frown remained.

He had barely made his way a dozen yards down the hushed corridor when he heard his name being called. The voice came from behind him. His body tensed and he swung round to see Gilbert Manville, suit still crumpled and, he thought unkindly, with a face to match. Carter didn't fraternize with the cast and so he hardly knew Manville. He thought of him as one of those performers who came alive briefly while on air, served their purpose and then shrank back into the shadows of mundanity. Carter's idea of hell would be to be stuck in a lift with Manville, whose whole personality was channelled into his various voices. The man himself had none.

'Sorry to catch you like this, Raymond,' he said approaching, deference and embarrassment fighting for control of his countenance.

Carter said nothing. Well, he really had nothing to say to this fellow, so why invent?

'I'd like to ask a favour.'

Carter placed the case containing Charlie Dokes down on the ground but still remained silent. He wondered how long it could be before he told this person to get lost.

'I know I have no right to ask you but . . . I am sort of desperate.'

'*Sort* of desperate . . . ?' Carter deliberately failed to keep the sneer out of his response. 'Perhaps you should see me when you are actually desperate.'

Manville was unsure how to respond to this barbed quip. Instinctively, he would have liked to punch the arrogant vent on the nose, but that would not do his cause any good.

31

'I need money. I need money badly, I'm afraid.'

'You are paid by the BBC, are you not?'

Manville winced. 'Yes but I'm not as careful with my pennies as I should be.'

Carter rolled his eyes. He had heard all about Manville's obsession with the horses — the gee-gees. How he spent most of his income on that dead cert which would make him a rich man — all those dead certs which turned out to be dead losses.

'It's my wife,' he said, taking a step nearer to Carter, causing him to step back. This, thought the ventriloquist, was taking on the dimensions of a Victorian melodrama. He envisaged Manville producing a violin at any minute to accompany his own sad tale.

'My wife is very ill. Dying, in fact. She is being cared for in a private sanatorium. She needs special treatment, you see.'

Carter saw but said nothing.

Manville nervously clasped his sweaty hands in front of him. 'The fees are rather steep, I'm afraid and . . . well, I've not been able to keep up with them.'

'That was rather careless of you, Manville. I presume you prefer to spend your time pouring cash into the bookies' pockets . . . '

'I bet on the horses in the hope I'll win enough to see Margaret all right. It . . . it just

32

hasn't worked out.'

'From what I hear, it hasn't worked out on a regular basis.'

Manville flushed and stared at his feet. 'I need a hundred pounds urgently. The sanatorium says I must take Margaret away unless I pay my arrears by the end of the month. The situation is making her worse. She is literally worrying herself to death.'

'That is a sorry state of affairs.'

Manville, failing to catch the note of dry sarcasm in Carter's words, was encouraged by what he thought was a sympathetic response and came to the crux of his plea. 'I wonder, Raymond, if you could see your way to lending me — I stress lending — one hundred pounds to help me out of this difficult situation. I assure you that I'll pay you back as soon as I'm able.'

Carter grinned. 'As soon as that elusive winner comes in first past the post, eh?'

'It would mean so much if you could see your way — '

'I'm sorry, Manville, I can't see my way. Only an idiot would lend an inveterate gambler a hundred pounds. It would be like throwing the money down the drain. No sooner had you got your greedy hands on the cash than you'd be off squandering it on some useless nag.'

Manville shook his head desperately. 'No, no. I assure you. It is for Margaret. For the sanatorium.'

'You should have thought of her before, shouldn't you? Didn't give her or the sanatorium much consideration while you were throwing your money away at the races. How many other suckers have you tapped for money, eh? You have a bit of a reputation as a scrounger: a ten-bob note here, a couple of quid there . . . a fiver. But now you're going for the jackpot. One hundred smackers.'

Manville took a step nearer, close enough for Carter to smell his sweat. 'Please,' he begged, his eyes moistening, 'I need the money for Margaret. I promise I won't gamble it away.'

Carter was tired of this now. He wanted to end this unpleasant and inconvenient inter-view. 'The answer is no. No, I will not lend you a hundred pounds. In fact, I will not lend you half a crown. No.'

Suddenly Manville stepped forward and grabbed the lapels of Carter's overcoat. 'I beg you. If not for me, for my dying wife. Please.'

Carter pushed the little man off him with a cry of disgust. 'Don't you dare touch me,' he snapped, anger now taking the place of disdain. 'I said no. And I damned well meant no.' Flicking his hands down his lapels to straighten them, he picked up the Charlie Dokes case, turned and walked away down the corridor, leaving the cringing and defeated Gilbert Manville frozen in a despondent posture.

'You bastard,' Manville said at length. His voice was quiet, a whisper almost but it was full of hatred and passion. 'You rotten bastard.'

★   ★   ★

Carter let himself into the flat with his own key. Evelyn Munro, wearing a cream silk dressing-gown, appeared in the tiny hallway holding a gin and tonic. She looked far from the demure girl she had appeared to be in the recording studio.

'You took your time,' she said coldly, moving past Carter into the sitting room. Sloughing off his overcoat and leaving his suitcase containing Charlie Dokes in the hallway, Carter followed her.

'I had a little business to attend to.'

'Oh?' Evelyn raised a quizzical eyebrow, as she lounged back on the sofa, her dressing-gown falling open to reveal that she had nothing on underneath apart from her underwear.

'Nothing that need bother you,' remarked

Carter casually, as he helped himself to a gin and tonic from the small drinks trolley. He took a quick slug and then leaned over Evelyn and gave her a gentle kiss on the forehead.

'It's a secret then,' said Evelyn, with thinly veiled petulance, the kiss having failed to melt the ice.

Carter threw himself down in the chair opposite her and took another sip of his drink. 'No secret from you, my darling. I've just been talking to Simmons about Keating.'

'That piss artist.'

Carter smiled. 'Language, Miss Munro,' he said, using his Charlie Doke's voice.

'Stop that. I've told you about talking like the dummy. You know it spooks me.'

Carter was tempted to continue with Charlie's voice and make some smutty comment about Evelyn's legs, which looked particularly desirable, but he knew that would really unnerve her. She hated the dummy and had insisted that whenever Carter called round to her flat, Charlie stayed in his case in the hallway.

'Sorry.'

'So . . . what about Keating? What have you said to Simmons?'

'I want the little drunk out of the show. He's unreliable.'

'That's a bit harsh, isn't it? I know he likes

a drink, but his monologues are funny and popular.'

'A bit too popular.'

'Oh.' It was Evelyn's time to smile. 'Frightened he might be sharing too much of Raymond Carter's limelight, eh?'

'You could say that. I've got to protect my interests, haven't I? Anyway, I've laid it on the line with Simmons. I want Keating out. So I reckon next week will be Keating's last. Then he can drink himself to death for all I care.'

'You get your way when you want to, don't you? I'd better watch my back, then. It could be me for the chop next.'

'You watch your back, Evie darling, and I'll watch your front.' He gave her a Groucho Marx leer.

She giggled as he moved to her side, kneeling down on the floor by the sofa, his hand slipping beneath the thin material of the dressing-gown to caress her breast.

'Ooh, Mr Carter, what are you about?' she purred in a little girl voice.

'With a bit of luck, I'm about to seduce you.'

'About time, too.' Evelyn snaked her arm around Carter's neck and gently pulled his face closer to hers so that she could kiss him. He responded easily and passionately. He still had difficulty believing his luck. Here he was about to make love to a beautiful young girl, twenty years his junior who wouldn't have given him the time of day two or three years ago when he was struggling on the halls. But that was Raymond Carter BAW — Before Al Warren. Before Al Warren had transformed his act and his life. He owed a lot to that young man, including indirectly the sexual favour he was about to enjoy. Carter was not naïve enough to think that Evelyn was actually in love with him, or even liked him that much. No doubt she saw him as a rung on her ladder to show-business success. It was good for her to have a headline name on her side. In practical and cynical terms, Carter knew that they were both using each other for their own ends but, what the hell, it was beneficial to them both and certainly he derived a great deal of pleasure from the arrangement.

They had both kept their affair a secret from the rest of the cast for Carter knew that such relationships had a habit of unsettling the dynamics of the team. He wanted nothing to jeopardize the success of his radio show. Besides, their affair was only just over a month old. It was really in the honeymoon period. He felt sure that one or the other of them would get bored with it sooner rather than later. It was not going to lead to a nice little cottage in the country with roses around the door and nappies on the line.

Evelyn rose from the sofa, allowing the dressing-gown to slip from her shapely frame. 'Let's go to the bedroom,' she murmured, and linking hands with Carter she led him away.

Once inside the bedroom, he began disrobing while she closed the door firmly, conscious that a few feet away in the hallway was Carter's case containing that horrid doll.

★   ★   ★

An hour later, Carter was smoking a cigarette in the sitting room and sipping a small gin and tonic. He was waiting for Evelyn to get dressed in the bedroom before they set out for the final rehearsal and the recording at the Paris studio. The love-making had been good — mutually enjoyable he believed — and he felt relaxed again after what had been a fairly stressful day. He was always tense on the day of a recording but those blasted messages — the threatening telephone call and the words scrawled on his script — had jangled his nerves further. He didn't know what they meant, but they were obviously some crank's idea of a nasty joke. As these thoughts were sifting though his mind, the telephone rang.

Evelyn hurried out of the bedroom in a light-blue dress that still needed fastening up the front. She snatched up the phone. 'Hello,' she said, a little breathless. Then she frowned and gazed over at Carter. 'It's for you,' she said uneasily, covering over the mouthpiece. 'How did anyone know you were here at my place?'

Suddenly the feeling of ease which had been blossoming within Carter wilted and died. He rose awkwardly, his features darkened by concern. 'I don't know. I told no one.' He held out his hand for the receiver.

'Hello,' he said briskly.

'Ah, hello my old friend.' It was Charlie Dokes's voice again. 'How was the little girlie? She's a lovely piece of meat, ain't she?'

Carter slammed the phone down.

'What's going on? What's the matter?' Evelyn's brow furrowed with concern.

'Some crazy idiot. I don't know. He's rung me before. Forget about it.'

'But how did he know you were here? That's what worries me. I don't want 'some crazy idiot' ringing my number.'

'I told you I don't know. He certainly didn't get the information from me.'

'You don't think you were followed?'

The words 'of course not' died on his lips. It was something he had not considered. But

40

now that he did think about it, he saw that it was a possibility.

'What does he want, Ray, this 'crazy idiot'?'

Carter shook his head. 'I've no idea. To upset me, I suppose.' He stared down at the telephone as though the instrument would reveal the answer; and on cue it rang shrilly, the sharp piercing bell seeming to fill the whole room.

'I'll get it,' said Carter. He lifted the receiver to his ear and listened.

'Now that wasn't very polite, was it, Raymond, old boy: slamming the telephone down on me?' It was the same voice. 'And here was me just ringing to do you a favour. To give you . . . a warning. It won't be long now, Raymond. Not long now before you go to that great theatre in the sky. You see, I'm coming to get you. I'm coming to kill you.'

3

My visitor entered hesitantly. As he surveyed the place, his expression changed from apprehension to dismay. It was clear that he thought he'd made a major mistake coming into this shabby little office with an even shabbier one-eyed bloke on duty. For a moment he looked as though he was about to turn on his heel and without a word make a bolt for it, but I rose quickly to my feet and extended my hand in readiness to shake his — and hang on to him. One of the first rules of being a private detective is to grab hold of prospective clients and keep them in your clutches until they cough up a fee.

'Good morning, I'm John Hawke. Do take a seat,' I said, with studied politeness. The honey trap worked. After a fashion. He looked too embarrassed to refuse my offer. With a certain amount of reluctance, the poor devil perched on the chair opposite my desk. He was quite a good-looking fellow. Well, he had the advantage of two eyes for a start. He also possessed regular features, a masculine square chin and a good head of neatly groomed hair, which was tinged with grey at the temples. I put his age around forty-five, but his skin was fairly smooth and without too many of the blemishes that time can give it. I could tell that there was a certain amount of humour in the blue-grey eyes although at the moment they stared at me with a mixture of embarrassment and uncertainty. There was also something faintly familiar about his face as though I'd met this fellow before. But where, I could not fathom ... for the moment.

'I'm not sure I should be here,' he said earnestly.

An opening I'd heard many times before.

'Well,' I replied, with what I hoped was reassuring warmth, 'something prompted you to visit a private detective this morning, something that's given you a bad night's sleep [the dark shadows under his eyes clearly indicated this] so perhaps it might be useful to get whatever's troubling you off your chest. I don't start charging until you hire me.'

A ghost of a smile haunted his lips momentarily. 'It's not your fee that makes me uncertain; I'm just not sure whether I'm making a mountain out of a molehill.'

'Let's find out, shall we? What do you think is the problem?'

'I think someone is going to kill me.'

'Well, that's certainly a mountain and not a

molehill. Have you any idea who this person is?'

'Not really.'

'And how do you know they intend to kill you?'

'Because they've told me.' He shook his head with frustration. 'Look, I'd better start at the beginning.'

'Good place.'

'I don't know whether you've heard of me but I'm Raymond Carter . . . ' He passed over his card, but I didn't need to look at it. I recognized him now.

'Of course you are,' I exclaimed foolishly. 'You're Charlie Dokes's keeper.'

'I suppose you could say that.'

'I have a little twelve-year-old friend who never misses your radio show and spends tuppence every week on Charlie's comic.'

Raymond Carter smiled indulgently. This wasn't what he was here for: to be told he had a young fan. Time to get down to business.

'OK, Mr Carter. Tell me about these death threats.'

'They only began yesterday. Only a couple of telephone calls. I suppose it could be just a crank.'

'Cranks can be dangerous. What does he say? It is a man, I suppose?'

'Well, that's part of the mystery. I'm not

44

sure because whoever it is uses Charlie's voice.'

I frowned. 'You mean he imitates . . . you? Your dummy?'

Carter nodded.

'What does he say?'

'He warns me that I haven't got much time left. Says my days are numbered. That sort of thing. And in the last one he said that he was coming to kill me.'

'All in the voice of your doll, Charlie Dokes?'

'Yes.'

'And you are absolutely certain that this isn't some kind of joke, some colleague pulling your leg?'

'It's not a very funny kind of joke, is it? No, I'm certain that this is serious. Whether it's a colleague, I'm not sure. I did find a written message on a page of my radio script yesterday at the studio.'

'What did it say?'

Carter reached inside his overcoat pocket, retrieved a sheet of paper and passed it to me. It was a typewritten page of script, but at the bottom scrawled in red ink in uneven writing, obviously a disguised hand, were the words: 'Not long now'.

'I had read the script at home and the message wasn't there then. But when I used it in the studio, it was.'

'The script must have left your possession at some point.'

'I probably put it down in the studio before the rehearsal began.'

'Well, that narrows things down. Whoever scribbled these words must have been present at the rehearsal.'

'I suppose so.'

'Have you any notion of who it might be? Is there anyone who has a grudge against you?'

'Not enough to want to kill me. But who can say? People harbour all sorts of feelings under the surface.'

'As yet you've not felt any direct physical threat.'

'The words, 'I'm coming to kill you' seem awfully physical.'

I sat back in my chair, allowing my finger to make a thin trail in the dust on my desk, while my mind did some assessing.

'Have you told anyone else about these threats?' I asked at length.

'No. I sort of didn't want to believe they were true, but having slept on it, I realize I need to do something about them.'

'Why have you come to me and not the police?'

'I suppose because . . . at the moment at least the whole thing is intangible. I want the matter to be investigated in a discreet fashion. I don't want the Press to get a whiff of this; it could be harmful to the act.'

I understood his motives, but I was well aware that no matter how discreetly one approached such cases, once someone began sniffing around looking for a potential murderer, curiosity is aroused, questions are asked and the truth had an unpleasant tendency to reveal itself.

'I'll look into the matter, if that's what you want?'

Carter nodded but his eyes remained uncertain.

'Well, let's start with a list of all those at the rehearsal yesterday who could have had access to your script.'

Carter reeled off the names with a brief description of each. There was his manager, Larry Milligan, producer Edward Simmons, scriptwriter Al Warren, cast members Evelyn Munro, Gilbert Manville, Arthur Keating, announcer Percy Goodall and special guest star Harry Mason.

'And you don't think that any of these characters has a particular grudge against you?'

'No, I don't . . . ' He paused awkwardly.

'Who?' I asked, picking up on his hesitation.

'Well, Arthur Keating won't be feeling too kindly towards me, I suppose.'

'Why?'

'We've rowed in the past about his drinking and unprofessionalism. He's known for some time that I've wanted him out of the show. In fact, I've now pushed for him to be dropped from the series. He is rather unreliable. Next week's show will be his last.'

'Do you think he's capable of these threats?'

'I'm not sure.'

'Well, Mr Carter, in one sense it all looks cut and dried. If one of these people tampered with your script, we must assume that they are the voice of doom. Whether they are serious about the threats is another matter.'

'I don't want to wait to find out.'

'Is there anyone on the list you think we can definitely rule out?'

'Yes. Larry, my agent, was with me at home, when I received the first phone call, so it can't be him. And . . . Evelyn . . . Miss Munro. She and I . . . We are seeing each other, if you know what I mean.'

I knew what he meant. However, in my book that didn't automatically erase her from the list of suspects. In fact, that sort of relationship often places the partner up there at the top.

'When's the next rehearsal?'

'Next Tuesday as usual.'

'I need to be there. To meet this gang of suspects.'

'I can arrange that.'

'Good, but I need to have a role, another persona. I can't be introduced as your private detective — that will certainly put our voice of doom merchant on the alert. I must be someone who can legitimately hang around with you without any suspicions being aroused. No one must know who I am. Not Miss Munro, or your manager.'

'That will be difficult.'

'It is essential. Couldn't I be your nephew, the son of your elder brother visiting London?'

'I don't have an older brother.'

'You do now.'

For a fleeting moment there was a flash of amusement in Carter's eyes. 'OK, if you think we can carry it off.'

'We can. Keep the details simple. I'm your nephew, John Hawke, whom you haven't seen for years and I'm down in London from . . . say Bristol, and I looked you up.'

'What do you do for a living?'

'Some sort of civil servant. I don't talk about my job. We'll keep that vague. I'll call on you next Monday morning to act out the charade in case anyone is watching your place.'

'And in the meantime?'

'I'll do my own digging around. If you receive any more threats, contact me immediately with the details.'

Carter nodded gravely and rose to leave.

'There is one other thing,' I said sharply.

'What's that?'

'The matter of my fee.'

★ ★ ★

After Raymond Carter had left, I made a cup of tea, treated myself to a digestive biscuit and had a big think. This was an unusual case but on the surface it seemed to be straightforward. There appeared to be a limited number of suspects and with a little investigation, I should be able to point the finger accurately. All I had to hope is that the phantom caller with the squeaky voice didn't actually carry out his threat before he could be identified and carted away. Of course, it could all be a rather nasty hoax, something concocted simply to put the wind up Carter. Perhaps he was getting too big for his ventriloquist's boots and someone wanted to knock him down a peg or two.

Or perhaps someone wanted to murder him.

I knew I had to treat this case with this

latter option in mind.

What I needed to find out was the reason why anyone should want to kill Carter in the first place, especially if it was a colleague. Carter must have really got under this person's skin to build up so much dark passion. It would seem that this wasn't a spur of the moment decision; our mystery man was planning this in a cold and methodical fashion, which to me suggested deep hatred, hatred that had built up over a period of time. Would a boozy little actor like Arthur Keating really kill someone because he had been kicked off their show? It seemed unlikely, but then not impossible. He had to be my first concern. It would be good to tick him off my list of possible culprits.

I began to feel a little like Agatha Christie's Poirot. He always ended up with a list of potential suspects and eliminated them one by one. The problem was I didn't have quite the same supply of 'little grey cells' that Belgian poseur seemed to possess enabling him to point the finger of guilt with ease. But what I did have were contacts and if I wanted to know anything about the show-business world there was only one man to see: Limelight Lionel.

4

I met Limelight Lionel as arranged in the Old Mitre Tavern, his favourite watering hole in Fleet Street. Lionel Dudley, to give him his proper name, was the entertainment gossip king of the Press world, who had a daily column in the *Express*. He had been around for ever, it seemed, and it was rumoured, jokingly, that Lionel's first job as a journalist was with William Caxton. No one knew how old he was. He looked ancient, but then he had looked ancient for years. With his white hair and gaunt, ashen features, he appeared as though someone had dipped his head in a tub of whitewash.

I had first encountered Lionel when I'd been a raw constable on the force just before the war and in a strange way we had taken a liking to each other. Maybe it was because he was a fellow orphan. His encyclopaedic knowledge of the world of entertainment was phenomenal and over the years he had been very helpful to me on several occasions. I hoped that this would be the case with my current investigation.

The Old Mitre was dark and sepulchral

and when I entered, just after noon, it was still reasonably quiet with only a few customers propping up the bar, journalists mainly moaning about deadlines and sub editors, while fuelling their creative urges. Lionel was in his regular spot, at the far end of the bar.

As usual a cigarette dangled from the corner of his mouth with at least an inch of ash on the end of it. He raised a hooded eye as I approached his favourite corner table on which stood two pints of dark ale.

'I got the drinks in, anticipating your imminent arrival,' he announced, in his croaky whisper of a voice. 'I told Roger the barman that you'd be paying for these . . . and the next round.' He waved a white skeletal hand at a jovial fellow behind the bar and pointed to me. Roger waved back and gave me the thumbs-up sign.

Lionel lowered his cigarette to the ashtray and raised a glass. 'Cheers,' he said, before downing nearly a third of it in one gulp. I responded with 'Cheers' but sipped a more demure portion of my pint.

Lionel sat back, a contented gleam in his eye. 'I never tire of communing with the ghosts of this place, Jonathan. You know Will Shakespeare and Ben Johnson were patrons of the Mitre. Their shades are still floating about the place. I just hope some of their glory rubs off.'

'I am sure when you go, they'll put up a plaque.'

'More than likely — 'Lionel Dudley got pickled here on a regular basis'.' He gave a strangulated dry cough, amused at his own joke and then suddenly his face turned serious and his rheumy old eyes fixed me with a basilisk stare. 'So, how can I help you, young Jonathan?'

'Two names. Two careers. I wondered if you knew anything about these fellows other than what I can glean by trawling through back issues of the Fleet Street rags.'

'Try me.'

'Raymond Carter.'

Lionel lit another cigarette and squinted his left eye as the smoke trailed past it.

'The current cat who's got the cream. In showbiz there's always someone who is the passing fancy and he's it at the moment. On film I reckon it's a tussle between Will Hay and George Formby. On radio it's Handley and Carter. Strange, isn't it that a vent act could be so successful on the wireless where the audience can't see the little doll and don't care a bugger if the vent's lips are moving or not?'

'It's the novelty maybe.'

Lionel nodded. 'And the scripts. This new fellow, Al Warren, is good. He approaches his material like the American writers, quirky: fast-paced, adult and witty.'

'So Carter is lucky.'

'They're all bloody lucky, my son. But, yes, Raymond Carter is luckier than most. He's been around for years and he was rotten for years. I saw him in 1939 and he was virtually booed off the stage. Don't get me wrong, he's a good vent. The dummy can be gabbing twenty to the dozen but his face is as stiff as a penis in a brothel. But his jokes. They were out of the ark. Since then he's ditched that dummy — a kind of naughty schoolboy — and got this saucy Charlie Dokes . . . '

'And a new joke writer.'

'Indeed.'

'What do you know of his private life?'

Lionel took another gulp of ale and then wiped his mouth on his sleeve before replying. 'Not much. Started out as personal dogsbody for Cyril Sarony, old time vent. Learned the tricks of the trade from him no doubt. Cyril is long retired. Last time I heard of him, he was in an artiste's home in Brighton. Don't know if the old bugger's still alive. Don't think Carter has ever been married as far as I know. String of girlfriends, usually chorus tarts after a bit of the spotlight. No scandal if that's what you're after. There's no dirt clinging to his coat tails. None that I'm aware of, anyway. Why do you want to know?'

'Can't say at the moment, I'm afraid.'

'Please your bloody self.' With an indignant growl, he downed the remainder of his beer and then indicated to Roger to bring another glass.

'What about Arthur Keating?'

For a brief moment Lionel's face lit up with a rare smile. 'Hah! Arthur rubberlegs Keating!'

'Rubberlegs?'

'It's a bloody wonder with all that alcohol inside him he can stand up.' At this point Roger plonked a fresh pint of ale in front of Lionel whose eyes twinkled at the irony and raised the glass as though examining the contents. 'Still, shouldn't laugh. There for the grace of Him Upstairs . . . ' He took a large gulp.

'Keating . . . ' I prompted.

'Keating . . . is a fool. He has the ability to be a great character comedian but the old demon drink is his master. I mean his little turn on Carter's show, The Hot Chestnut Man, is a minor triumph of performance and delivery, but every so often the voice falters, the words slur slightly and those with a keen ear for these sort of things — like yours truly — can tell that he's not completely in charge of his tongue. The alcohol is.'

'Is there any dirt clinging to *his* coat tails?'

Lionel shook his head. 'He's never sober long enough to do anything naughty.'

'He's about to lose his job on Okey Dokes. That's going to make him cross, isn't it?'

'Is he? Poor old bugger. Make him cross? Make him feel sorry for himself, more like. It certainly wouldn't be the first time he's been given the boot because of his drinking.' Lionel took another gulp of beer. 'Now tell me, young Jonathan, you wouldn't be asking these questions out of casual interest, would you? What's afoot? If Raymond Carter's in a bit of bother, I want to be the first to know.'

'You will be the first to know, I promise, but at the moment it's all a bit tenuous.'

'I can work with tenuous.' He grinned mischievously. 'OK, I won't press you any further, but keep me informed. And buy me another pint before you go, there's a good lad.'

★　★　★

As I walked out into the grey November daylight, I felt I was not a great deal wiser. It seemed that there were no skeletons in

Raymond Carter's cupboard and it appeared that Arthur Keating was a harmless old drunk and could be crossed off the list of suspects. However, not for the first time in my detective career, I was wrong.

5

In his dressing room at the Palladium, Raymond Carter was applying make-up in readiness for the evening performance when the telephone jangled shrilly. Charlie Dokes was propped up on a chair by the makeup bench.

'Oooh, I've got that ringing in my ears again,' the doll quipped.

Carter wiped his hands on his handkerchief and reached over for the phone. And then he hesitated. For a moment, his fingers hovered over the instrument and his body stiffened with apprehension. Since the second threatening message, he had become nervous about taking calls. Then a pang of annoyance at his own timidity struck him and with a swift, jerky movement he snatched up the receiver. 'Hello?' he said briskly.

'Raymond? It's Edward, Edward Simmons here.'

Carter felt the knot in his stomach loosen. 'Hello Edward. What can I do for you?'

'I'm sorry to bother you before your show, but I wanted to catch you tonight. I've a bit of news. You'll not be pleased, I'm afraid.'

'Oh?'

Simmons hesitated a moment before continuing, 'Yes. It's . . . it's about Arthur Keating. I'm afraid he won't be leaving the show, after all.'

'Oh yes he is. I just won't put up with that old soak any longer.'

'I'm sorry, but you'll have to. There is no way I can fire him. I'm afraid it's all laid down in his BBC contract. He has not transgressed any of the conditions. He could cause an awful stink if we tried to go ahead with his sacking. He said as much when I called him into the office today. He can be a cantankerous so and so if riled. However, to be fair, I have to admit he is quite within his rights. And he knows it. Quite honestly, Raymond, I have to tell you that the powers that be are not happy with your desire to get rid of him. They see his Chestnut Man routine as an asset to the show. They want him to stay. And, I'm afraid, stay he will.'

Raymond didn't know what to say. For a moment anger robbed him of words.

Simmons continued, 'I know this is not what you wanted to hear, Raymond, but I've had my orders. I fought your corner for you but in this instance I lost. You know that I always try to do my best for you when I can. After all, Okey Dokes is my baby. I was the

60

one who came to you with the idea in the first place.'

Carter mumbled his acceptance of this fact.

'Look, Raymond, the best advice I can give to you is to grin and bear it for now. There's only another eight shows left to go this time around and I'll personally guarantee Mr Keating will not be signed up for the next series.'

'This is not the end of the matter, Edward.'

'I'm afraid as far as the BBC is concerned, it is.' The voice was relaxed and smug.

'Thank you for letting me know.' Carter replaced the receiver before Simmons had a chance to respond.

The ventriloquist gazed at his sour reflection in the make-up mirror. 'Damn!' he barked.

'Temper, temper. You've a show to do tonight. People to amuse,' piped up Charlie.

Carter shifted his chair and stared down at Charlie. 'You're the one who amuses the people, Charlie. I'm just your dummy.'

★   ★   ★

Half an hour later, Raymond Carter walked on to the stage of the Palladium Theatre to a wave of enthusiastic applause from a packed house. Charlie's head, garish and shiny in the spotlight, revolved from side to side as though surveying the audience, his eyes gyrating as his mouth opened and closed viciously in savage amusement.

'Hey, Carter,' he piped, when they had reached the microphone at centre stage, 'how did all these drunks get into my room?'

The first laugh of the evening. It was good to get that over with. Now Raymond could relax. He gazed down at the first few rows of seats, the only rows where he could make out the faces clearly. As he surveyed the array of smiling punters staring back at him, he saw one that he recognized. A crumpled ruin of a face with a large, bulbous, red nose and bright piggy eyes. It was Arthur Keating, sitting in the middle of the front row bearing a broad facile grin, his features bathed in the rosy glow of the footlights. When he saw that he had caught Carter's eye, he raised a shiny metal hip flask in the gesture of a toast and then thrust it to his lips. The bastard, thought Carter, he's come here to gloat. He thinks he's got one over on me. And for a brief moment Charlie Dokes lost all his animation.

★   ★   ★

It was nearing midnight when Arthur Keating staggered up the three flights of stairs to his tiny flat in Hallam Street where he'd lived since his divorce some twenty-five years ago. He was in a good mood and it wasn't solely down to all the alcohol that he had imbibed that evening. He was savouring his triumph over that jumped-up vent Raymond Carter. Like some bloody Roman emperor, he'd thought that all he had to do was thrust his thumb down and announce 'Get rid of Keating' and they would — they could. Well, they bloody well didn't 'cause they couldn't. He'd shown that pompous bastard a lesson. Keating grinned again as he searched for his key. Oh, he thought, I wish I had a picture of Carter when he clocked eyes on me lording it on the front row of the Palladium savouring my triumph. It really put the bastard off his stride. It took him at least a minute to regain his composure. There's nothing worse than a vent who's struck dumb. Keating laughed at the notion, causing him to stagger forward and slump against the door of his flat, which gave way easily against his weight. With a gargling cry of surprise, he fell across the threshold. For a moment he lay still and tried to steady the seesaw motion of the floor. After a while, he managed to clamber unsteadily to his feet. A thought came to him through the miasma of inebriation: why was the door open? He was sure he'd locked it on his way out earlier that evening. Hadn't he?

He staggered into the tiny cluttered sitting room and switched on the table lamp but nothing happened. The room remained in darkness.

'You keep late hours, don't you, Arthur?' A high, piping voice came from the shadows.

Arthur shook his head rapidly. He couldn't be sure he'd heard it. Was it the drink fooling him? There were times in the past when he'd heard voices conjured up by the alcohol. Was it happening again? But those teasing cadences . . . he knew them so well.

'You've been on the booze again tonight, Arthur. That's how you view the world, isn't it, Arthur? Through the bottom of a glass.'

No, he was not imagining it. The voice was in the room. And he recognized that voice.

It belonged to that damned doll. That Charlie Dokes.

'What the hell do you want?' Keating cried angrily, throwing his arms wide, an action that unsteadied him and he stumbled backwards into a table.

'What do I want? I want you, Arthur. Or more precisely, I want you to die.'

Keating peered into the darkness. He could just make out the vague shape of a man and that blasted dummy.

'You can't frighten me, Carter. I'm not

leaving that show.'

The man shape moved, the outline blurring in the shadows.

'That's what you think,' said the high, piping voice. 'You've dropped your chestnuts in the fire for the last time.' Keating was suddenly aware that someone was very close to him. He could hear them breathing and then he felt two hands grasp him around the neck and press with great force and ferocity against his windpipe. He tried to scream but he could not.

'Say 'night, 'night, Arthur. Sweet dreams.'

Keating could neither move nor struggle. His mouth opened and closed noiselessly as saliva seeped out of one corner and trailed down his chin. In a fierce and frightening moment of revelation cutting through the haze of alcohol around his brain, Arthur Keating realized that he was actually going to die and there was nothing he could do about it. The life was being squeezed out of him. His vision began to fog and falter while his body grew limp. Just before Arthur Keating slipped into the sleep of death, he fell forward. The last thing he saw was the shiny, cruel, implacable face of Charlie Dokes, its mouth open in a static grin.

6

The ringing telephone broke the intense silence of Raymond Carter's bedroom. Like the shriek of some ferocious banshee it shattered his dreamless slumbers, dragging him into unwilling consciousness. For some moments he lay on his back and stared into the unrelieved blackness that seemed to press in on him while the cogs in his brain slowly cranked into action. Then instinctively he reached out like a blind man feeling for the switch of the lamp on his bedside table.

All the while the telephone screamed for attention.

He turned on the lamp and the room formed itself like a mirage around him. Subconsciously, he noted that the alarm clock indicated that it was just past 2 a.m. Still in a post-sleep, zombie-like state, he dragged the receiver to his ear.

'Hello,' he mumbled.

'Hello there, my dear Raymond. So sorry to wake you up.'

Icy fear stabbed his heart and in an instant all vestiges of sleep vanished from his brain. Now he was fully awake, alert and frightened.

It was that voice again. That whining, insinuating, threatingly creepy voice. It was his voice. His voice as Charlie Dokes. His doll was speaking to him. Carter felt incapable of reply. He just sat there resting on the pillows, the telephone clamped to his ear, like a man in a trance. What he wanted to do was to slam the receiver down and cut the demon off, but he knew he couldn't. He knew he had to wait, to listen, to hear what the voice had to say. To hear what Charlie had to say.

'You're not very chatty this evening,' the caller said at length. 'Cat got your tongue, eh? What a *purrfect* excuse.'

'Who are you?'

The voice laughed. 'You don't need me to tell you that, do you, Raymond? It's your little friend, Charlie.'

'What the hell do you want with me?'

'I've brought you a present.'

The words did not make sense. 'Present?' he muttered mechanically, his mind frozen with fear.

'A gift from me to you. Out of the kindness of my wooden heart. If you go to your front door you'll find my present to you waiting on the doorstep. Special delivery. I hope you enjoy it.'

'What . . . ?' Carter began, but the telephone went dead, a deep burring sound filling the sudden silence. Slowly, he replaced the receiver, a great sense of unease swamping all other emotions. It was like some kind of nightmare, but he knew that he was awake. This was no frightening dream. This was real. He would have loved to have ignored the call, switched out the light and settled down under the blankets. But he knew he just couldn't. He had to find out if there was 'a present' on the doorstep. And what the nature of this gift was.

Full of apprehension, he threw back the covers, slipped out of bed and struggled into his dressing-gown. With the movements of a somnambulist he made his way through the house to the front door. Nervously, he unlocked and opened it, allowing the harsh cold November air to waft into the hallway. He shivered violently. And pulled the dressing-gown around him more tightly. Stepping on to the porch, he stared out into the darkness with no idea what to expect. His gaze eventually fell upon a dark shape on the ground just beyond the doorstep. At first he thought it was a large sack, but as he crouched down to examine it, he gave a gagging cry of horror. This was no sack. The object before him was a body. It was curled up tightly in a foetal shape, the head obscured within the folds of a large tweed overcoat. It was the body of a man. This was his present: the special delivery.

Without really knowing what he was doing, Carter leaned forward and gently pulled back the lapels of the coat in order to expose the face. Two dull, pig-like eyes, motionless in death, stared up at him, while the fleshy mouth was agape in a silent scream.

Raymond Carter was now paralyzed with fear. His body froze as he crouched over the corpse, staring uncomprehendingly at the dead face before him. It was a face that he recognized.

A face that he knew.

It was the face of Arthur Keating.

7

Despite the strangeness of my occupation and the unusual hours that I'm sometimes forced to keep, I'm rarely telephoned in the middle of the night by a distraught client. They tend to harass me during the daytime only. And I can say with great certainty that I'd never been called up in the wee small hours by an hysterical ventriloquist ranting on about finding a corpse on his doorstep. Not that is until the night Raymond Carter phoned. It took me some time to calm him down sufficiently to get any kind of coherent story out of him. He was jabbering on, the words ill-connected with sense. Eventually, I managed to elicit a brief, staccato telegram-like version of events. The warning voice had called again saying that he had left a gift for him which had turned out to be a dead body dumped on his doorstep. It was Arthur Keating, one of the performers on his radio show, the man whom he had tried to have removed from said radio show. It didn't need a Sherlock Holmes to appreciate the implications of this very dodgy situation.

'I'll come over straight away,' I said, stifling

a yawn. Well, what else could I say? This was looking more and more like a case for the police, but Carter was still my client and as such it was my duty to do my best for him. And I had a living to earn!

I dragged on some clothes, washed the sleep from my eye and set out for Bentley Mews. It was 3 a.m. The streets were damp and cold but despite the war, there were always some pedestrians around the city no matter what time of night or the season — lonely silhouettes who passed you by in the gloom. Shift workers wending their way to or from their work; soldiers, sailors and airmen on leave determined to squeeze every ounce of pleasure out of their limited time in the city — and maybe their limited time on earth; girls on the game hoping for one last trick before heading for their own bed and a proper undisturbed sleep; and the pampered rich to whom the war was but a mere irritation, emerging from the various drinking clubs that had proliferated since 1939 in cellars and private houses, to make their way home to their well feathered nests.

And thankfully there was always the odd solitary cab trawling the streets for trade. I managed to grab one of these motorized ghosts at the corner of Oxford Street and Tottenham Court Road and within fifteen minutes of leaving Hawke Towers I was ringing the bell of Raymond Carter's mews house. He'd obviously moved the corpse indoors as I'd suggested and there were certainly no bloodstains or any other signs to indicate that a dead body had lain on his doorstep.

The chimes had barely stopped bing-bonging before the door was wrenched open and an ashen-faced Raymond Carter dragged me indoors without a word. There on the hallway floor was the offending article: the unwanted corpse.

He was lying on his back, his vacant eyes staring sightless at the ceiling. The mouth was agape and a swollen purple tongue peered tentatively from the aperture. Kneeling down, I examined this unwelcome guest. He was a short, stout chap of around sixty and had been dead for some time. His skin was cold to the touch and rigor mortis was setting in. There were no wounds to the body that I could see apart from severe bruising around the neck which would suggest that the fellow had been strangled. There was little else to be detected by the naked eye. It was, as I'd thought, a job for the police. I had already considered the possibility, that Carter himself could be the killer and that this was an elaborate set up, involving me as an unsuspecting participant, to give him some kind of alibi. However, I had rejected it — for the moment at least. It was too contrived and unnecessary. If Carter had wanted to get rid of Arthur Keating why do it in such a melodramatic fashion? I know he was in show business, but that would be a step too far. Having a dead man planted on your premises is certainly not the way to deflect suspicion. And why involve a private detective, increasing the chance of being found out? I wasn't sure how good an actor my client was, but he seemed genuinely terrified and distraught by events. He stood by me as I examined the body, white-faced, clutching a tumbler of whisky which remained untouched, and shivering as though he was in the throes of a severe attack of double pneumonia.

I took Carter through to the sitting room, sat him down, instructed him to take a large gulp of the whisky to help settle his nerves and then tell me in detail exactly what had happened that night. He obeyed my instructions to the letter, reciting in dry emotionless tones the events that led up to him telephoning me, although I have to admit I was none the wiser after he'd finished. There was nothing in what he told me that came within a hundred miles of what we professionals call 'a clue'. However, what was clear was that whoever was making these threats against Carter had cranked the dial up several notches. This was no longer a matter of harassment or even blackmail. Cold-blooded murder is in the red zone at the top of the dial.

After finishing his account, my client flopped back in his chair and stared at me, waiting, I expect, for words of comfort, wisdom and explanation. I could not oblige. I knew there was only one course of action now and it was one that Carter feared.

'I'm afraid I shall have to call the police, Mr Carter . . . '

He opened his mouth to object but I held up my hand to stop him.

'If I don't I could be accused of attempting to pervert the course of justice. But apart from that, how would it look if you didn't tell the cops about a dead body in your house? And the body of a man you have issues with. A big fat finger with the word guilty stamped on it would eventually come around pointing in your direction. It could well be that the murderer himself will tip off the police if you try to sweep things under the carpet. You are innocent so don't act guilty. Although things may get tricky for a while, in the end you have nothing to fear.'

'To be accused of murder. That's what I

have to fear.' Now Carter became animated. Slapping the whisky tumbler down on the floor, he rose and began pacing up and down. 'Can't you see how even the suspicion of this could ruin me? Can't you see the headlines: Well-known Entertainer on Murder Charge?'

I could see the headlines.

It would seem that this is exactly what our mystery voice wanted. He was not only chipping away at Carter's sanity but his fame and fortune as well. It was an expertly calculated and executed plan.

'It need not be as bad as you suggest. If you had intended to kill Keating, you would hardly leave his corpse at your house and then ask a private detective around to examine it.' I didn't fully believe my own words. I knew that in many cases the police jumped to convenient and obvious conclusions whether they were the right ones or not. There was a war on after all and domestic crime needed to be cleaned up quickly and efficiently.

Carter dropped back down in his chair and ran his fingers through his hair. 'I know that you're right . . . but . . . it's all so unfair.'

I'm sure Arthur Keating would agree with you, I thought. But I kept that one to myself.

I glanced at my wristwatch. It was just coming up to 4 a.m. Still very early but really we couldn't wait for daylight before I made the call to Scotland Yard. Then I had an idea. They do bump into me now and then.

I told Carter to get dressed while I made a phone call. With a mooching reluctance he vanished into his bedroom and I took a few moments to take a more detailed observation of my surroundings. Pressed into choosing one word to describe the nature of Carter's little mews place, I would have plumped for 'opulent' as the most appropriate adjective. The sitting room was filled with expensive and stylish items, ultra modern sofas and sideboard, a gleaming drinks trolley, the latest oak-encased radiogram and what looked like a couple of ancient and valuable oil paintings. These were trappings of success, which were all down to the little wooden doll which sat amidst the splendour like a small god. I brushed away a small pang of jealousy and set about my task.

As I crossed to the telephone I couldn't help but smile at the thought of rousing my friend Detective Inspector David Llewellyn from his beauty sleep. Well, it was the unfortunate lot this night: Carter had been dragged from his slumbers; as a consequence so had I and now it was the turn of Inspector Llewellyn, whom I knew was not at his charming Welsh best in the early hours.

The phone was answered after the third ring.

'Llewellyn,' barked a grumpy and groggy voice.

'Hawke,' I responded in kind. 'Did I wake you?'

'Johnny, is that you?'

'It's me.'

'Yes, you did bloody wake me. Are you mad, man? Have you any idea what time it is?'

'Certainly. It's 4 a.m.'

'Is this some kind of weird joke, Johnny, because I warn you I am not in the mood.'

'It's no joke, I promise. I need your help.'

David groaned. 'What kind of scrape have you got yourself into now?'

'It's to do with a client. I need to report a murder.'

'Well, why don't you ring the duty desk at the Yard?'

'Because I want you to handle it. I need some sensitive hands on this one.'

'Flattery doesn't work on me at this time of the bloody morning,' he snapped back.

'Honestly, David, this is a bit tricky . . . '

'It always is with you, boyo.' He sighed heavily. 'Look, ring me back in five minutes. Give me time to grab a fag and a cuppa. Then I can take the call downstairs. There's no point in my wife having her night's sleep ruined as well as me.'

I did as he asked and when we spoke again, David sounded more alert and less tetchy.

'Right, tell me the story from the beginning,' he said.

I complied with his instructions and he listened without interruptions.

'Bloody hell, you pick your clients don't you?' he announced, with a bleak chuckle when I'd finished.

'Can you help? I want to keep tabs on this case. I don't think my client had anything to do with Arthur Keating's death and I'd like this affair to be kept from the papers for the time being at least.'

'Listen, Johnny, neither you nor I are King Canute. We can't keep the tide of the Press at bay. Something will sneak out. It always does. After all, this Keating character is a performer on the radio. He's not Joe Soap round the corner. He will be missed. Questions will be asked and answers will be found — not necessarily the ones you want. All I can say is that I'll do what I can . . . within the bounds of my official capacity. I know you think Carter is innocent, but *I* don't know that, do I? I have to treat this murder as I would any other.'

'I understand. I appreciate your help though.'

'Hey, you don't think he's putting the blame on Charlie Dokes, do you?' David gave a throaty chuckle.

In a sense I suppose he was.

'What now?'

'Stay where you are. Make sure your fellow does not tamper with any evidence and I'll be with you shortly. It will give me great pleasure to drag Sergeant Sunderland from his slumbers to bring him along with a couple of uniformed fellows for an initial look around before we get the body taken away to the Yard for an autopsy.'

While I'd been on the phone, Raymond Carter had dressed and covered the dead body up with a sheet.

'What now?' he asked, his pale face drawn and haunted.

'We wait for the police,' I said wearily, lighting up a cigarette.

8

Peter was dressed and ready for school by 7.30. It wasn't his favourite place in the world to go, but after all he had experienced in his short life it was tolerable at worst and sometimes quite enjoyable. As a small London school, it was filled with pupils not unlike himself, orphans or kids with only a mum or a dad at home, a parent who wasn't prepared to see their youngster being sent off into the country supposedly for safety's sake. Peter had been an evacuee and sent down to Devon. He had hated it. There in the country he had been the oddball orphan with the funny accent and ill-fitting hand-me-down clothes, the target for bullying and abuse. The other kids had made his life a misery and the grown ups had been oblivious to his torment. In the end, he'd run away and come back to the city to be with Johnny, his one-eyed friend. It was Johnny who had rescued him from all that evacuee nightmare and he, along with Nurse Susan McAndrew, had taken the place of his phantom parents. He'd never known his dad and he'd run away from his neglectful mother a couple of years before.

She was barely a memory now. It was a part of his life that he avoided revisiting.

Today Peter was ready for school much earlier than normal. As a rule he was like Shakespeare's schoolboy — a snail to school — but today was Thursday and this was special. It was the day when he could call at the newsagent's shop on his way to school and buy his weekly comics. This little venture was funded by Johnny who understood his joy and fascination with his picture papers; in fact they would sometimes read them together. Peter took *Radio Fun* and *The Beano*, mainly because his pals at school did, but his real top two favourites included *Tiger Blake Weekly* featuring his all time hero, the dare-devil adventurer, Dennis 'Tiger' Blake in a complete story in every issue. There was more writing in this paper than the others. It wasn't really a comic as it was packed with tiny print and the pictures were only used as illustrations to the text. It took Peter nearly a week to finish this one. But he delighted in savouring the exciting stories. It seemed that every week, Tiger Blake came near to winning the war as he cracked another Nazi spy ring or parachuted into Germany to rescue an Austrian scientist and his secret formula which would ensure success for the allies. Then came his best comic of all: *Charlie Dokes's Fun Paper*. This contained cartoon capers of many of the radio favourites along with two strips featuring 'the woodpecker's friend, Charlie Dokes and his pal Raymond Carter'. They were great fun and Peter read these first. Peter was also an avid listener to the wireless and he chuckled with delight every Wednesday night at 8.30 as he listened to Charlie's antics in the 'Okey Dokes' radio show.

The Horner Sisters, Edith and Martha, who looked after Peter and in whose house he lodged, knew by now that on Thursdays he would be ready for school a good half an hour earlier than usual so that he could race to the newsagent and have a read of his comics on the way to school. It amused the spinster sisters to see the eagerness with which their young charge downed his breakfast in order to speed off to the newsagent. On other weekdays, sometimes they had to call him down more than once and prise him from the house with moderate force to be sure he reached school on time.

But not on Thursdays.

The sisters had grown very fond of Peter. They had, by accident, become like surrogate aunts to him, part of the small circle of adults who cared and shared responsibility for the boy. They did more than house and feed him; they gave him a real sense of stability and domestic comfort. For the first time in his life he felt safe and loved. In return, he was no real trouble to the sisters and although he behaved as all twelve-year-old boys did, harbouring a few naughty traits, he also had a shy, polite manner and a surprisingly mature consideration for others that was endearing. As Edith Horner doled out his comic money, she observed that, 'Charlie Dokes is on at the Palladium in the West End. You ought to ask Johnny if he can get you seats.'

Peter felt a tingle of excitement. 'Crikey,' he exclaimed, his eyes widening with pleasure at the possibility of seeing Charlie Dokes in the flesh . . . as it were. 'That would be super,' he said, pocketing his comic money.

Peter felt sure that he could persuade Johnny to take him. He was well aware that in certain situations he had ways and means of manipulating his best friend — for that's how he viewed Johnny — into doing things. It certainly was not the case with Nurse McAndrew: she was more wary and canny. Peter liked her a lot, but he knew that she was much more strict and censorious than the relaxed and malleable Johnny.

The thought of sitting in the stalls of the Palladium and seeing Charlie Dokes on stage put an extra spring in Peter's step as he made his way to school, via the newsagents.

'You were very energetic last night,' observed Evelyn Munro with a sly grin as she applied her make-up in the dressing-table mirror.

The man in the bed behind her stirred, propped himself up on the pillow and reached for a pack of cigarettes on the bedside table before replying. 'The same could be said for you, sweetie.'

'Always happy to oblige a real man.'

'Thank you ma'am,' He gave a mock salute, before lighting a cigarette. 'Old Carter not servicing you as you would wish, then?'

Evie pulled a face in the mirror. 'You could say that,' she said, without a trace of embarrassment.

'I don't know how you put up with him. Why don't you ditch the creep?'

'Because of my career, darling,' she replied with an affected flourish. 'I've had more work and attention than ever since I've been on the show and I know it's because old Raymond has been putting good words for me with various producers. Just being seen around him gets you noticed. With any luck, I'll be on at the Palladium with him before the end of the run. I've sown the seeds. A suggestion here a hint there. Playing on his vanity.'

'Honey, you should get top billing at the

Palladium just for sleeping with the fellow.'

Evie smiled. 'Once I've really established a career for myself, that's when I can give Raymond the boot and then it'll just be you and me.'

'How cosy,' said the man without emotion, as he blew a series of smoke rings into the air.

Evelyn turned around and faced him, her face suddenly serious. 'You know that's what I really want, don't you? And you're the man to help me. You will, won't you?' There was a note of desperation in her voice now.

'Of course I will,' he replied absentmindedly, as he studied his hands. He flexed the long fingers and smiled at the memory of the satisfying task they had performed the previous night.

9

It was around nine in the morning when I wandered into Benny's café. It was wonderful to be back in familiar surroundings with the buzz of normality around me. Wartime normality that is. I was famished and desperate for some grub washed down with a mug of steaming hot dark-brown tea. Trade was brisk and the place was crowded. Benny was scuttling around the tables, like a man with his pants on fire, delivering breakfasts to his customers and scooping up dirty plates with practised aplomb. In recent months his trade had increased so much that he'd found it necessary — much to his own chagrin — to take on some help in the kitchen. 'Now I've got staff to pay for, my profits will plummet,' he moaned to me. His 'staff' consisted of a plump jovial lady of some seventy years called Doris. I never learned her second name and I don't think Benny did either. Doris appeared one day almost like a fairy godmother and she stayed. Now I reckoned Benny couldn't do without her. She became the heart and the engine of his establishment. As for Benny's profits plummeting, the reverse was the case. He never discussed anything as vulgar as finances with me, but it didn't need a business expert to see that the café was on the up and up. With Doris in charge of the cooking, the quality of the meals had improved also and the news got around. Even with the deprivations of rationing she could turn out a very decent shepherd's pie and her scones were a delight. However this morning I had my mind on eggs and bacon.

Benny saw me enter and hover by the till. With a broad grin, he waved me to a corner table. As I sat down, he flapped the tablecloth with his tea towel, sending a shower of errant crumbs flying into my lap rather than dispersing them.

'Johnny, my boy, good to see you,' he greeted me, oblivious that he had littered me with breakfast detritus. He leaned forward, a concerned look replacing the grin. 'But you look pale and decidedly thin. You need building up.'

This, I knew, was a none too subtle reference to the fact I'd not been in the café for nearly a week. As a friend of the old fellow, I was expected to support his establishment by visiting it every day. Size-wise, he wanted me to be Oliver Hardy, but I was more content as Stan Laurel.

'I've been up half the night . . . ' I said, by way of explanation of my peaky features.

'I knew you looked poorly. Malnutrition is just around the corner.'

'On a case.'

'Ah, so now you're an all-night detective.'

'Seems like it. So I'd appreciate tea and a plate of your finest bacon and eggs.'

'I got a few mushrooms I could slip on there too. Help prop open the eyelids, eh?'

I flashed him a toothy smile and he gave me a friendly squeeze on the shoulder before bustling off to the kitchen. I sat back in my chair and lit up a Craven A, suddenly feeling very tired, the hours of lost sleep overcoming me. My limbs ached and my head throbbed. I just wanted to sleep for ever, or at least forty-eight hours. But I knew I couldn't. As I watched the smoke from my cigarette corkscrew its way lazily to the ceiling I forced myself to review the night's events.

After I'd telephoned David, Raymond Carter had contacted his manager Larry Milligan to give him a potted version of events. I could not help catching the gist of their conversation. I could not help it because I made a point of staying in the room and listening. It seemed that Milligan was not pleased with the news. He was angry with his client for keeping him in the dark about the telephone threats and Carter's attempt to get Keating the sack. I couldn't catch everything that Milligan was saying on the other end of the phone, but from Carter's glum expression and his halting delivery which was being interrupted on a regular basis by the voice at the other end growing ever more strident, it was obvious that Milligan was in the process of blowing his top.

But then again, Milligan could be a good actor.

As he put the telephone down, Carter looked at me glumly and announced, 'He's coming over now. I'm afraid he doesn't really approve of you.'

I shrugged and gave a tight grin. 'Very few people do.'

'Well, I don't care what he says. I want you to stay on the case. Especially now.'

He cast a glance towards the hall door, beyond which was the still cooling corpse of Arthur Keating.

'That's fine by me, but you realize that ungainly bundle of trouble, I refer to your unwanted parcel out there, has put the kibosh on our little scenario where I was to play the role of your unassuming nephew. Now I'm going to be your private detective. That's going public. Sadly, people are very wary of the breed and tend to clam up and hold back.

It just makes getting at the truth a mite more difficult.'

Carter said nothing. But the sigh which caused his body to shudder was eloquent enough.

Milligan arrived before the police and taking time only to throw me a sour glance set about interrogating his client. He was a big, well-groomed man, with luxuriant hair neatly swept back and glossy with pomade. I reckoned that although he couldn't have reached the age of thirty yet, his sideboards and the neat Clark Gable moustache were touched with grey. He had an assured manner worn almost like a lapel badge which seemed to say I can cope with anything you throw at me and if it gets too tough, I can walk away from all this. Check my contract.

Although Milligan must have dressed in a hurry, he was immaculately attired in a well-cut three-piece brown tweed suit with a yellow silk tie and matching pocket handkerchief. There must, I suggested to myself, be money in this managing business. I looked down at my own crumpled pinstripe affair with some dismay. More money than in the detective game anyway.

He took a quick look at the corpse of Keating in the hallway. He gave a cry more of disgust than dismay and returned to the sitting room. Slipping a silver cigarette lighter from his pocket and lighting up a small cigar, Milligan paced the carpet while he continued to question Carter about 'this most unfortunate affair'.

'And you have no idea who might be making these threats? Or why?' he asked.

Carter shook his head.

'No man is without enemies, Raymond. There must be someone you've upset in the past.'

'Not enough to want to kill me because of it. It's quite clear that whoever murdered Keating did it in order to drop me in the dung. It takes a peculiar . . . a strange mind to carry out such a plan. It suggests insanity — wouldn't you agree, Mr Hawke?'

We'd been over this ground between the two of us before Milligan arrived. To my mind insanity was too easy an answer. There was cunning and cold-bloodedness here which required a clever and determined mind rather than a mad one. But Mr Manager was right, whoever had killed Keating and dumped him on Carter's doorstep had a deep hatred of the ventriloquist.

I shrugged my shoulders in response to the question and then realizing that perhaps this wasn't an adequate response, I added, 'It's possible. But madmen are usually more obvious. I suppose *you* have no idea who might want to harm Raymond, do you, Mr Milligan?'

He raised an eyebrow in surprise — surprise I suspect, that I'd had the nerve to address him directly.

'Of course not!' he snapped, and puffed peevishly on his cigar.

'That was rather a quick response. You said yourself that no man is without enemies. For example, there must be many jealousies in the world of show business . . . '

'Well, yes there are . . . but it's a big leap from jealousy, or harbouring a grudge against a particular artiste, to actually committing murder.'

'But some do make the leap.'

'Maybe, but I know of none. My client is well respected in the profession.'

Milligan had changed his tune very quickly. Only moments before he was badgering Raymond Carter to come up with a name of someone who might have it in for him. Now I was getting the public face, the official stance, in readiness no doubt for the police and possibly the Press. Something told me that I did not like Mr Milligan terribly much.

He loured over Carter in the armchair like defending counsel. 'What we have to make sure is that the police do not link you publicly with the murder. It could do you irreparable harm.'

'That's easier said than done,' I suggested. 'The dead body is here in the house.'

Milligan groaned. 'If only you had phoned me first,' he said.

'What good would that have done?' asked Carter.

'We could have moved the body. Thrown it in the river or something.'

'I'll pretend I didn't hear that,' I said.

Milligan threw me a dirty look, but I didn't catch it.

At that moment there was a heavy hammering on the front door in accompaniment to the bell ringing insistently.

It was the police in the shape of Inspector David Llewellyn, Sergeant Sunderland and two bulky constables. I obliged with the introductions. David nodded briskly, very much in professional mode and not at all like the relaxed drinking pal I was familiar with. Without further ado, he pulled back the sheet and examined the body, coming to the same conclusions as I had that the fellow had been strangled.

'OK, lads, take him out,' he instructed the constables. 'We'll get him to the Yard for a proper medical examination.'

The two uniformed officers carried the

body out from the hall to the waiting vehicle.

'Right, Mr Carter, I think it's time we had a little chat. I want to hear all about it,' David said, leading the pale-faced ventriloquist back into the sitting room.

Sitting with his hands resting limply in his lap and staring at the carpet, Raymond Carter recalled the events of the past few days, the phone calls, the message on the script and finally the discovery of the body. David listened intently, while Sunderland made notes. When Carter had finished, David chewed his lips for a while digesting the information he'd been given and then he turned to me. 'What's your take on this?'

'The obvious scenario. Someone's out to damage Mr Carter's reputation,' I said simply, not wanting to discuss my ideas on the case in any detail in front of my client and particularly his pompous manager.

With a sudden movement, David rose to his feet. 'Right, well, I'm afraid you'll have to come down to the Yard with us to make an official statement, Mr Carter, and then, for the moment, you'll be free to go.'

Before Carter could respond, Milligan chipped in, 'I'll need to come along, too, to protect my client's interests.'

A ghost of a smile softened David's features. 'You can bring the ruddy doll as well

94

if you like,' he said, nodding towards the chair in the corner where Charlie Dokes was sitting, an unnerving silent witness to all that had taken place in the room. As I gazed at that immobile wooden face with the knowing eyes and malevolent fixed grin, I fully expected it to make some sarcastic comment, but for once Charlie remained silent.

While Sergeant Sunderland escorted Carter and his limpet manager to the police car outside, David and I had a few quiet words together.

'You reckon he's telling the truth, eh?' my friend asked.

'About the body, certainly. Only an idiot would dump his murder victim on his own doorstep. I know a clever idiot might do it to put us off the scent, but I don't think that this is the case here. Carter has much more to lose than gain by Keating's death.'

David nodded in agreement. 'You say that he's telling the truth about the body, implying that he wasn't about the other things. What d'you mean?'

'I'm not sure. But it stands to reason that if someone is desperate to hurt you, desperate enough to murder, you would have some idea who it might be. It can't be a complete stranger, can it? There must be something in his past. Someone . . . '

David frowned but did not reply.

'One thing is certain, I don't think it stops here,' I continued. 'Whoever our murderer is, he's not done yet — not until he has destroyed our friend, Raymond Carter.' Instinctively, I glanced over at Charlie Dokes. 'Perhaps the dummy knows the answer,' I said.

★ ★ ★

By the time I had run these events through my mind, Benny had returned with my breakfast. 'When Doris knew it was you, she scooped up an extra rasher,' he said.

'Give her a kiss from me.'

'I will do nothing of the kind. She'll think I'm some kind of flirty old man.'

'I reckon she knows that already.'

Benny laughed and flushed a little. Just then the door of the café opened as two customers entered, allowing a sharp draught of November chill to sneak in with them.

'Busy, busy,' beamed Benny, eyeing the couple. 'See you later, Johnny,' he said, moving swiftly to greet his new customers.

Without further hesitation, I set about appeasing my hunger. After a long tiring night, this was just what I needed: warm bacon — brittle and lean just as I liked it — a runny fried egg mopped up with a couple of slices of toast lightly smeared with something approaching the colour and consistency of margarine but not quite reaching the taste. The whole glorious ensemble was washed down with scalding hot tea. Ah, the simple pleasures. A feeling of relaxed contentment swept over me and, for a brief interval, dead bodies, threatened clients and even the war seemed far away and irrelevant. Of course, such moments are fleeting and by the time I was indulging in a post-prandial cigarette, the cold, harsh fingers of reality were already beginning to squeeze the sense of cosy languor out of me. I had an investigation to carry out: people to see and if possible a murderer to find before the devious devil took it in to his head to kill again.

As I left Benny's café, with these thoughts in my mind, the sumptuous hot breakfast I'd enjoyed was lying like lead in my stomach.

10

It was nearly noon when Raymond Carter returned home from Scotland Yard. They had kept him and Larry waiting around for ages in a damp and draughty room with the dimensions of a cupboard before Llewellyn had interviewed him and then he'd made his statement. On Larry's advice he had not involved the services of a solicitor. 'The fewer outsiders that are involved at this stage the better,' Milligan had advised, unable to keep the growl out of his voice. The ventriloquist had been too tired to raise any disagreement.

Carter was asked the same questions he'd been asked at the house and he had given the same answers. It was a weary and wearing process. He could understand why some people might confess in such a situation just so that it could all be over. It was like some kind of mind-numbing repetitive torture. Eventually they had let him go with the veiled understanding that, 'No doubt we will need to speak to you again, Mr Carter.'

Milligan and he parted company just beyond the gates of Scotland Yard. 'Get some rest and put the whole business out of your mind,' said Milligan.

'Easy advice to give; not exactly easy to administer. Not after the night I've had.'

'Work at it. At least you can be content in the knowledge that your desire to get Arthur Keating out of the show has come about. You won't have to put up with his drunken antics any more.'

Carter pulled a pained expression and went off in search of a cab.

★   ★   ★

Once indoors, Carter slumped down on his sofa clutching a large glass of whisky. He took a long hard gulp, enjoying the feeling of fire in his throat. It was somewhat painful and therefore in a strange way rather pleasing. He took another mouthful and the whisky went down the wrong way. He began to splutter and cough, ejecting some of the alcohol in a fine spray.

He slumped back with a grin at his own incompetence.

'Steady as she goes, Cap'n,' said Charlie Dokes, from the chair in the corner.

'And you can shut up for a start.'

'Well, that's up to you, of course. You're the chatterbox . . . *really*. I'm just the one who gets all the laughs.'

'I said shut up.'

'And, of course, I don't get arrested for murder.'

'Just shut up, will you!' Carter barked furiously.

'You've got to shut up first,' said the doll.

Suddenly Carter gave a snarl of rage. He rushed across the room, snatched up the dummy and began shaking it.

Charlie Dokes's immobile face stared defiantly back at Carter. And then the mouth dropped open emitting what sounded like a faint giggle.

A strange irrational fear took hold of Carter. What was happening to him? Did he make the blasted doll giggle . . . or did Charlie do it on his own? Was the creature taunting him?

How could he consider such a thing? Charlie Dokes was an inanimate doll made of wood and papier mâché.

And yet the bastard had a mind of its own.

It was time he was silenced.

Fury seized Carter and he grabbed the doll by the neck as though he was trying to strangle it. So violent were his actions that the head came away from the doll's body which slipped to the floor.

'Now look what you've done,' said Charlie,

as Carter staggered back on to the sofa still clutching the dismembered head.

Tears sprang to his eyes and misted his view. 'Now look what you've done,' he sobbed in his own voice.

★ ★ ★

Some thirty minutes later, more sober and much chastened, Carter reunited Charlie's head with the rest of him and checked that there was no damage done. He refrained from apologizing for his actions because for the moment he couldn't bear for the doll to speak back to him.

Carter had just propped Charlie up in his usual chair when the doorbell rang. He groaned. Who is it now he thought? After the morning he'd had he just wanted to have some rest — a sleep. He had a show to do tonight. He had to go on a stage in front of hundreds of people and be funny while at the same time being suspected of murder. These thoughts pummelled his brain as he made his reluctant way to the door.

It was Al Warren — bright and breezy as usual. 'Hello, there. Mr Carter, sir. I've just called round for an autograph and a cheese sandwich and maybe a big gin and tonic and if you have one of those pretty showgirls to spare . . . 'Warren stopped his patter when he observed the tired, grey features of Carter gazing back at him.

'Say, you look as though you've been up all night.'

'That's because I have.'

'Those pretty showgirls, eh?'

'It's not a joke, Al. Arthur Keating has been murdered.'

'What!'

'Come into the sitting room. I'll get you that drink and fill you in.'

When Carter had recounted the events of the previous night to yet another audience, he sat back with a sigh. He had cut out all the information about the warning phone calls and the death threats. That, he reckoned, needed to be kept private for now. Only he, Larry, the police and Johnny Hawke knew about that side of the affair. And the bastard who was making the calls, of course.

Even as he ran these names through his mind, Carter was shocked how the circle had grown so big in a matter of a few days. A few hours really.

Al Warren said nothing for a while. He just sat clinking the ice against the side of his glass. 'That's rough,' he said eventually, his expression registering an awareness that his response was somewhat inadequate. 'Let's hope they catch the devil who did it post haste.'

Carter nodded. 'And it wasn't me!'

'No, of course not. I know you didn't care for the fellow, but I don't see you as an axe-wielding murderer.'

'He was strangled.'

Al smiled. 'There is that, too. Actually I came round to discuss next week's show, but I reckon you've got other things on your mind at the moment. We can leave it for a day.'

'Look, Al, I trust you with the show. Just for once let's skip the discussion. You do what you like with Charlie . . . '

Instinctively both men turned to the dummy in the corner.

'I had some ideas about those pretty showgirls as well,' said Charlie.

'You're far too young, my lad,' said Al. 'And, besides, your performance in the bedroom is somewhat wooden.'

Carter laughed. For the first time in a long while it seemed.

'I appreciate your trust . . . ' said Al, his expression suddenly darkening.

'Al, without you I wouldn't be here today. Remember when we first met? I was dying on my feet with material that Moses had gathered on his way to picking up the Ten Commandments. Your bright ideas and your clever scripts got me where I am.'

'Why, thank you, kind sir.' Al appeared embarrassed and covered this by taking a large gulp of gin.

'I mean it,' continued Carter, recent events loosening his emotions. He was fully aware that this funny chap with the strange mid-Atlantic tones was the main reason he was the success that he was and he was conscious that perhaps he did not acknowledge it enough, especially to Al himself.

'Well,' said Al, in a brisk tone, appearing embarrassed and really wanting to get back to the matter in hand, 'I intend to run with that idea I mentioned last week about you trying to raise some cash to take your girlfriend out for a meal in a swanky restaurant by checking Charlie into a pawn shop and then losing the claim ticket.'

Carter grinned. 'That seems fine.'

'Of course, I'll have to write some extra material to fill Arthur's spot, but I'll need to speak to Edward, our beloved producer, about that.'

'Sure.' Just at the moment Carter didn't care and the tone of his voice clearly indicated as much.

'Well, I reckon I'll mosey along and let you get some rest.'

'Thanks.'

Al rose, but before leaving the room, he went across to Charlie and ruffled his synthetic hair. 'Bye, young man. Be good.'

'Where's the fun in that?' said Charlie.

After Al had gone, Carter decided that he would actually go to bed and try to grab a couple of hours' sleep. As he slipped under the covers he found his mind wandering back to Al Warren. He not only admired the young man's talent, he envied him, too. He was such a bright uncomplicated fellow. He was English, but had spent the first twenty years of his life in California, hence his strange drawl and easy attitude to life. Nothing seemed to ruffle his smooth feathers. As a youngster Warren had loved American radio and listening to all those quick-fire cross talk comedy shows; these had given him the grounding and inspiration to become a scriptwriter himself. After some minor success in the States, he'd travelled to Britain to try his luck. But, Carter mused, it was the fact that Al had lit upon a clapped-out vent act to try out his magic that made Carter really the lucky one. Whenever he contemplated his sudden rise to fame and success, a dark unnerving thought always crept into his mind: what if Al deserted him? What if his Svengali got a better offer or just grew tired of churning out gags for a wooden dummy?

What would Raymond Carter do then? Oh, yes, there were other scriptwriters, but no one quite like Al Warren.

He tried to brush away these unsettling worries and slipped further under the covers. In the end tiredness won the day and he found himself beginning to doze, his mind smoothing into a blank canvas. He was just surrendering to the realms of deep sleep when he was brought to full consciousness with a start. The phone bellowed at him from the bedside table. It was like the cry of a wounded animal demanding attention. Answering the telephone had now become a frightening ordeal for Carter. For some moments he let it ring, hoping, praying that it would stop. But it didn't. The fierce jangling noise stabbed like a knife into his brain until he could take it no longer and in a sudden jerky movement he snatched the receiver from the cradle and held it to his ear, his heart pounding in his chest.

'I know you're there Raymond. I — can — hear — you — breathing.' It was the voice of Charlie Dokes. He gave a little characteristic giggle before continuing. 'I won't keep you long, my friend. I just wanted you to know that I haven't finished with you yet.' Another giggle and the line went dead.

Carter sat up in bed for some moments,

still clutching the receiver, his knuckles white with the pressure of his grip. At length he put the phone down and slowly got out of bed. His mind was numb with a kind of frustrated despair and he walked zombie-like towards the door. He needed another drink. That's all he could decide at the present.

As he made his way across the sitting room towards the kitchen, he automatically cast a glance to the chair where Charlie Dokes was sitting. But he wasn't sitting there. The chair was empty. Carter felt his chest tighten and his legs grow weak. What on earth was happening? Where was Charlie? His head swung round, frantically surveying the room, his eyes finally lighting upon the dummy, those dark lifeless eyes were staring, Carter thought, straight at him in an accusing fashion. To the ventriloquist's horror, he saw that Charlie was now sitting on a chair next to the telephone.

11

After leaving the womb-like warmth and comfort of Benny's café I padded my way round to Broadcasting House. The walk and the sharp winter air were excellent stimulants to my thought processes, further enhanced by a good smoke. I reckoned that my field of suspects was a fairly narrow one. Whoever was playing nasty games with Raymond Carter must have been present at the rehearsal for his last radio show as they had scrawled the warning message on his script. Already one of those present had been eliminated from my enquiries — literally. If it was the killer's intention to knock off the other members of the team one by one, he would rather obviously reveal himself eventually. This was highly unlikely and I didn't really want to wait to see if this happened. It wouldn't do my reputation as a keen-minded sleuth much good for a start. However, I knew this was an improbable scenario. Carter was the real target of hate and I felt sure it wouldn't be long before the killer made an attempt on his life. Above all, I must prevent that from happening.

What didn't encourage me as I ran the names of the possible suspects through my head was the realization that I really didn't have an inkling which one of them could be the murderer.

Well, I had to start somewhere and so I thought I'd have a few words with Edward Simmons, the producer of the programme. He could fill me in with details of all the cast while, I hoped, revealing something of himself.

As I strolled up Regent's Street towards Langham Place, the imposing curved edifice of Broadcasting House hove into view, like some great landlocked vessel. Thank God, I thought that the Jerries had failed to destroy this valuable establishment. Not that they hadn't tried and in 1940 they had scored a hit but thankfully the damage was minimal. The frontage still bore the blackened scars of the raid, but the building and its service survived. It was the lifeblood of the nation, providing news and information to the population as well as stress-relieving music and entertainment. Without the radio, the war, hell though it was, would have presented a far grimmer prospect.

Spinning my fag end into the gutter, I passed between the portals of the great institution. The foyer of Broadcasting House is opulent: marble walls and pillars reaching high to the decorated ceiling. It has all the hushed glamour of the very best of hotels. I was stopped by a tall fellow with the chest of a buffalo dressed in a commissionaire's uniform. He asked to see my papers and enquired what my business was at the BBC. He was polite but wary. I reckoned that one wrong word or gesture and he'd have had my arm up my back and out on the pavement before you could say Tommy Handley.

On establishing that I was kosher — or as kosher as a shabby, one-eyed private detective in a cheap crumpled suit can be — he directed me to the enquiry desk. Here a plump-faced young woman with bulging cheeks and pursed bee-stung lips peered at me through a pair of thick bifocal spectacles. She looked like a bossy goldfish. I explained that I was a private detective investigating the murder of Arthur Keating and I wanted to speak with the producer of the Okey Dokes show, Mr Edward Simmons. The girl's cheeks bulged even more. ' Mr Keating is dead?' she said, her voice rising in pitch.

'I'm afraid so.'

'How dreadful. He was such a gentleman. He always raised his hat to me when he passed.'

I nodded in a sympathetic manner.

'How . . . how did he . . . pass away?'

'I'm not at liberty to go into details, I'm afraid.' I leaned further forward and lowered my voice to a harsh whisper. 'It's all rather hush hush.'

Her fish eyes widened with excitement. 'Really!' she said, matching my scratchy croak. 'How fascinating.' I could see from the dreamy look on her face that the mixture of death of a radio performer and a private detective seemed to have tipped her over into the realms of fantasy.

'Mr Simmons?' I prompted, attempting to bring her back on track.

'Oh, yes,' she said quickly, resuming her business-like pose. 'I'll ring him and see if he is free.'

She turned round to the little switchboard behind her and plugged in a line. Before long she was holding a brief conversation with someone — Simmons no doubt — but her back was still towards me so that I couldn't hear what she was saying.

Finally she swung round. Her face had resumed its officious immobility. 'Mr Simmons says he's very busy but if you'll go up now he can give you five minutes.'

Five minutes! We'd barely have got the formal introductions over with before he was showing me the door. Well, it was a situation

I'd encountered many times before. Folk are reluctant to give me much of their time but very rarely do they refuse to see me at all in case their actions appear suspicious. But I had my methods of extending interviews to as long as I wanted.

I grinned back at Miss Goldfish. 'Five minutes will be fine. Where do I go?'

Her eyes rolled erratically. 'Oh, this place is a warren. I'll get Gareth to take you to Mr Simmons's office.'

I expected Gareth to be a fresh-faced errand boy just out of short trousers. Instead he was the oldest man on the planet. His body had curved with age into the shape of a question mark. It would be wrong to say he moved at a snail's pace; that would be insulting to snails.

'You got some snout?' asked Gareth, in a wheezy Cockney drawl as we made our way towards the lift.

I passed him a cigarette. 'Ta, mate. They pay me peanuts here, y'know. I make some of it up by cadging fags and stuff. You ain't got any spare food coupons as well, 'ave you?'

I grinned surreptitiously. 'Sorry, no.'

'Pity that. Another fag then,' he said, ushering me into the lift.

I obliged.

'Mr Simmons was it?'

'Yes.'

'That's third floor, corridor seven, room 6a. You'd never find it on yer own.' He emitted a chesty chuckle. 'We've had folk in walking around this building for days trying to find their way out. It's like the Hampton Court maze.' His laughter increased, shaking his frail frame so much I feared that he would fall over.

The lift whirred to a stop and we got out. Slowly but not all that surely Gareth led me down a series of dimly lighted corridors until we reached a door marked '6a'.

'This is Mr Simmons's office. I'll wait here until you finished and then take you back.'

'Oh, that's not really necessary,' I said.

'Look, mate, you're my responsibility. We don't want you wandering around 'til the war's over looking for the exit, do we?' His ancient face split open with a hoarse roar of laughter. 'Let me out, let me out,' he mimicked.

I could not help but chuckle.

'I'll have your fag while I wait,' he added.

I knocked on the door and a high-pitched cry followed seconds later. 'Come in.'

It was a tiny room with several metal filing cabinets on which were piled reams of paper which at a casual glance looked liked scripts. There was a tiny desk behind which sat a young man with unruly nut-brown hair and the inquisitive peer of a benevolent short-sighted owl. He was dressed in a tweed jacket and wore a brightly coloured bow tie which I feared may light up and whiz round at any second. Despite his rather flamboyant appearance and hesitant manner, I guessed that Mr Simmons was no one's fool. I assumed you needed talent and a steely determination to become the producer of the most popular comedy show on radio at such a young age.

As I neared his desk he rose and thrust out his hand in a friendly fashion.

'Ed Simmons,' he said. 'You must be Hawke, the private 'tec helping to look after our boy.'

'John Hawke,' I nodded, shaking his hand.

'Do take a seat. I will help all I can, of course, but we'll have to be brief. One of our cast members . . . oh, well, of course you know. That's why you're here, I suppose. I've already had the chaps round from Scotland Yard this morning asking questions.'

David didn't waste much time.

'About Arthur Keating's murder, yes.'

Simmons winced at the word 'murder'.

'I'll try not to take up too much of your time, Mr Simmons, but of course we both want to help Mr Carter and get to the bottom of this unpleasant business.'

'Of course. Of course.' He nodded his head nervously and his mop of hair flapped backwards and forwards as though it had been caught in a stiff breeze. 'I'm not sure I can help you that much. I only have what you might call a professional relationship with Mr Carter. We don't meet socially or anything like that. I've only known him for about six months, since I started work on the Okey Dokes show.'

'I gather he came to see you privately yesterday about Arthur Keating.'

Simmons twisted his mouth awkwardly. 'Yes. In the light of events that's rather unfortunate. They had never really hit it off, those two. I don't think it was personal just professional rivalry. Raymond thought that Arthur was unreliable because he drank more than was good for him or his performance and was mugging too much on the show and . . . well . . . '

'Getting too many laughs.'

The eyes narrowed behind the glasses. 'I suppose you could put it like that. Raymond is very nervous about his career. He has been around a long time and spent many years in the wilderness and then at the age of forty-something he suddenly becomes what you might call a star overnight. I think he's terrified that it all may, equally, disappear overnight as well. If he sees any threat to his position, he must do something about it.'

'And he saw Arthur Keating as a threat.'

Simmons pursed his lips in a sudden movement and his bow tie stood to attention. 'In a way. It has happened many times before in this business: a supporting player stealing the thunder from the star. I think Raymond saw Arthur as getting too popular in his spot for comfort. Keating was an old soak, of course, but he never disgraced himself on air, which is the important thing.'

'So Raymond asked you to sack him.'

'He insisted.'

'And you agreed.'

Simmons shook his head. 'I produce the show. I make those decisions.' Suddenly, for a moment, the amiable, soft-faced young man disappeared to be replaced by a hard-faced bully. And then Simmons grinned awkwardly as though he realized he had unwisely let the mask slip. 'Besides I couldn't,' he said casually. 'I work for the BBC and have to abide by their contracts. Arthur was signed up for the full series. There was no way I could drop him now . . . not without the most terrible legal kerfuffle. No, Arthur Keating had to stay.'

I got the impression that if Simmons had

116

wanted Keating out, he'd have been out, despite his BBC contract.

'So Raymond Carter killed Keating in frustration to ensure that he wouldn't appear again on his radio show.'

'My God, is that what you think?'

I permitted myself a thin smile. 'No, that is not what I think, but I suspect that is what the murderer wants us, and the police in particular, to think. Tell me, is Raymond Carter well liked by the cast and crew?'

Simmons hesitated for a moment before replying. It was as though the question had completely foxed him. His face had lost its animation and his brow furrowed, putting a good five years on him. 'I honestly believe that they have no strong feelings either way. Raymond is a fairly quiet and private man. It's that rather nasty dummy of his that does all the talking.'

'But the dummy *is* Raymond.'

'Well, yes, I suppose he is, but he really seems to have a different personality from Raymond.' He shook his head as though puzzled at this strange confession and then cast an embarrassed smile in my direction. 'However,' he said after a pause, 'if you are asking me if anyone disliked Raymond enough to set him up for a murder charge then I would have to say no. To be honest the man is rather a blank.'

'But you dislike Charlie Dokes . . . '

'I detest him. I simply do not see the appeal of the blasted doll. He's rude, objectionable and has no saving graces.'

'You talk about him as though he were real. As though he has an independent personality.'

'I'm aware it's crazy, but yes, that's how I think of him. Oh, I know he is fuelled by the clever scripts that Al gives him — Al Warren our script writer — but there is something about Charlie that is eerily self sufficient. I suppose it is as though Raymond Carter had a split personality.'

Oh, oh, I thought, this is uncharted psychological territory and I don't have a map or a compass. I don't even have an inkling. But the worrying thought suddenly struck me that all I had to go on in this whole business was Raymond Carter's word about the phone calls. He could have made the whole thing up as a smokescreen for murder. Of course I had seen the script with the warning message scribbled on it, but Carter could quite easily have written that himself. What if it really was Charlie Dokes who was making these phone calls? What if Carter was really speaking to himself — one half of a split personality threatening the other? I had witnessed for myself how master and dummy had engaged in banter. And now here was Simmons making the point that he saw Carter and Charlie Dokes as two separate entities — two separate individuals. It would be a neat case for Dr Freud rather than Johnny Hawke. But there was the certain matter of a dead man. Charlie couldn't have been responsible for that also . . . could he?

I felt a headache coming on. Nevertheless, I had to probe further.

'What is Carter's relationship with Charlie Dokes like?' I felt rather stupid in asking the question but now we had wandered into surreal-land, I might as well.

The answer was equally bizarre. 'They get on well enough. Of course Charlie's character was essentially created by Al. Before Charlie came on the scene, Raymond had been touring the halls for years with a dummy called Tommy Trumble. He was a completely different kettle of fish from Charlie. Tommy was a simpleton who always got the wrong end of the stick, misused words and never really understood what Raymond was talking about.'

'Whereas now Charlie is the smart one.'

Simmons nodded. '*Très* smart.'

'Where is Tommy now?'

'Who knows? In a dustbin somewhere. I'm

sure that Raymond hasn't got him. He wouldn't want to be reminded of his years of failure. And I suspect Charlie wouldn't allow his rival to be around.'

I lit a cigarette to give me a moment to contemplate the nature of this weird conversation in which we were discussing two ventriloquist's dolls as though they were real, as though they had motivations of their own, as though they were human. It was time to direct things back to the mundane.

'What about friends? Does Raymond have many?'

'Friends? Not really. Not that I know of anyway. There are his associates, of course. He spends a fair bit of time with Larry Milligan, his manager and Al. It's strange, but despite his youth, Al has been a mentor to Raymond. With his scripts he's guided him up that fickle ladder to stardom.'

'What about girlfriends?'

Simmons stroked his chin and his eyes twinkled. 'I can't be sure, but I have a feeling that he's 'seeing' our soubrette in the show.'

The word soubrette was a new one on me. It sounded nice. I assumed this to be the pretty singer, Evelyn Munro.

When I mentioned her name, Simmons gave me a vague nod.

'Is it serious?'

'Oh, I doubt it. There's nearly twenty years' difference in their ages. I would think our Evie is hitching a ride on a star wagon for the time being — but then I'm rather a cynical bastard. That sort of thing helps at the BBC.' He glanced at his watch in a theatrical fashion, almost as if he was following a stage direction. 'I think that's about as much as I can tell you . . . and I really have rather a lot on.'

'That's fine,' I said stubbing out my cigarette in an enormous glass ashtray on his desk. 'If you think of anything else, please get in touch.' I handed him one of my cards. I knew it would be in the wastepaper bin within seconds of my leaving the room but I had to go through the motions. You never know.

Gareth was waiting for me when I left Simmons's office. He was sitting on a chair opposite the door and looked for all the world as if he was asleep, but as soon as I emerged, he raised himself slowly into what was for him a standing position.

'Follow me,' he said, addressing my chest and then creeping forward down the corridor.

By the time I left that maze of a building Gareth had cadged further two cigarettes from me.

12

When Raymond Carter eventually answered the door, Evelyn Munro could tell that he was far from sober. His stance was uncertain and she could smell the whisky on his breath.

'You took your time coming round,' he snapped by way of greeting, as he swayed gently like someone on a rickety escalator. 'No doubt you've heard what's happened. That bastard Keating has got himself killed.'

Evelyn brushed past him and walked into the sitting room. Carter wandered in after her.

She turned on him, her face flushed with anger. 'Thanks for the welcome! If you must know I stayed away deliberately, in case the police were here. I didn't want to add to your problems. But I've been ringing you for the last few hours and there's been no reply.'

'I've stopped answering the phone. It seems . . . to give me a headache.'

His words were slurred and his eyes partially glazed.

'My God, Raymond, you've a show to do tonight. How much have you had to drink?'

Instinctively his eyes wandered to the bottle

of Scotch on the sideboard. It was half empty. 'Not enough,' he mumbled. And then in the same inebriated mumble, Charlie Dokes who was still positioned by the telephone, echoed the words; 'Not enough.'

Evelyn felt a hot surge of annoyance and frustration at Carter's stupid drunken behaviour. She could, of course, leave him to his fate. The Arthur Keating murder story had not been picked up by the Press yet, but Carter's failure to perform at the Palladium would certainly make the papers and then it wouldn't be long before some clever soul connected the two events, coming up with a damaging equation. It was the path to self-destruction. Family entertainment and murder don't mix. Show-business fame and public approval were fickle and sensitive. They were easily blown away by the winds of rumour and implication. For this to happen now was too soon for her. She hadn't finished with Carter yet. She needed him to be useful to her for a little while longer. She wasn't prepared to let that potential slip through her fingers so easily. And apart from that — if there were any scandal it may very well reflect badly on her. Some savvy creep from the gutter Press would dig up the truth about their relationship and no doubt embellish it in the process.

Grabbing his arm roughly, she dragged him towards the kitchen. 'You've done with whisky for today. We've got to get lots of black coffee down you. Sober you up. You and that damned doll of yours have to go on stage tonight and make people laugh.'

Carter allowed himself to be manoeuvred by Evelyn into the kitchen where he slumped down on a wicker chair. The one small part of his brain that had retained a vestige of clear thinking and common sense knew she was right. And besides he hadn't the energy now to fight back. The whisky had brought on an overwhelming sense of drowsiness. He just wanted to sail away on dreams and leave the real world of complications and pain behind. He was almost asleep by the time Evelyn handed him his first cup of coffee. She had to hold it up to his lips to get the scalding liquid into his mouth. Like a baby he took the coffee, mug after mug of it, until slowly the first flags of sobriety were seen fluttering on the far horizon. Eventually he was able to take the mug in his own hands and drink unaided.

As the coffee gradually nullified the effects of whisky, Carter began to feel foolish and guilty. He glanced at his watch. It was five o'clock. He had just under an hour before it was time for him to leave for the theatre. He ought to get himself ready — change his clothes. Impulsively, he rose to his feet and immediately sank back down again. His legs weren't quite ready yet.

Evelyn shook her head, her face registering a mixture of disgust and dismay.

'Can you get me a cigarette?' he asked, his voice still shaky around the edges.

'After you've drunk another cup of coffee.'

He half smiled. 'Are you trying to drown me?'

'I think I'd like to,' she said, handing him another mug. 'What on earth has got into you, Ray? Are you on some sort of suicide mission?'

He shook his head. 'I just got a bit down about Keating's death and how it might damage the show . . . start rumours.' Even affected by alcohol as he was, he was still certain that he didn't want Evie to know about the phone calls. The fewer people who knew about those infernal things the better.

'Getting pie-eyed and missing a show is hardly going to do you any good in the eyes of the public or the police.'

He nodded vigorously and took a gulp of coffee. 'Now how about that fag?'

She snapped open her handbag and retrieved a packet of Senior Service. She lit a cigarette and passed it to him. He gave a sigh of pleasure as he inhaled hard, feeling the soothing smoke billow into his lungs. 'I think I'm beginning to feel human.'

'Well, there's a first time for everything,' said Evie, mimicking the voice of Charlie Dokes.

Carter dropped the mug in shock.

'Now, look what you've done,' she said.

'Why did you do that?' cried Carter, staggering to his feet, his eyes wide with fear.

'Do what?'

'Talk like Charlie. You talked like Charlie.'

Evie seemed puzzled. 'It was a little joke, that's all. What's the big deal?'

'You sounded just like . . . just like him.'

Evie laughed out loud. 'So? Hey, Raymond . . . maybe it wasn't me. Maybe it *really* was Charlie.' And then going into the dummy's voice again, she added, 'What d'you think about that, Ray, old boy?'

This last little touch caused Carter to snap. The trauma of the phone calls crashed down on him, galvanizing his body. He stepped towards the girl, his mind now chillingly clear and his legs functioning as normal. In a careful and precise fashion, he hit Evelyn across the face.

She staggered back in shock and let out a sharp cry. In truth it was a cry of surprise rather than pain. She had never expected

126

Raymond to hit her ever and certainly not for a little joke. The man must be off his head.

As soon as he had done it, Raymond Carter regretted his actions. He knew immediately that he had been dangerously foolish.

'I'm sorry . . . Evie. I'm . . . sorry. I didn't mean to . . . '

'Didn't mean to, eh? Well, you bloody well did, didn't you?' She glared at him, her eyes moist with tears — but they were not tears of sadness or regret but tears of anger. 'But I'll tell you this, you crazy bastard,' she continued, her voice steady and low, 'you won't get another chance to do what you just did.' She snatched up her handbag and hurried from the room. Carter rushed after her into the hall. She was struggling into her coat, her anger making it more of a chore than it should have been.

'Please don't go, Evie. Let me apologize properly. Don't leave me. I need you.'

'You should have thought of that before you became so free with your hands. No man gets a second chance to hit me, not even the great Raymond Carter.'

She hurried to the door and was out into the street before he could react coherently and say something sensible in response. As the door slammed, the sound echoed in his brain like a roll of thunder.

Carter stared at the door for a while, not knowing what to do. Eventually he wandered back into the sitting room as though in a trance. What the devil was happening to him? Within a few days his whole world seemed to be crumbling and crashing around him as though it had been hit by one of Hitler's air raids. Somehow he'd been dragged from the Elysian fields into a dark and dangerous side road where his fate was uncertain. He didn't know who the hell he could trust any more. In a daze he picked up Charlie Dokes and slipped his hand inside. The head turned and the eyes moved as though to gaze at him.

'Cheer up,' the doll said. 'Worse things happen at sea.'

Carter grinned in spite of himself.

'I've got to get you ready, Charlie old boy. I've got that bloody show to do tonight, or the fat will really be in the fire.'

'Ready when you are, old man.'

Carter laid down the dummy on the sofa and was making his way to the bathroom to splash cold water on his face when the telephone rang. It was now a sound that he had come to dread. His whole body stiffened and he found himself clenching his fists with fear. He cried out as though in pain. He wanted to bellow, 'Leave me alone.' But he didn't. Instead, like an automaton, he turned and walked back into the sitting room and stood by the shrieking instrument. For a moment his hand hovered and then gently with an aching heart he lifted the receiver and placed it by his ear.

13

The warm beery fug hit me with some force as I pulled open the door of the Guardsman pub. It enveloped me like the welcoming arms of an old friend. The chill November air that had been freezing me to the marrow was instantly forgotten and I felt my body not only relax but expand with relief and pleasure.

It was only six in the evening but the place was already crowded with punters easing the rigours of the day with booze, cigarettes and inconsequential conversation which buzzed around the place. I squeezed my way through the throng to my usual corner to discover that David Llewellyn was already ensconced there and halfway though a pint. He looked ghastly, rather like the ghost of Jacob Marley, wrapped as he was in his voluminous trench coat with a complexion like the morning ashes in the grate and dark semi circles hanging below his bloodshot eyes. It struck me that I must look in a similar grim half-dead condition, or maybe even worse given that I'd been up somewhat longer than my friend. To test this assumption, I tried to catch a glimpse of myself in the mirror behind the bar, but the smoke and dim lighting and jostling customers prevented me from getting a good look at my phizog. It was for the best, I reasoned. I felt sure I looked like an extra from a Bela Lugosi zombie picture. I certainly felt like one.

On my arrival, David ordered a fresh drink for himself and a pint for me. 'When I've finished this, I'm heading home for bed.'

'I think I might join you,' I said.

He smiled and raised an eyebrow acknowledging the spark of a joke in my response. We were both too weary to pick it up.

'What news have you got?' I asked.

He sighed, inflating his cheeks and then releasing the air. 'Nothing of significance I reckon. As we suspected, Arthur Keating was strangled. He died around midnight. I've spoken to his radio producer today.'

'Edward Simmons . . . so have I.'

'And I've seen Percy Goodall, the announcer on the show. But learned very little. Our friend Carter doesn't seem to arouse much feeling in folk either way. People don't appear to hate him, but they don't fall over themselves to be in his company either. He's a bit of a blank. However Simmons seemed to think that Gilbert Manville, the chap that does all the funny voices on the show harbours a bit of a grudge against our Raymond. Maybe you'd like to follow that up, boyo.'

I nodded. Any lead is better than no lead. David passed me a scrap of paper. 'This is where he lives,' he said. 'Not far from your gaff. A flat in the Euston area. Let me know how you get on.'

'Sure.'

'Another thing. Both Simmons and Good-all were of the opinion that maybe Carter and the girl singer Evelyn Munro might be a little closer than they let on.'

'Ah, Evelyn Munro. The soubrette.'

David returned my smile. 'My, we are picking up the showbiz lingo, aren't we?'

I touched my hat in mock salute.

'Well, call her what you will, I'll be meeting her tomorrow so I'll see if I can get the low down on her relationship with Mr Dokes's keeper.'

'I got a hint of that as well. I suppose if they are in a torrid affair . . .'

''Ere, Mr Hawke, watch your language.'

' . . . it might present a motive.'

'How come?'

'For someone who is jealous of the liaison. Someone who wants Miss Munro for himself.'

'Tenuous but possible.' David took a sip of his second pint. 'Tell me, Johnny, what's your take on the Keating murder? I can't see Carter being the killer, can you?'

I shook my head. 'It seems unlikely, but not completely out of the question. I've been in this game long enough to know you cannot eliminate any possibilities, however improbable, until you really know the truth. However, I rang Carter about an hour ago to check on things and he took ages to answer the phone and when he did, he sounded like a terrified schoolboy. Unless he's up for an Oscar, I reckon this phantom caller has really got him well and truly spooked.'

'I hate dealing with theatricals. You can never tell where you are with them. Their working lives are filled with falseness and sleight of hand. It spills over into their real world too. But, you know what, Johnny, if I'm honest I reckon we won't get any further with this case until something else happens, something that helps to indicate some kind of a pattern. All we have now is a series of threatening phone calls that no one has been a witness to — and a murder. Not much for an investigation to take flight.'

Unfortunately, I had to agree with David. We might have been presented with a small cast of suspects but there was no clue whatsoever as to the identity of the culprit or what the motive was. However, I suspect that our mystery foe was having a right old time winding up Raymond Carter and he would continue the process rather than go for Carter himself. That little entertainment could wait. But I had no idea what his or her next move was going to be and gazing at my fellow zombie whose eyes were flickering with tiredness over his beer glass, neither did he.

We left the pub together, abandoning its strange protective warmth and emerging into the bitter Stygian gloom of a winter's evening. We shook hands as we prepared to part and wend our individual ways.

'Now, I know you, Johnny Hawke,' said David, waving a good-natured finger at me. 'I don't want you keeping any useful information to yourself so that you can unmask the murderer in a dramatic fashion like they do in the pictures. Remember this is a police investigation first and foremost, so you keep me in the frame, all right?'

'Yes, sir.' I stood to attention and gave him a mock salute. He threw me a sarcastic glance and disappeared into the darkness of the night.

It was still quite early. I thought it might be useful to make a call on that flat in the Euston area and see what Mr Gilbert Manville had to say for himself. And so I took myself along to 34 Croxfield Mansions. The word 'mansions' was a serious misnomer. These flats were only a few notches up from slum dwellings. I wondered what a radio performer was doing living in such a place. But then he wasn't a big star like Raymond Carter, just a fairly anonymous feed.

It was a tenement style building with the flat in question on the second floor. It was reached by traversing a twisting stone staircase which stank of mould and urine. On reaching the second floor, I made my way along the balcony dodging under the various lines of damp washing strung out there until I eventually came to number 34. I knocked hard on the door but there was no response. I reckoned that this was not going to be my lucky night. I waited a few minutes, knocked again, waited and then threw in the towel on this particular venture. It was obvious that the fellow was out. As I turned to make my way back, running the gauntlet with the soggy washing, a shadowy figure of a man appeared out of the gloom before me. He was shambling and short of breath.

'What do you want?' he asked. The tone was puzzled rather than brusque.

'Mr Manville?' I said.

'What's left of him.' The voice was blurred with alcohol.

'I'm a detective investigating the death of

Arthur Keating and I wondered — '

'Arthur's dead? My God. How?' He seemed genuinely shocked and upset. But then he was an actor.

'He was murdered. Strangled.'

'Christ!' Manville staggered a few paces. 'You'd better come in.' He fumbled with his keys and opened the door of his flat.

The place was a tip inside. Papers, scripts were scattered everywhere. Cups of half-drunk tea decorated the tiled mantelpiece and dining-table. I could see into the kitchen area where the sink was piled high with dirty crockery, while a small mound of empty tin cans and food packets littered the work surface. I thought my place was untidy but it was a palace compared to Manville's gaff.

'It's a bit of a mess, I'm afraid,' he said observing my glances. 'I shall need to clean the place up a bit. Margaret's coming home in a few weeks,' he mumbled, more to himself than to me. With a violent gesture, he tossed a series of papers from the sofa to floor in order to clear a space for me. 'Take a seat, Mr . . . Mr?'

'Hawke. John Hawke.'

'Would you care for a beer? A Guinness maybe?'

I shook my head. 'I'm fine, thanks.'

'You don't mind if I indulge.'

'Not at all.'

He wandered into the kitchen, returning some moments later with a bottle of Guinness. He cleared a space in the armchair opposite and flopped down in it. 'So, Mr Hawke, what do you want to know?'

'I really want to talk to you about Raymond Carter.'

'I thought you said Arthur Keating was dead. What's Carter got to do with it?'

'I believe that someone is trying to frame Mr Carter for Keating's murder.'

'Wouldn't surprise me if Carter had done the old bloke in.'

'Why do you say that?'

Manville's face twisted into an expression of deep hatred. 'Do you know the man? Have you met him? He's a cold-hearted bastard. Wouldn't lend me a hundred quid to save my Margaret's life. She's slipping away from me and they've told me that if she leaves the sanatorium, they don't give her longer than three months.' He shook his head sadly and took a gulp from the bottle.

I'm used to piecing together random comments into a comprehensible whole from the characters I interview in the course of my investigations — especially the ones whose emotional equilibrium is tilted even further off the level by the intake of alcohol. With some gentle probing and minor leaps of reason, I was able to knit together the strands of Manville's tale. In simple terms: his wife was in a sanatorium, dying of consumption, but Manville could no longer maintain the payments to keep her there. He had approached Carter for a loan to help him out but 'the miserable bastard' had refused. So Margaret had to come home. I gazed around me at the squalor of the flat and felt something of the despair that Manville was feeling. If I had the hundred pounds, I would gladly have passed the money over to him.

'Where were you last night?' I asked, moving the subject back to Keating's murder.

'Last night?' Initially his tired brain had trouble with the concept. 'Oh, I was with Margaret. I stay at the sanatorium a couple of nights a week if I can. They make up a camp-bed in her room for me. I've only just left, a few hours ago, then I called in for a few drinks in town.' He paused and rubbed his hand over his face as though he were trying to reshape it into something or someone else. 'Who killed Arthur did you say?'

'I didn't,' I said. 'The investigation is still ongoing.'

'Oh, I see. Well I hope they catch the bastard.'

Well in my considered estimation, the

'bastard' certainly wasn't Manville. He was a wreck of a man, with an imminent tragedy about to engulf him. Of course I'd pass on the info to David and he could check up on the sanatorium story, but I was convinced. I reckoned that we could eliminate Mr Manville from our lists of suspects. I hoped I wasn't being naïve. I left the sad fellow still sitting amid his personal debris, sucking on a bottle of Guinness.

As I made my way back towards Tottenham Court Road, it crossed my mind to take myself down to the Velvet Cage, the night club which on occasion became my second home. Here I could indulge in a night cap, while catching the first set of Tommy Whittle and his group. But in the end I felt so weary that even the thought of a good Scotch and some cool jazz couldn't tempt me from the prospect of a reasonably early night in my little lumpy bed back at Hawke Towers. And so I wandered home, allowing my mind to drift over the events of the last forty-eight hours.

I felt a tinge of guilt when I was reminded of David's words about keeping him in the picture. Of course I'd tell him about my encounter with Manville but I wasn't yet prepared to share my own thoughts and theories about the case and I wouldn't be in a hurry to inform him about my visit to Brighton tomorrow which I hoped would help me assemble a few more pieces of the puzzle. I didn't like to divulge details until I had something concrete. I guess David knew that.

The telephone was ringing when I arrived home. It was Peter.

'Hello, Johnny,' he cried breathlessly, when I lifted the receiver. 'I thought you weren't going to answer.'

'I've only just got in. This is a bit late for you to be ringing, isn't it?'

'It's only nine o'clock. I go to bed at half past. Are you on a case?'

'Sort of.'

'Is it murder?'

'Now you know the rules, Peter. You don't ask me about my cases and I don't ask you about school work.'

'Oh, well, I got ten out of ten in a mental arithmetic test today.'

I grinned. 'Good boy. But I'm not trading on that piece of information.'

'I wish you would. You know I want to be a detective like you when I grow up.'

'With ten out of ten in maths I think you should be aiming a little higher: a scientist or a professor maybe.'

Peter mulled this over for a moment. 'Yeah,

that would be good.'

'Indeed, Professor Peter. I like the sound of that. You could invent a formula to make Hitler disappear.'

There was a snort of laughter. 'Did you hear Okey Dokes the other night?'

At the mention of the radio show I felt a tingle down my spine. I knew that it was a coincidence but it unnerved me for an instant. 'No, I didn't. Was it good?'

'It was great, Charlie really makes me laugh. Miss Horner says that Charlie Dokes is on at the Palladium. Can . . . can we go and see him?'

When I didn't reply immediately, Peter added, 'Oh, please, Johnny. I really would like to go.'

'I'll see what I can do.'

'This Saturday . . . ?'

I grinned at the dark irony of this request. The thought struck me that I could classify a seat in the stalls at the Palladium as research. I reasoned that it would be useful to see the man in action.

'Oh, please,' came the plaintive wail squeaking out of the receiver.

'As I said, I'll see what I can do,' I said, my grin broadening.

'Oh, thanks, Johnny. That would be smashing,' he responded, with unbounded enthusiasm, as though the whole thing was arranged and set in stone.

We talked a little longer about inconsequential things and then it was time to say goodbye.

'Don't forget about Charlie at the Palladium,' was Peter's parting shot.

'I won't. Goodnight, Professor Peter, and God bless.'

Well, I pondered, as I stripped ready to climb under the covers, there's one little soul going to bed happy tonight. I doubted if Raymond Carter would sleep as soundly.

14

I had been down to Brighton several times before the war and had fond memories of the town. I remembered it as being imbued with a constant carefree holiday atmosphere: the bold garishness of the shops catering for the seaside trade with the brightly coloured beach balls and buckets and spades in containers spilling out on to the pavement, the flashing coloured lights and raucous hurdy-gurdy noise of its fun fair contrasting with the soothing and hypnotic rise and fall of the tide on its crunchy shingle beach, the elegance of the famous pavilion and what seemed, in retrospect, constant warm sunshine. For a young lad it was a magical place where worries were sloughed off and replaced with swimming trunks and a kiss-me-quick hat, ice cream and saucy postcards. In those days everyone in Brighton seemed to have a smile on their face.

Not so in the November of 1943.

As I made my way from the station to the sea front, a pale winter sun struggled through grey clouds as though attempting to bring a lightness to the dull streets, trying to capture its old glamour, but these scant rays could not eradicate the effect that the war had wreaked on the old seaside town. The boarded-up shops, the bomb-damaged buildings, the tense, hunched posture and grim faces of the folk who passed me by in sullen silence told all too vividly of the demoralizing effects that the war had brought the people and the place. Along the promenade where once the ranks of gaily coloured deckchairs had flapped in the warm breeze there were now rolls of rusting barbed wire barriers strung out in stark regimented fashion and bleak signs warning people off the beach. Above me wheeled the shrieking seagulls, the only signs of the old normality. The grim face that Brighton now wore was the new normality — thanks to Adolf Hitler.

I found a little café and warmed myself up with a mug of tea. As I sat by the window staring out across the road and beyond to where the sky met the sea, my hands clasping the mug in both hands, savouring the heat it produced, I was surprised how sad I felt at seeing the old place in such a state. I knew that things would be different but I really hadn't expected so radical a change.

My destination was Sunset House in Hove, a retirement home for variety artistes. I showed the address to the café owner. He gave me directions with the assurance that I could walk there in about half an hour, which was fine by me. The exercise would do me good and despite everything else he'd done old Adolf had not been able to eradicate the benefits of breathing in the sea air.

The café owner was pretty accurate for within thirty-five minutes I approached my destination. Sunset House was a large stuccoed villa, placed on a quiet stretch of road opposite the sea. It must have been something quite splendid in earlier days when it was no doubt a luxurious seaside dwelling owned by some rich fellow. Now there was an air of shabbiness and neglect about the place. Paint was peeling here and there; the lawn was overgrown with moss, and weeds were invading the path that led up to the front door.

I stood on the porch and glanced at my watch. It was nearly eleven o'clock. I rang the bell, which was answered by a young girl in a maid's outfit. She looked a little startled when she saw me. A lot of young girls do, I'm afraid. Despite the war, they're not used to seeing a youngish chap with a black eye-patch. I suppose it can give me a sinister and rather foreboding appearance.

I raised my hat and smiled as charmingly as

I could. 'My name is Hawke. Mrs Connor is expecting me.'

Mrs Connor was the matron of this establishment. I had spoken to her on the telephone the day before and explained that I wished to speak to one of the residents, Cyril Sarony, in connection with a murder enquiry. She seemed quite alarmed at first, not wanting anyone in her charge to be upset with talk of death and murder, but I had worked hard to set her mind at ease, assuring her that I would be gentle, considerate and discreet.

The young girl bade me enter and led me down a featureless hallway to Mrs Connor's office; here she knocked lightly on the door. 'Come in,' cried the voice I recognized from our telephone conversation.

'Please wait here, sir,' said the girl, before disappearing into the room. She emerged a few moments later with erratic swiftness like the white rabbit from *Alice in Wonderland*.

'Mrs Connor said you'd best go in.'

Mrs Connor was a large lady floating to the top end of her forties. She was dressed in a bright floral dress which may have fitted her beautifully when she was about a stone lighter but now it seemed to be imprisoning her ample figure rather than gracing it. Her face was heavily made-up with powder and lipstick. She leant over her desk and extended a podgy hand to me. I shook it. It was cold and slightly damp.

'Gladys Connor,' she said briskly but not unkindly, and then, like the young maid, did a double take after catching sight of my eye-patch.

'A war wound, Mr Hawke?' she enquired, waving me to a seat.

I nodded. It was a convenient reply. It was a subject I really didn't want to discuss. It was tedious for me to explain that it was an accident with a faulty rifle when I was training to join the army at the start of the war. If that hadn't happened, I'd have been fighting Hitler in uniform rather than plodding the streets as a private detective. I quickly cast these dark thoughts aside.

'How exactly can I help you, Mr Hawke?' Mrs Connor smiled at me but it was a professional smile. There was no warmth behind it.

'Well, as I explained on the phone yesterday, I just want a chat with Mr Sarony about the old days and his friendship with Raymond Carter.'

'And this is in connection with a criminal investigation.'

I nodded again and passed her one of my cards.

Mrs Connor frowned and some of the powder on her forehead flaked a little. 'But what has Cyril Sarony to do with a crime in London? He hasn't left Brighton in about five years. He can barely walk now.'

'It's only background information I'm after. I'd just like him to reminisce, that's all. I won't mention anything about crime. I don't wish to upset him.'

Mrs Connor's professional expression softened. 'That is essential. Cyril is rather frail now and I don't want him disturbed in any way. However, if it's just a chat about the old days then that's fine. It's what he loves. It's what they all love in here. Their life was the stage and the only bit of living they get to do now is to relive the past.'

I was beginning to warm to Mrs Connor. The stiff and starchy exterior was melting away and the real caring persona beneath was making an appearance.

'Why don't you introduce me as a reporter who's doing a piece about old-time music hall stars and then there's no suspicion of the real reason for my visit?'

'That's an excellent idea,' beamed Mrs Connor, rising from her chair. 'Very well, come along then. I'll take you to meet Cyril. He'll be in his room now. He doesn't usually emerge until lunchtime.'

She took me through a large lounge area where about a dozen or so of the residents were sitting around; some playing cards, others reading, a couple chatting, and one poor old dear was staring mournfully at the wall. Most ignored our passage through the room, but a couple of the ladies turned their heads in my direction and gave me a sly coquettish smile, as for a brief moment they were young girls again. My patch didn't seem to bother them.

On entering Cyril Sarony's room, at first glance it appeared to be empty. This impression was supported by the fact that Mrs Connor had knocked and there had been no reply. The room felt cold although there was a meagre fire struggling for survival in the grate. The walls were bare apart from a couple of yellowing theatre posters and a mottled mirror. There was a single bed, a desk, a table with a radio on it, a large wardrobe and a winged armchair facing away from us towards the window. How sad, I thought, to live a long and productive life only to end up here a virtual prisoner in these bleak, dingy quarters. Suddenly, there was a slight movement in the large armchair.

'Who's there?' A croaky voice emerged from the depths of the chair.

'He's rather deaf,' muttered Mrs Connor

conspiratorially, as she led me round the front of the chair to introduce me to its occupant.

Cyril Sarony was skeletally thin, his body shrunken with age. He was almost completely bald apart from a few uncombed stubborn wisps of white hair that sprouted from the side of his head. His face was shroud white, but it possessed two of the brightest blue eyes I'd encountered. They were like azure diamonds shining forth from those pasty features.

Mrs Connor introduced me as a reporter as arranged and left me with him. 'Don't tire him, please. No longer than half an hour, eh?' she murmured on departure.

I nodded in agreement.

We were left alone. Cyril Sarony grinned. 'Nice to meet you, young man,' he said, his voice and demeanour belying his aged appearance. 'Before we start, let's have a little nip, eh? There's a bottle of good brandy in that cupboard and a couple of glasses. Let's warm our cockles, shall we?'

I retrieved the brandy and poured him a glass. 'Good lord, young man, don't be stingy. Let's have a good measure. This is a bit of a celebration. I don't get many visitors these days . . . ' He gave a wry chuckle. 'To be honest, I don't get any at all.'

He beamed and took a generous sip before

emitting a dry, throaty chuckle. 'It warms the cockles, it does. It warms the cockles. Now then young man . . . '

'Call me Johnny.'

'I will. I will. And you must call me Mr Sarony.' He chuckled to himself. 'Sorry. My little joke. That's what Tim always used to say: 'my little joke'.'

'Tim?'

'My dolly. I was a vent act you know. Quite an attraction in my day. Before you were born.'

'That's what I wanted to chat to you about. Your vent act and how you helped Raymond Carter.'

The eyes dimmed and the mouth turned down at the corners. 'Oh, him,' he said disdainfully.

'You know that he's a great success now.'

'Oh, yes, I know that.'

'Do you listen to his radio show?'

Cyril Sarony made a disparaging noise in his throat. 'Pah! A vent act on radio. How ridiculous is that? The whole point of a vent act is to see a man — see a man, mind you, make a wooden doll talk and no matter how much you stare at him you can't for the life of you see his lips move. On radio they could just be two different men — who's to know? And the crime is that Carter is a very good

151

ventriloquist. And so he should be. I taught him all I know.'

'How did you come to meet?'

Cyril Sarony's pale features softened into a smile. 'It was years ago, my boy. Just after the Great War. Can't say for sure. My memory is still as sharp as it ever was, but I've never been good on dates. I was quite successful, me and Tim that is. We weren't quite headliners but certainly not in the wines and spirits department — that's down at the bottom of the bill. 'Cyril Sarony With Tim, His Talking Doll' — that was my bill matter. Not brilliant, was it? But the act did fine. Here, top up my glass with a drop more brandy, son: this talking is making me thirsty. Yes, that's right. Full to the top.'

'Now then, how did I meet Raymond Carter? Well, it was at the old Hackney Empire. Of course, in those days London was crammed with theatres. As I said it was just after the war and folks were desperate for entertainment. They just wanted to laugh and sing again after all the misery of that bleedin' war. There was hardly a night when we didn't have a packed house. Raymond was a young shaver, around twenty I should guess. 'Course he went under the name of Frank Palmer then. He was a stage hand and he was fascinated by ventriloquism. He used to

152

watch me from the wings every night and came to chat to me in between shows. He was eager to learn the techniques and the tricks. I know how he felt. I'd been the same as him when I'd been younger. My father was a vent too and he'd schooled me in the art — and it is an art, young man. It takes skill, patience, dedication and hours and hours of practice. And even then it's not given to everyone to succeed. I think ventriloquism chooses you, rather than the other way around.

'Anyway, to cut a long story short, Raymond sort of became my pupil. It didn't take long for me to realize the lad had a natural talent for it. A gift, if you like. He picked things up with ease. He used to practise on Tim as well, getting used to the mechanics of the doll. It's not all talking with your mouth closed, you know: you have to co-ordinate eye, head and mouth movements, too. And never keep your dolly still for more than ten seconds or that's how he'll come across to the audience — as a bleedin' wooden doll. He's got to live, you see. You've got to convince them he's alive.'

There was a crack in the old man's voice and he took a large gulp of brandy to cover his embarrassment.

'I remember the day Raymond came into my dressing room carrying a large suitcase.

153

He'd gone and got his own doll. He'd been up to Smallbone's magic shop in town and had his own dummy made. And they weren't cheap even then. Well, that week after a few practices with me, I let him come on stage towards the end of my act so that the dolls could indulge in a bit of cross talk together. It went down a treat. I suppose it was the novelty of seeing two vents on the stage at the same time — two men who said nothing but their dollies were going at it hammer and tongs. It was something really different. We did it again every night that week and got the same reaction. At the end of the engagement, I decided to take on Raymond as my junior partner. He was more than happy to accept my measly offer of twenty-five per cent of the take. He was now in show business. And that's when he changed his name.'

The old man paused for a moment, those brilliant eyes misting over as though he was visualizing the moments all over again.

'So, Johnny,' he said at length, 'you can imagine what happened. Gradually Raymond took over more and more of the act. He didn't stay on twenty-five per cent for long. Well, he was a lively, good-looking lad and I was an old codger approaching sixty. He had more appeal to the audience, especially the ladies. Oh, and he did have a way with the ladies. You know what they say about sailors having a lady in every port — well, he was the same with the chorus girls. More than one sometimes in every theatre. Then he slipped up. Got one of them pregnant. Silly blighter. Still, he did the decent thing and married the girl. Nice little thing; Sally was her name. It was about this time he told me that he had decided to go solo. He thought I was holding him back. He'd got his eye on the West End, he said. That was a real slap in the face for me, I can tell you. After all I'd done for him. I wouldn't have minded if he'd done it with some kindness, but he just dropped it on me like one of Hitler's bombs. Bang! You're out of the act, go and plough your own furrow. I know it's silly and sentimental — I expect it's the brandy talking — but I used to think of him like the son I'd never had. I didn't have kids of my own; I was married to the theatre, you see. But I looked on Raymond that way.'

The old man's bright eyes moistened. 'Brandy always does this to me,' he said, trying to effect a grin as he wiped an errant tear away with his sleeve. 'You can top my glass up again, lad. In for a penny, eh?'

I poured a little more of the brandy into his glass without comment. I had no intention of saying anything that might interrupt his flow.

'So, off he went with wife and his little son

ready to climb the heights of the show-business ladder of fame, leaving me to try and make something of what was left of my career. But times were changing. People didn't seem as amused as they once were with a man and a dummy on stage. They needed more novelty. More brashness, I suppose. I struggled along for a bit and then I gave up and worked as a kind of talent scout for a booking agency for a while until I threw my hat in altogether.' He coughed a little on purpose and I could hear his chest rattle. 'My health let me down in the end. Still my compensation was that Raymond had the same problems with his act as I did. He didn't change with the times, y'see, and the bookings fell away. In time he was just an also ran on the variety bills. He began to drink and became unreliable. But I didn't feel sorry for him because just after leaving me he did the nastiest thing a man could do.'

I leaned forward affecting an interest. Well, I wasn't affecting it, I was really interested, but I wanted to demonstrate that fact to Cyril to make sure he carried on with his revelations. He took a sip of brandy before continuing.

'He left his wife and young 'un and went off with one of his blasted chorus girls. He just dumped them. Like he dumped me. Left them without a penny. Well, the girl, Sally, his wife, was distraught. The fool really loved him, y'see. Oh, he had charm when he wanted to. He could switch it on and off like a tap. I tell you, he could have given that Jekyll and Hyde some lessons in the art of being two-faced. It was tragic. Sally couldn't get over losing the bastard so she topped herself. Slashed her wrists. He didn't even go to the funeral. That's your Raymond Carter for you. When it came down to it, all he cared about was himself. He just used other people for his own convenience and satisfaction.'

Cyril Sarony sat back in his chair with the air of a man who had finished his tale. But there was more that I needed to know.

'What happened to the child?' I probed gently.

Cyril shrugged. 'I don't know. What I do know is that Raymond had nothing to do with the little lad. He refused to accept any responsibility for Sally or the child's future. It was as though they had never existed. He cut them from his life. I believe he persuaded himself that they had never existed. I told you he was a bastard.'

'How old was the baby when Sally died?'

'About one or two, I reckon.'

'And what happened to the chorus girl that Raymond went off with?'

Cyril's face split into a wide grin and he gave a slight chesty laugh. 'She fell by the wayside. Like they all did. No doubt there've been dozens of tarts in his bed since then. Even now in his forties he's a good-looking chap, isn't he? I see his picture in the papers. I bet he's still sniffing round the girls.'

'What happened to Raymond in the thirties?'

Cyril shrugged. 'He played the halls. Second-rate venues up and down the country. He struggled like we all did then. He scraped a living, I guess. Then like a bleeding miracle, he pushed the stone away from the mouth of the tomb and stepped into the limelight once more. Big time.'

The anger that this evoked in the old trouper set him coughing again and with great effort he sat forward and expelled a gobbet of phlegm into the fire grate where it hung there hissing and sizzling.

'It couldn't have happened to a slimier toad.'

'When was the last time you saw Raymond Carter?'

'The last time I saw him to speak to was in August 1920. And he did the talking. He told me to get lost. That I was all washed up and he would no longer be associating himself with me. I've seen him a couple of times since

— on the stage. I hate the man, Johnny, but I've got to give him his due: he's a mighty fine ventriloquist. And the words stick in my throat to admit as much.'

'I understand.'

'I hope you'll print the story in your paper. It's time his adoring public knew what a termite he is.'

I nodded positively, but did not commit my lips to the lie. I felt bad about lying to the old man, but I was only doing my job, wasn't I? 'And you've really no idea what became of Raymond's son,' I said, keeping myself on track.

Cyril shook his head. 'I haven't got a clue — but wherever he is he's better off not knowing who his father is.'

'Well, thank you for your time, Mr Sarony . . . ' I said, realizing that as far as the case was concerned I had squeezed this particular lemon dry.

'Oh, you're not going so soon, are you? I was so enjoying our little chat.'

I felt a pang of guilt as I noted the desperate sadness in his eyes. I had taken him, momentarily, back to the good old days, *his* good old days, allowing him to revive memories of a time when he was performing, when he still walked out on a stage to engage with people, of a time when he mattered.

Now I was dragging him back to the drab present and abandoning him there — abandoning him in this tiny, shabby room with a misty view of the sea and nothing to look forward to but further decay and death. For a brief time I had allowed him to pass through the door into his warm and colourful past and now I was shutting that door and not even providing him with a press cutting he could treasure.

'I'm sorry but . . . ' I muttered, embarrassed by my own ruthlessness.

Suddenly, Cyril smiled. 'That's all right, young man. You have things to do, I know.' Without warning he rose unsteadily to his feet. 'But you won't leave without saying goodbye to Tim, will you?'

Without waiting for my reply — which was fine because I really hadn't got one — he moved in a stiff awkward fashion to the large oak wardrobe by the bed. On opening its creaky door he extracted a large suitcase. With some difficulty he undid the clasps and lifted the lid, revealing a ventriloquist's dummy — a red-cheeked fellow dressed in a faded green and red striped blazer and white flannels. He wore a jaunty, schoolboy's cap. Cyril lifted the doll out and began operating him: the eyes swivelled, the head rotated from side to side and the wooden mouth

160

clapped open and shut.

'This is my Tim,' said Cyril, proudly. 'Say hello to the young gentleman, Tim.'

'Hello, young gentleman,' said Tim, Cyril's aged lips quivering somewhat as he did so.

I nodded politely and somewhat bizarrely I found myself addressing the wooden doll. 'Hello, Tim, I'm pleased to meet you.'

'I've got something to ask you,' said Tim, the eyes flickering from side to side. 'Why would you find a cashier in a police station, eh? Tell me that.'

I smiled. This old chestnut had passed me by. I indulged Tim. 'I don't know. Why would you find a cashier in a police station?'

'He's there to count the coppers,' said Tim, with gleeful satisfaction and produced a high-pitched giggle which transferred itself to Cyril.

'He's a monkey, isn't he?' said Cyril.

I smiled and nodded.

'Goodbye then, young man,' said Tim. 'But one last word. I hope when you write your piece about Raymond Carter you'll tell the truth, the whole truth and nothing but the truth. It's time people knew what he was really like.'

By the time Tim had finished talking, his lips had stopped moving and the words were coming directly from Cyril Sarony.

A few minutes later I was walking along the promenade, breasting a sharp and blustery wind from the sea as I made my way back towards the town centre and the railway station. I had learned quite a lot and the trip had certainly been worth it in terms of the case. Why then did I feel so depressed?

15

'You're up bright and early,' said Larry Milligan, as with accustomed ease he pushed passed Raymond Carter into the hallway of his client's mews house. He surveyed the ventriloquist who was smartly dressed in sports jacket and flannels. 'I fully expected you to greet me still slopping about in your pyjamas and bearing a face like a wet weekend,' he observed sardonically, throwing his overcoat on to the sofa.

'Yes, well, I've a busy day ahead of me. I've decided it's time I got my life back on track.'

Larry gave him a grim smile. 'Glad to hear it. You got coffee?'

'In the kitchen.'

'So,' said Larry a few minutes later, perched on one of the stools in Carter's kitchen, cup of steaming coffee in hand, 'what has brought about this change of perspective? I left you jittery and maudlin yesterday and today you're buzzing like Donald Duck on heat. I gather there have been no more telephone calls.'

'Oh, yes, there have. I got one last night. But by then I'd had enough. I just put the phone down and cut the bastard off. If he cannot spill his venom into my ear he can't poison me, can he?'

Milligan pursed his lips. 'Very poetic. And logical, I suppose.'

'If I don't let this fellow get to me, then his purpose is defeated. He's already caused enough trouble in my life; I'm not going to let him continue.'

'Bravo, say I,' said Milligan, before taking a tentative sip of the steaming coffee. 'Does that mean you'll be giving your one-eyed Sherlock Holmes the heave-ho as well?'

Carter shook his. 'No. Hawke stays on the case. I still want to get to the bottom of this business. There is a murderer behind it after all. I'm not stupid enough to think I'm safe just because I'm not taking the calls any more. We'll see what happens next, but one thing's for sure: I'm determined not to start cringing when the telephone rings. Now, unless you have some pressing business matter to discuss, I must ask you to drink up and leave me to get on. I have a pretty girl to placate.'

'Evelyn? You've fallen out?'

'A little more than that. I don't want to go into details. Let's say I upset her mightily and I've got a fair amount of grovelling to do.'

'Do you want my advice?'

'No.'

'Well, I'm your manager so you're going to get it anyway. Let her go, Ray. She's a two-a-penny singer who's trying to grab some of your spotlight for herself. My nose tells me she's bad news.'

'Your nose is in danger of being bloodied by my fist,' snapped Carter. 'You're employed to look after my professional life, Larry, so keep your meddling fingers out of my private one. When I need a wet nurse, I'll let you know.'

Milligan shrugged. 'I'm only trying to help. As I've told you before, Ray, people at the top of the show-business tree don't have private lives. As long as you're in the main spotlight, you belong to the public.'

'I'm my own man and always have been.'

Milligan raised an eyebrow but said nothing. There was a lot he could say but he was well aware that it would be pointless. He was used to performers who, having sniffed fame, believed they knew best. Milligan knew differently. If Carter wanted to push his own personal handcart to hell, then let him. Certainly he would not be hitching a ride. Milligan poured the coffee down the sink and moved into the sitting room where he scooped up his overcoat and headed for the door. 'I'll see you later,' he murmured, without turning round.

'What are you doing here?' Evelyn Munro's reception was as cold and harsh as a winter blizzard.

'I've come to make amends — to apologize for being a first-class idiot. There's something I need to explain to you. Hear me out, please?'

'Explain? There's nothing to explain.' She did not budge from the threshold of her flat.

'Give me ten minutes, that's all.'

She gazed at his face for some moments, her mind whirring with possibilities. Suddenly she looked a little nervous. Carter took her hand. 'Please,' he begged.

Evelyn cast a glance back into her flat and then relented: 'Five minutes,' she said.

Sitting with Evelyn on her sofa, smoking several cigarettes, Raymond Carter told her the whole story in detail: the phone calls, the threats, the lot.

'And so,' he concluded, 'when you impersonated Charlie yesterday, I just snapped. I wasn't thinking. It wasn't Raymond Carter who slapped you but some foolish nervous wreck.'

Evelyn appeared genuinely shocked by Carter's revelations. 'And you think whoever is threatening you over the phone was responsible for Arthur Keating's death — his murder?'

'There's no doubt. And I could be next.'

She slid her hand forward and took hold of his. 'Oh, Ray, why didn't you tell me this before?'

'I'm not quite sure now. I just wanted to keep the whole thing secret, I guess. Part of me was . . . I don't know . . . embarrassed, I suppose, ashamed by it.'

'That doesn't make sense. You're not responsible for the actions of a madman. Oh, come here.' She leaned forward and planted a kiss on his cheek.

'Then I'm forgiven?' he said.

She gave him a dry smile. 'I guess so.'

'It was a shock to my system and knocked me for six for a time. But now I'm determined that this creep — whoever he is — is not going to get to me . . . is not going to destroy me.'

'Of course not, darling.'

Another kiss. Carter hadn't expected the reconciliation to be so swift, so easy.

'What about the police? What do they think?'

Carter shrugged. 'I don't really know. I suppose at the moment I'm the main suspect in the frame for Keating's murder. But they've no real proof, so I guess they're watching and waiting to see what happens next. I know I can't rely on them. That's why I've got my own man on the case.'

Evelyn reached over and retrieved a packet of cigarettes from her handbag, and extracted two, passing one to Carter. 'What d'you mean, your own man?'

Carter flipped his lighter and lit the cigarettes. 'I've got a private detective working for me.'

Evelyn giggled. 'How exciting. How very Hollywood. Does he look like Humphrey Bogart?'

Despite himself, Carter grinned. 'Hardly, he's a young chap with an eye-patch, but I reckon he knows what he's doing.'

'What's his name?'

'John Hawke.'

Evelyn turned her head and blew a cloud of smoke over Carter's shoulder.

'How interesting,' she said, evenly. 'Let's hope he comes up with the goods.'

Carter grinned and cast an eye towards the bedroom door. 'I was thinking that perhaps we should celebrate our reconciliation in appropriate style.' He stroked the back of her hand gently.

'Oh, I'd love to, Ray, but I've got such a busy morning. Not just right now, eh?' She cast a glance at the bedroom and smiled awkwardly. 'Some other time. Soon.'

Carter thought she looked nervous, but he wasn't about to press the matter. He knew that he had some ground to make up with Evie and pushing her into bed before she was ready was not the best of tactics.

'Come and see me after the show tonight,' he said. 'We'll have a little supper on the town and then perhaps you'll come back to my place for a nightcap.'

'That sounds lovely.' She kissed him again, but just as he was about to hold her in his embrace, she rose briskly, straightening her dress. 'But, my darling, I've got to get myself ready now. As I said I've a busy day.'

Ray gave a theatrical moan. 'Very well. I'll just use your bathroom before I leave, is that OK?'

Surprisingly she did not answer, but he made his way there all the same. While he was washing his hands he thought he heard the outer door of her flat close. Maybe she had another visitor. Apprehensive, he waited and listened for the sound of voices. He didn't want to compromise Evelyn, or more particularly himself, by being discovered visiting her flat. There were no voices, but nevertheless he left the bathroom quietly and peered around the sitting room door. Evelyn was sitting on the sofa with her make-up mirror applying some lipstick. She looked up as she noticed Carter's head appear round the door and smiled. 'What are you doing, skulking around my flat? You look like a very well-dressed burglar.' She giggled at her own conceit.

He grinned sheepishly back at her. 'I thought I heard a noise, someone in the flat.'

'Drat those mice. I shall have to get them some slippers. Oh, Raymond, don't be silly, there's no one here. You must relax, otherwise you'll end up a gibbering wreck.'

She moved to his side and put her arms around him. He felt the seductive warmth of her body and smelt the faint sweet aroma of her eau de cologne.

He kissed her forehead. 'I'll try,' he said softly, with a sudden realization of how difficult it was going to be to ignore his feelings of insecurity and uncertainty. The morning bravado he had mustered about the phone calls was already receding. The thought insinuated its way into his mind that maybe he wasn't strong enough for all this. For years he had thought of himself as a tough fellow, emotion-proof, but perhaps he had been kidding himself. Either that, or he had not really been put to the test before. He had been the one calling all the shots, making the decisions, but he was most certainly being put to the test now and on current form he wasn't handling things at all well.

Evelyn gazed at his sad features and gave him a reassuring hug before pulling away. 'Now then, weren't you about to depart?'

'Guess so.'

The telephone rang and without thinking his body stiffened and he felt his mouth go dry. Evelyn saw the effect this had on him and squeezed his hand.

'You're in my flat now, Ray. And it's only the telephone. It'll be Monty, my agent. Just a mo.' She moved to the telephone on a small table against the wall and lifted the received from the cradle.

'Evelyn Munro,' she whispered seductively, glancing over at Carter with a smile. Then her features darkened and her brow creased in a surprised frown. She clasped her hand over the mouthpiece. 'It's for you,' she said simply.

'Me?' cried Carter, louder than he intended. The old fear returned and his legs began to feel unsteady. 'Who is it?'

Evelyn shrugged. 'He says he's a friend.' She held out the receiver for Raymond to take it.

He did not move.

She held out the receiver closer to him. 'Come on, Ray. Don't be frightened.'

But he was frightened and all logical arguments and prevarications had gone from his head. In fact, his eyes and his mind focused solely on the black Bakelite telephone receiver that Evelyn held out like a supplicant.

It was a friend, she'd said, but he really didn't have any friends. And certainly no one who would know he was in the flat of Evelyn Munro, apart from Larry that is, and he wouldn't ring him here and he wouldn't classify himself as a friend anyway. Theirs was a strictly business arrangement.

'I'll put the receiver down, if you like,' said Evelyn. There was no mistaking the disappointment in her voice.

'No, that's my job,' Carter snapped, snatching the receiver from her and clasping it to the side of his head.

'Hello. Raymond Carter.' His voice was firm and aggressive.

There was silence on the line at first and then through the sibilant hiss Carter could detect a faint chuckling. It was mocking and high-pitched. He was about to replace the receiver when the caller began to speak. To Carter's horror, he heard the voice of Charlie Dokes.

'Hello, there, Ray old chum. How's tricks? Got the little girlie into bed yet? You being a naughty boy again, are you?'

A sharp, fierce pain rippled across his chest and for a moment he thought he was going to faint. His legs began to give way and he staggered backwards, dragging the telephone to the very edge of the table until it was in danger of crashing to the floor.

'What is it, Ray?' asked Evelyn, alarmed at Carter's behaviour.

'It's him,' he muttered.

Evelyn snatched the receiver from his limp grasp. 'Hello, hello,' she called down the phone. 'Who is this? What do you want?'

Ruffling his hair, Carter stood back watching her intently, wondering what she was hearing.

'He's hung up,' she said at last.

'What did he say?'

She shook her head as she replaced the receiver. 'Nothing. I heard nothing.'

'But it was him. Using Charlie Dokes's voice. The same bastard.' Carter's eyes widened with fear as he realized the full implication of the call. 'My God, he's watching me closely. He seems to know my every movement . . . '

16

I sat by the window on the noisy, rattling train on my way back to London, staring out at the passing panorama of fields and houses, houses and fields, with the occasional factory and river thrown in for variety but without really seeing a thing. My mind was fully occupied, digesting the details of the Raymond Carter story as passed on to me by Cyril Sarony. If I was to believe what I was told — and there really was no reason not to — Mr Raymond Carter emerged as the bastard son of Jekyll and Hyde. Obviously beneath that smooth and apparently sensitive exterior beat a heart of lead. To ditch your young wife and child and have nothing more to do with them takes more than the average streak of cold bloodedness. It puts you up there with Attila the Hun. In my encounters with my client, he had presented himself at worst as Mr Bland and at best a fine fellow, who, to his astonishment and surprise, found himself being persecuted and threatened. If his treatment of Sally, his wife, and his little boy, as well as old Cyril Sarony himself, was anything to go by, over the years Raymond

Carter must have created enough enemies to fill a medium-sized football stadium, all ready to do him ill. In that sense the field of suspects was wide open. Well, in theory anyway.

As the train neared Victoria, my mind was still reeling with the implications of my discovery. It certainly opened several new avenues to consider and investigate. I calmed my feverish thoughts and acknowledged that despite Cyril Sarony's revelations and the different complexion they placed on the case, the likely candidate for making the death threats, and indeed the person who had murdered Arthur Keating, was still someone connected with the Okey Dokes radio show. However, now there were greater possibilities for nailing down a motive — the reason this mystery caller had for trying to destroy Carter's career and, presumably, ultimately, the man himself. The thought struck me that Carter might well have a suspicion as to who this avenger was, but didn't want to confess it because it would reveal some unforgivable past behaviour of his — something that would show the bastard up for what he was: a bastard.

I had to have this out with him. No investigator can work effectively if his client is keeping details from him. And I was certain that there was even more that I should know. Mr Carter had better cough up or, before he knew it, he could end up on a stone slab in the morgue. The more I thought about Carter, the more I came to realize that he was the dummy, the figment, the wooden-headed front man, and the sniping, nasty, unscrupulous Charlie Dokes was really my client.

I could see that fixed grin, the baleful gorgon eyes darting feverishly from side to side and that champing shiny mouth that snapped noisily as it opened and closed. That was the real Raymond Carter. The man who handled him was merely an empty husk.

★   ★   ★

It was late afternoon when I arrived back in London. I incarcerated myself in a foul-smelling telephone box outside the station and called Carter. The phone rang for an eternity before it was answered, or rather before the receiver was lifted at the other end. But no one spoke. I had the image of a white-faced Raymond Carter holding the receiver tentatively to his ear in fearful anticipation of another death threat. Having learned what I had about him, I was very tempted to adopt the voice of Charlie Dokes and meet his expectations. It would have

176

given me the greatest pleasure to make him squirm. I grinned at the thought. However, common sense won the day.

'Mr Carter, it's John Hawke,' I said.

'Oh, hello,' came the reply. The relief in the voice was tangible.

'I think we need to speak soon.'

'Yes, of course. Have there been any developments in the case?'

'In a manner of speaking.'

'What are they?'

'It can wait until we meet.'

'Very well, if you insist.' His timidity had been sloughed off now and I could hear the assertiveness growing in his voice. 'I have things to tell you also. I think I'm being followed. The devil seems to know where I am, where I go, what I do.'

'I'll come over to your flat now.'

'No, I'll be setting off for the theatre in half an hour. Come to the Palladium and see me in my dressing room around six this evening. I'll tell the stage doorkeeper to expect you.'

'I'll be there,' I said, and put the phone down.

Time for a drink to fortify me, I thought, as I heaved open the recalcitrant door of the phone box. My usual haunt, The Velvet Cage wasn't too far a slog to Argyll Street, home of the Palladium, I reckoned. I'd call in there

177

and treat myself to a slug of whisky before facing the demon ventriloquist.

An hour later fortified by two slugs of whisky — one always leads to another — I made my way past the entrance to the Palladium, and turned left down Great Marlborough Street to the stage door. I knew this part of London well, having tramped the streets hereabouts on numerous investigations, mainly petty affairs involving infidelity or unpaid debts, the bread and butter employment of a glamorous private eye.

The stage doorkeeper looked just like George Robey. It could well have been George Robey down on his luck. There he was, the Prime Minister of Mirth with two thick eyebrows which appeared as though they had been drawn on his face by a broad piece of charcoal; these were accompanied by two red spots of colour on his cheeks and a couple of twinkling beady eyes which gazed at me with undisguised animosity. I had obviously interrupted his quiet time with a bottle of stout and a sports paper.

'Artistes only round here, mate. Shove off.'

Charm personified.

'I've come to see Raymond Carter. I'm expected. The name is Hawke.'

Mr Robey gazed at me as though I were a German paratrooper who had just dropped in. He did so while chewing something unidentifiable in a vigorous fashion.

'Oh, yeah?' he said at last, his eyes returning to his paper.

'Yeah,' I replied adopting his tone and attitude. 'Now are you going to give me directions, or do I have a word with my good friend Arnold Phillips?' I had noted the name of the manager above the main entrance to the theatre as I'd passed. The mention of his employer did the trick. Robey put his bottle down, flashed me an awkward smile and leaned forward and pointed down the corridor. 'Down there to the end, turn left, up the stairs and you'll find Mr Carter's name on one of the dressing rooms.'

I raised my hat. 'Most kind,' I said, with as much sarcasm as I could muster.

★   ★   ★

Raymond Carter, dressed in a voluminous towelling robe, admitted me to his dressing-room without a word of greeting.

'I got the impression from your phone call that you'd made some progress. Is that right?' he asked, somewhat petulantly, after he had sat down at the make-up mirror to finish getting himself ready for the show. Charlie Dokes was sitting on a stool at the side of the table, his baleful eyes gazing at me with what seemed spiteful malice.

'I think so,' I replied vaguely, sitting down on the only vacant chair in the room.

'Well . . . ?' said Carter with a trace of irritation in his voice. He turned to me, his face shiny with greasepaint, full of anticipation.

'Today I went to visit an old friend of yours: Cyril Sarony.'

Carter's face darkened. 'What on earth for?'

'A little background detail,' I said evenly.

Carter gave a scornful laugh and returned to his make-up. 'Oh he'd give you that all right. You'll need to take a few sacks of salt with anything he told you. He's a bitter old man who never got over the fact that I left his failing act to go on my own over twenty years ago. He was a second-rate talent with a third-rate act.'

'You didn't just leave the act though, did you? There was the little matter of a wife and child as well. You left them, too.'

'If you believe Sarony I did. Sally was an alcoholic and a neurotic. She left me, disappeared, and then within months she had committed suicide.'

'And the child?'

'I don't know. I don't know what happened

to him. I tried to find him but . . . I couldn't. I think Sally's mother took him away. But I'm not sure. I know I tried to find out where she'd gone but she had vanished.'

It was smooth and rehearsed, but he was lying. I was sure of it. Just as I was sure that Cyril Sarony had told me the truth. Carter had been glad to be rid of the burden of old wife and new child. They were baggage not wanted on his journey.

'Don't you think it still haunts me: the fact that I lost a son? But it was all a long time ago. There's no point in raking over old coals. This has nothing to do with the matter I'm employing you to investigate.'

'Are you sure?'

'What does that mean?'

'Someone hates you, Carter. Someone hates you enough to kill in order to make your life difficult. And in time he'll come for you. Now he has a damned good reason for this and I believe you know the reason.'

Behind the sheen of make-up, Carter's face fought to find the appropriate expression with which to respond to my accusation. In the end, he settled for a frustrated glare. 'I never said I'd led a blameless life. To survive in show-business you've got to be a bit ruthless from time to time, but I swear there's no one . . . no one I can think of who would actually . . . want to *kill* me.'

'I think you are being naïve. Or perhaps you want me to believe you are naïve.'

'That's nonsense.'

'There must be someone . . . someone connected with the radio show whom you have upset in some way, in some mightily significant way, that has prompted them to take some drastic action.'

Carter shook his head. 'There's no one, I — ' He froze mid sentence, his eyes flickering erratically.

'Oh, yes there is,' I said softly, sitting back and taking out a pack of cigarettes. 'Why don't you tell me? Telling the truth can be quite uplifting, you know.'

He shook his head a little as though he was a mite confused. 'I'm not sure. It's just a thought that's all.'

'Well, share the thought, Mr Carter.' I lit up a cigarette and waited.

'Percy Goodall, the announcer on the show. I first worked with him on *Variety Fanfare* about eighteen months ago before I had my own show. I just had a regular guest spot. We got on quite well at first.'

'And then . . . ?' I knew there had to be an 'and then'.

Carter avoided my gaze. 'I had a bit of a thing with his wife.'

Now we're getting somewhere, I thought. 'I think you'll have to be more precise. You mean you had an affair with her.'

Carter nodded. 'An affair sounds rather grand and serious. I slept with her a couple of times.'

'If I were her husband I'd probably regard that as rather grand and serious. I think you'd better tell me the whole story.'

'There's not a lot to tell. Her name was Gloria. I was introduced to her at the end of a *Variety Fanfare* series party. She is a good ten years younger than Goodall. A small, pretty brunette with a very nice figure. She had worked in Bourne & Hollingsworth when they'd first met. I reckon she was impressed that an important person like a posh radio announcer had taken an interest in her. She was a little stage struck, if you know what I mean.'

I knew what he meant.

'And she was even more impressed when a rising radio star paid her attention.'

Carter couldn't help himself: he smiled at the memory. 'She was all over me at the party . . . and Goodall didn't seem to mind. Well, he didn't show it, at least. Then a couple of weeks later we bumped into each other in the Strand. I took her for a drink and things just developed from there. You can hardly say I seduced her. She was as eager as I was.'

'How very nice for you. I suppose you never stopped to think that you were leading the girl into adultery.'

'Not really. I'm not sure I was the leader. It was a joint venture, if you like.' He shrugged casually. 'Anyway the whole thing only lasted a few weeks.'

'Goodall found out.'

'Well, yes he did, because the silly bitch told him. She thought she was in love with me. Wanted to divorce him and marry me. She had delusions of being the wife of the famous radio star Raymond Carter.'

'So you dumped her.'

'I certainly did. She was OK in bed, but that was it. There was not a lot going on upstairs.' He illustrated the point by tapping his temple with right forefinger.

Now here I was seeing the real Raymond Carter for the first time: arrogant, self-seeking and unscrupulous. The model as described by Cyril Sarony. He was happy to take someone's wife to bed with him for self-gratification but once she began to get serious he abandoned her — ruining two lives for his own pleasure.

'What happened?'

'Goodall came to see me and begged me to

184

stop seeing Gloria. He'd been drinking and was maudlin and pitiable. I told him that I had already said my goodbyes and I wanted nothing more to do with the stupid cow. Then he tried to take a swing at me, but he was too drunk to do it. Next thing I knew he was crying his eyes out. I got him a taxi and bundled him off home.'

'How very considerate of you. Where is Gloria now?'

'You'd better ask Goodall. She left him a few weeks later. I expect she's back behind a counter at Bourne & Hollingsworth.'

'What's your relationship with Percy Goodall like at the moment?'

'Professional. He's the announcer on my show. I'm the star. We don't talk unless it's about some aspect of the script. It's all very civilized.'

'Any more skeletons in your cupboard that I should know about?'

'I don't regard this incident as one of my skeletons. It's just something that happened. As I said, Gloria was as eager for it as I was.'

Nicely expressed, I thought. I wondered if the sentiment appeased Goodall.

'However, if you are thinking that Percy Goodall is the fellow who's been threatening me and who murdered Arthur Keating, I reckon you're barking up the wrong tree. He hasn't the nerve or the guts.'

'Maybe, but hatred, concentrated hatred, built up over time, can prompt a man to do many things that under normal circumstances he wouldn't.'

'You didn't see him that night, blubbering in front of me. He's a spineless individual.'

I let the matter lie. 'You said you had some news for me.'

His face darkened. 'Yes, I have. It seems that the murderer knows my movements. He must be following me. I went round to Evelyn Munro's flat this morning and he telephoned me there. That's the second time he's done that. The first could have been pure luck on his part ... but ... Well, he must be watching me. Watching and waiting.'

'He used Charlie Dokes's voice?'

'Yes. It was the same kind of banter. The only way he could have known that I was at Evie's ... was if he'd followed me.'

'Who else knew you'd be there?'

'No one ... well, except my manager, Larry Milligan.'

'Your relationship with Miss Munro ... is not strictly professional?'

'I take her out now and then.'

I can spot a euphemism like that from a mile off, so I cut to the chase. 'You're sleeping with her?'

Carter did not reply in words, but his expression gave me the answer. So, another piece of information that had been denied me. The flame of indignation billowed and roared within me. My gut reaction was to throw in the towel now. What was the point of trying to protect my client and discover the identity of the person who was threatening to kill him, if said client was determined to keep me in the dark about key pieces of information relating to his past and present private life? On top of this, I was beginning to dislike Mr Raymond Carter intensely. But common sense overruled these defeatist thoughts. If I turned down all cases in which I didn't care for the character of my client, I wouldn't get much employment. Apart from that I was caught up in this affair and I had become determined to get to the bottom of it.

'Has she any old flame, someone from a past relationship who might have a gripe against you for taking his place with Miss Munro?'

'None that I know of. There have been boyfriends in the past, I guess, but as far as I'm aware nothing serious.'

'Are you sure there is nothing else you have forgotten to tell me?' I asked.

'Nothing that's relevant,' he snapped back.

'Let me be the judge of whether it's relevant or not.'

'Nothing.'

I didn't know whether to believe the slimy toad, but I reckon that's the best answer I was going to get. Before I could reply, there was a sharp rap at the door and then it burst open and a young man breezed in, grinning.

'Oh, sorry, I didn't know you had company,' he said, his voice tinged with mid-Atlantic tones.

'I think our business is done for the moment,' I said, eyeing up the young man.

'This is Al Warren, my scriptwriter,' said Carter. 'Al, this is an old friend of mine, John Hawke.' The lie slipped out with ease.

'Hi there, John, pleased to meet you.'

'Likewise,' I said shaking his hand.

'Sorry to interrupt, but I've got a few new gags for the opening spot in the second half, Ray.' He brandished a couple of sheets of paper. 'I thought it was getting a bit dull. You could try them out tonight and see how they go.'

Carter took the sheets without looking at them. 'Yes, I will. I agree that spot is not getting as many laughs as it should.'

It was time for me to go. I clamped on my hat and made my way to the door.

'I'd better let you finish getting ready,' I

said, glancing at my watch. 'It's only thirty minutes to curtain up.'

'Don't let me drive you away,' said the young man, smiling.

'No, no. I've got to go. Our business is done for now. But I'll be in touch.'

'Please do,' said Carter, throwing me a meaningful glance.

'By the way can you arrange for two seats in the stalls for tomorrow night's performance?'

Carter seemed a little surprised by my request and then, with a faint smile playing about his lips, he glanced over to Charlie Dokes. 'Seems like you've got a couple of new fans, eh, Charlie.'

'That's no surprise to me,' replied the inanimate dummy. 'Enjoy the show, Mr Hawke. The tickets'll be waiting at the box office for you.'

A few minutes later I was out on the street again glad to be breathing in the fresh, untainted, cold night air. I felt that it was cleansing my mind and body from the contaminations of the last thirty minutes or so; from the slippery ambivalent nature of my client, a man to whom a lie came so easily to the tongue, and the crazy world he inhabited in which wooden dolls spoke to you and even threatened murder. It was good to be rubbing shoulders with anonymous humanity, to be part of the real world again. I felt my body relax as I made my way back to the office and to what I thought would be an early night. But fate had other plans in store for me.

17

I headed for Prior's Court, my office, my home and my haven where I could shut out the naughty world for a while. However, when I was less than half a mile away, I suddenly felt in need of another drink to ease my passage into sleep and so, as I passed a scruffy little pub called the Lord Nelson, the noise from within and the smell of ale that lingered on the pavement outside the door lured me inside. Once within its boozy, smoky clutches, the establishment didn't release me until I'd downed a couple of pints of cheap bitter.

I resumed my journey home now less sober and less steady on my feet, but feeling a lot happier. The night was invigoratingly cold and a pale half-moon watched over the city providing a meagre light by which to navigate my route. The streets were very quiet: there were hardly any pedestrians about and just a couple of vehicles purred past me in the gloom, their shaded headlights carving a little amber pathway in the darkness. By the time I was approaching Hawke Towers, I had left humanity behind. I was alone, the only person left on the planet, clip-clopping his unsteady way along the empty street to home and what I hoped would be a refreshing night's sleep. I had managed to squirrel away all thoughts of the Carter case until the morning and I felt relaxed and at ease.

However, as I turned into Prior's Court something suddenly deflated my balloon of contentment. Call it sixth sense if you will, but I knew immediately that something was wrong, something was not as it should be. It was like someone had walked over my grave, as an old sergeant of mine used to say. The hairs prickled on the back of my neck and instinctively my body tensed. Something imperceptible brought my senses to attention. Whether there was a slight sound, a movement in the shadows or sense that I was no longer alone, I did not know. All I did know was that my personal Radar had picked something up and had warned me to be on the alert. I shook my head to dislodge the soft cushion around my brain created by the alcohol.

Instinctively, I froze on the spot and listened. Like an animal I sniffed the air for danger. But there seemed to be nothing — nothing more tangible than the usual muted night sounds. For a fleeting moment I thought I had been imagining things and then there was a slight movement in the black void before me. It was just a gentle rustle of clothing as though someone had shifted position or taken a step nearer. Whatever it was, I was certain there was someone beyond my sight, out there in the darkness, someone who no doubt meant me ill.

'Who's there?' I asked automatically. It was a silly question in one sense, but it informed whoever it was waiting there in shadowy ambush that I was aware of their presence.

From out of the blackness came a little high-pitched giggle.

I waited in the gloom, my nerves beginning to tingle.

'It's a lovely evening, Johnny,' came a disembodied voice. It was a voice I recognized. It was a voice that sent a chill to my heart and a flush of perspiration to my brow. It was the voice of Charlie Dokes.

I was lost for words. What could one say in reply? I was too puzzled and apprehensive to conjure up some coherent response or even some witticism, so I said nothing.

'Cat got your tongue, eh, Johnny? Little meddling Johnny.' The sound now seemed to be coming from another direction. Either the devil was moving around or he was throwing his voice. Instinctively, I took a step forward towards the sound and I heard a shuffling in the gloom as though my phantom friend was shifting position again.

'I've come to get you, Johnny,' said the disembodied surreal, squeaky voice. 'I'm sorry, but I've got to put a stop to your interfering ways before you ruin my party.'

Another direction again.

Behind me this time.

I swung round just in time to catch the shape of the figure as it approached me. At first it was just a shadowy silhouette, hardly any lighter than the darkness from which it emerged, but, as it came closer, I could just about make out the features. I peered hard at the face and then my heart did a fierce leap into my mouth. I was staring into the shiny, clown-like face of Charlie Dokes. There he was: red-lipped rictal grin, bold gorgon eyes and vivid painted cheeks.

The dummy had come to life.

It had grown into human form.

And it was moving towards me.

Coming to get me.

For a moment, my mind could not cope with this prospect, one that was at once too fantastic and yet terribly real. I was for a brief time held rigid, unable to move, my body mesmerized with the horror of this apparition.

The garish face shimmered before me like

a macabre mirage and inanimate though the features were, they seemed to me to project an aura of cruelty and malevolence. Involuntarily, I emitted a sharp guttural cry of fear. How could this be, my mind screamed, as I took few clumsy steps in retreat? But the thing kept coming, the eyes holding me with their maniacal scare.

As though in some bizarre dream, that grotesque face came nearer and nearer, forming itself with greater clarity out of the shadows. It did not utter a word but I could hear the thing breathing, breathing heavily. Before I knew it, the creature was almost upon me. Then I saw the knife. It was raised above his head and glimmered palely in the dim moonlight.

As the blade began to descend, at last my instinct for self-preservation took over and I dodged sideways to escape the blow. I wasn't entirely successful. The knife caught my right arm and sliced into the material of my overcoat — my lovely warm overcoat. My assailant giggled. It was the repulsive Charlie Dokes giggle and the sound of it made me shudder. And then he came at me again, but now I was ready for him. I bent low and head butted him in the stomach as hard as I could. To my delight I heard him groan as the wind was banged out of him. He staggered back and again I saw that surreal face clearly. Of course, I informed my now sober brain, this is a man wearing a mask, not some supernatural thing from the pit. But I also told myself that this man in a mask intends to kill me.

He returned, the knife held before him, but this time he anticipated my move sideways and I felt a sharp pain in my thigh.

A hit. A palpable hit.

Strangely, the overwhelming emotion I felt on receiving a wound was anger. The bastard had torn my overcoat and now he had hurt me. He had gone too far. I roared with rage and ran towards him as they had instructed me during bayonet practice, although, of course, in this instance, I didn't actually have a bayonet to aid me. Now it was his turn to retreat and try to avoid my advance. I grabbed the hand that held the knife and thrust it upwards, shaking his arm as hard as I could in an effort to force him to drop it. I had almost succeeded when he pressed his body against mine and kneed me in the groin, causing me to release my grip.

I groaned and stumbled awkwardly, but managed to retain my balance. Again the blade descended and again my overcoat suffered a further breach. On the shoulder this time. If I survive this assault, I pondered wildly, I'll be wandering around London with bruised privates, wearing a coat of rags and tatters.

Without a pause, he came at me once more. This time I employed a different tactic. Instead of trying to dodge out of his way, I rushed towards him again, but this time I quickly side-stepped to the right when I drew close. As I did so, my hand shot out towards my assailant's face, or more precisely to the garish mask that he was wearing.

'Let's see who you are,' I yelled fiercely, my fingers finding purchase on the edge of the mask. As I tugged hard at the shiny papier-mâché visage glinting in the thin moonlight, once again the knife penetrated the sleeve of my coat and I felt the sharp stab of pain in my arm as I received a second wound.

I gave a yelp as the blade sliced into my flesh, but I maintained my grip on the mask and tugged even harder. So hard in fact that I began to fall backwards. Suddenly I felt myself losing my balance but I held on to the recalcitrant mask, and found that I was hauling my assailant down with me. With a most un-Charlie-Dokes-like deep-throated grunt, he heaved himself back from me in order to maintain his own equilibrium. As he did so, I managed to drag the doll's mask away from his face.

Released from my grip, he stumbled away into the darkness and I fell to the ground, crashing down on my wounded arm. For a very unpleasant moment, I saw a very bright ack ack display of lights flash before my eyes while my arm felt as though it had been stabbed with a red-hot poker. Stifling a moan of pain, I picked myself up, but by now my assailant had disappeared. Without his disguise his vulnerability had been exposed and he had evaporated into the night. As I steadied myself, I could hear his footsteps fading into the distance. I swore softly. I hadn't managed to get a look at his face.

I took a few deep breaths and tried to bring my heart rate down to somewhere approaching normal. As I did so the pain in my right arm asserted itself with a regular rhythmic throb. I'd better get home and examine the wounds to my arm and thigh and, I thought, wryly, survey the damage to my overcoat. I was about to turn and stagger the last few yards to Prior's Court when a thought struck me. For a few moments I searched in the shadows until I found it. The mask — the grinning gargoyle mask of Charlie Dokes. The mask worn by the killer. I scooped it up and hobbled homeward.

18

'You've been a very careless boy, haven't you? A very careless boy indeed,' the voice sniped at him.

He wiped the sweat away from his forehead before replying, 'I guess so,' he said, looking away into the darkness.

'You nearly got caught. Exposed yourself.'

The head turned and the eyes stared accusingly.

'I know. I know. Let it drop, will you?'

'How can I? I ask you. How can I? You call yourself a mastermind. You nearly ruined everything, you fool,' said Charlie Dokes, his mouth snapping noisily.

19

On reaching home, I stripped off my clothes in order to examine my wounds. It was a painful process because the ritual required so much movement from my gashed arm, that I moaned and groaned each step of the way. I'm not keen on pain.

At last, stripped down to my underclothes, I took on my medical duties and inspected the damage. The gash on my thigh was quite narrow but fairly deep. It could probably do with some stitches, but I wasn't about to take myself off to hospital for that. I was a big boy now. I didn't need a nurse to kiss me better — although the fleeting thought of it aroused me slightly. A feminine embrace and a pair of warm lips on mine would be an ideal restorative. Shaking such notions from my tired mind, I took down the first aid tin. I reckoned that if I bandaged the wound on my leg tightly it would heal itself sufficiently in a week. The cut on my arm was more painful but less serious. I bathed it in Dettol and stuck some cotton wool on it held down with a big strip of Elastoplast. I certainly couldn't have bandaged it one handed.

Although the two wounds ached unpleasantly, guaranteeing that I wouldn't get much sleep that night, I was thankful that I had escaped comparatively lightly from the little skirmish. It had been bizarre and frightening. I wouldn't forget very easily being attacked by the figure of Charlie Dokes. It was the stuff of childhood nightmares, but I had experienced it. The one positive aspect of the encounter — how circumspect that word is — was that it indicated that I was getting close to some unpleasant truth and the killer — for I must assume it was indeed he who had attacked me — wanted to eliminate me before I came any closer to it. This thought filled me with mixed feelings. I was pleased that I had in some way unnerved the fellow, but I didn't relish the fact that I was now on his list of potential victims. However, I felt so weary and in such discomfort that neither contemplation stirred my emotions to any great degree. All I cared about now was to escape the cares of the world by having a good kip.

So, once I'd finished ministering to my wounds, I took myself off to bed. I lay on my back — the position which caused the least discomfort — and waited to be scooped up into the arms of Morpheus. He took a long time coming. While I tried to let my mind drift off into sleep, my two wounds were sending throbbing Morse code messages to each other. Sometime around three in the morning I finally drifted off.

When I awoke, the pain started immediately. Both wounds pounded indignantly. They were not going to let me forget their presence or the way I'd allowed my body to be damaged in such a violent fashion. I decided not to examine the cuts in case they depressed me further. I would just have to grit my teeth and get on with things — the damage would heal in time. So I gritted my teeth and set about the awkward and often painful task of dressing myself and carrying out my morning ablutions. Finally, after much jerky movement and a series of stifled groans, I was ready to face the world. As I sat over what I laughingly called breakfast — a cup of tea, a slice of burnt bread scraped with a sheen of margarine, and a cigarette — I examined the mask that I had ripped from my assailant's face the night before. It was finely crafted — from papier mâché — was a clever representation of Charlie Dokes's ugly mug. On the inside of the mask was a signature. It was tiny and I had difficulty making it out with my naked eye. I retrieved my Sherlock Holmes magnifying glass from the sideboard drawer and gave it a closer examination. It looked like 'Max Summers'.

'That could come in handy,' I murmured to myself, but before I could let my thoughts wander down that particular avenue, the telephone rang.

It was Peter, wanting to know what time I was coming round today. Of course, it was Saturday. I'd forgotten.

'I've one or two errands to carry out this morning,' I said, trying to sound cheerful, 'so I reckon it'll be sometime in the afternoon before I can make it.'

Peter groaned. 'I wanted us to have a game of football in the park this morning. It'll be too dark by the time you get here.'

'I'm sorry about that, but I'll make it up to you. I'll take you into Town for a nice tea and then ... ' — I paused dramatically and chuckled — 'and then, I'll take you to the Palladium to see Charlie Dokes.'

'Really! Do you really mean it?' Peter virtually shrieked down the phone with uncontained excitement.

'Certainly do,' I said beaming. 'That's better than a kick about in the park, eh?'

'You bet.'

'See you later then, OK?'

'Can't wait. Come as soon as you can,' he said, and I pictured him as he replaced the receiver in the hallway of the house where he stayed. He would be grinning from ear to ear, his young face flushed and his eyes wide with pleasurable anticipation.

Checking my watch for the time, I lifted the receiver again and dialled. It was a bit of an off chance but I knew that Limelight Lionel worked six mornings a week and could invariably be found at his desk between the hours of nine and when the pubs opened. After that it was anyone's guess where he'd be.

I was in luck.

'Good morning, Johnny. You got some juicy gossip for me I hope?'

'Not yet, I'm afraid,' I said, bending the truth a little. 'I'm afraid I'm after a little information again.'

Lionel gave a dry chuckle. 'You know I do this kind of business in the Old Mitre. Information comes at a liquid price, my son.'

'I'll just have to owe you. You know you can trust me.'

'Maybe, but I'm rather thirsty now.'

He was playing with me and I went along with the game.

'So, what do you want to know this time?'

'I've got hold of a theatrical mask. Very nice. Very well executed. The maker's name is on the inside: Max Summers. Have you heard of him?'

Lionel chuckled again. 'Max Summers?

Certainly have. One of the best in the business.'

'Where does he hang out?'

'Four pints and a whisky chaser . . . '

'A steep price for an address, Lionel.'

'Steep price, maybe, but where else you gonna go for this info?'

'Point taken. It's a deal.'

'Max has a shop on Henrietta Street, near Covent Garden. Don't leave it too long before you pay your dues, Johnny boy.' With that parting shot, he put the phone down.

★ ★ ★

I walked to Henrietta Street thinking the exercise would do the wound to my thigh some good. Whether it was beneficial or not, I wasn't sure; I just knew that it hurt like hell. By the time I had reached my destination, I was limping because of the pain. My composure wasn't helped by the additional discomfort from the wound to my arm which throbbed in sympathy with its partner. I must have made a strange sight: a one-eyed limping man in a tattered and sliced overcoat grimacing at every step, slowly patrolling Henrietta Street.

As I neared the Charing Cross Road end of the street, I came across a small shop front

205

which was full of masks. The sign above the door read MASKS UNLIMITED. Below it in very small lettering I read: 'Prop. M. Summers'. Good old reliable Lionel. I went inside. The shop was tiny. There was room for two customers only before a narrow counter, behind which was a small display cabinet containing half-a-dozen masks and a door leading off to the rear of the premises. There was a little handbell on the counter. I rang it.

A voice called from the inner recess of the shop, 'Coming.'

And sure enough, the owner of the voice came. It was a pretty young woman with short cropped glossy dark hair that framed her face and the most amazing grey eyes, like those of an enigmatic cat. She was dressed in a pinstriped pencil skirt and a neat black cardigan that was buttoned almost to the neck. Her face was powdered to a pale ivory and enlivened by her bright red lipstick. She flashed me a broad smile of greeting. Sadly, I was wise enough to recognize that this was a practised smile given freely to all prospective customers and not something meant especially for me. And indeed, why should it be? I must have looked a strange fish indeed with my tired face, my limp, eye-patch and coat of threads and tatters. Certainly not someone to arouse the interest of an attractive young lady.

More's the pity, I thought, for I found this attractive young lady particularly alluring.

'Good morning,' she said, politely. 'How may I help you?' Her voice was soft and mellifluous and tinged with accent. She was French.

'I'd like to have a word with Mr Max Summers, the proprietor.'

At my request, her long fingered right hand fluttered around her mouth in a feeble attempt to stifle a laugh.

Her action was so delightful and refreshingly natural that I found myself smiling too. I didn't really know why. 'Have I said something funny?' I asked gently.

The girl nodded, her eyes still brimming with amusement and then she giggled again, but this time she made a greater effort to contain herself. 'I am sorry,' she said, blushing slightly, 'you see *I* am Max Summers, the proprietor.'

'Max . . . ?'

'Short for Maxine.'

'I see. I apologize for jumping to conclusions.'

'And I apologize for laughing at you.'

'Then we are even.'

This time she flashed me a genuine smile. I luxuriated in the warmth of it.

'So, how may I help you? You are wanting a

mask of some kind?'

'It's information, really,' I said, pulling the Charlie Dokes mask from the innards of my tattered coat. 'I believe this was made here.' I passed it to her.

She gave it a cursory glance. 'Oh, yes, I remember it well. It was made to look like the doll from the radio show. I was given a photograph to work from.'

'Could you tell me who asked you to make the mask?'

For the first time, Maxine Summers' sweet face lost its smile. 'Oh, dear no. I cannot betray a customer's confidence.'

I leaned on the counter and lowered my voice to a conspiratorial whisper. 'This is very important, miss. I am a private detective working on an important case. It's a matter of life and death.' I passed her one of my cards which she read very carefully, her lovely features registering the change from surprise to uncertainty.

'I don't know . . . ' she said shaking her head slightly.

'It's just the name I want. I wouldn't ask you if it wasn't vital to the investigation.'

She hesitated further, but I knew that she was weakening. It was time to add a little pressure. 'I only want the name. There's no real harm in that, is there? It's either tell me, or I'm afraid I'll have to go to the police and you wouldn't want that, would you? Great big coppers clumping up and down your premises. Looks bad for business too,' I added. I was not particularly proud of this particular turn of the screw, but I had to be prepared to upset the pretty Maxine in order to get the name.

And from the change in her expression, I could see that indeed I had upset the pretty Maxine. 'Very well,' she said coldly and then disappeared into the back of the shop, leaving behind the faint lingering smell of her perfume. She returned a few moments later with a small ledger which she consulted, holding the pages away from me so that I could not see them.

'The customer who bought the mask was a man called Carter. Raymond Carter.'

My mouth gaped a little. What the hell was going on here? I just stopped myself from asking Maxine if she was sure, if she had given me the correct name. But of course she must have — even though it didn't make sense. Why would Carter buy such a mask and — more particularly — was it really him who wore it last night in order to attack me? My mind juggled with these thoughts while I repeated the name to Maxine to make sure that I really heard correctly: 'Raymond Carter.'

She nodded and closed the ledger.

'Well, thank you, Miss Summers. I really appreciate your help.'

'Will that be all?' she asked sharply, sending an Arctic breeze in my direction. There were no smiles now. She looked stern and disappointed and, of course, I knew why. I had bullied and threatened her into doing something she didn't want to do, something that was against her principles and now she hated me for it. And I hated myself too.

I couldn't think of anything to say or do that would make her think better of me, this shabby one-eyed man with a ragged coat and bullying manner. And I wanted her to think better of me. Desperately so.

'Could I buy you lunch . . . as a thank you for helping me?' I said suddenly. Where that came from I had no idea. My lusting subconscious had temporarily taken over my brain and tongue and acted on impulse. Normally I would have been too shy to make such a suggestion to a young, attractive woman.

She looked aghast at the very idea of it. There was no hesitation in her reply. 'No,' she snapped disdainfully, her eyes flaring with anger.

I tried a little harder. 'Please. I feel awful about putting you on the spot like this, but it is terribly important. I'd like to . . . express my gratitude.'

The gates remained closed. 'Thank you, Mr Hawke, but I really do not want to take lunch with you. To be honest, you are the last person on earth with whom I should wish to take lunch. Goodbye.'

I have never been quite sure where the phrase 'a flea in my ear' originated, although I know what it means and on this occasion I experienced the sensation first hand. In fact, if it is possible the delightfully gamine Maxine gave me several fleas in my ear with her fierce and flinty rejection of my offer of lunch.

'I'm sorry. I hate dining alone,' I said.

'And you must do that so often,' she replied, her eyes narrowing with sarcasm.

'Keep my card. You never know when you might need a detective.'

'Goodbye, Mr Hawke.'

Within moments I was back out on to the streets in the cold November wind but strangely it was less chilly than the inside of Masks Unlimited.

20

Al Warren stood in the open doorway of Larry Milligan's outer office and skilfully tossed his trilby across the room so that it landed neatly on the hat rack.

'And for my encore . . . ' he cried, bowing from the waist down.

Madge Dailey, Milligan's secretary, a large blonde-haired lady who wore a permanent world-weary expression, looked up from her desk with indifference. She gave Warren a brief raise of the eyebrow which eloquently informed him that she had seen the trick before and that she wished that he wouldn't perform it every time he came to the office.

Warren took no notice of her silent censure. 'Is he in?' he asked cheerfully.

The eyebrow went up again. 'He's here and that's why I am. Even though it's Saturday. He's got me typing up some complicated contract.'

'Good, I need to see him.'

'Ah. Ah!' She held up her hand to halt his progress across the room towards the door of Milligan's office. 'You can't just barge in. I'll announce you.' With a nimbleness that defied her substantial bulk — Warren reckoned at least sixteen stone — Madge Dailey sprang to her feet, squeezed her ample figure round the end of the desk and made her way to Milligan's door where she tapped gently before opening it. Popping her head round the door she said, 'Al Warren is here to see you.'

Warren heard Milligan emit a low moan of irritation.

'Charming,' observed Warren quietly to himself, before announcing loudly, 'it's quite important, Your Highness.'

'Come on in,' came the reply.

Warren smiled broadly at Madge and entered Milligan's office. It was a small room but elegantly decorated. The walls were filled with photographs of Milligan's past and present clients. On his desk was a large framed picture of Raymond Carter and Charlie Dokes. The doll was in the foreground, dominating the photograph, its shiny face peering out into the world with that unnerving fixed grin which Warren thought gave the features a look of arrogant malevolence.

One other photograph caught Milligan's eye. It was lying casually on Milligan's desk. It was a picture of Evelyn Munro.

'I can only spare you a few minutes,' said

Milligan, before Warren had a chance to sit down.

'I reckon five minutes will suffice — from my side of things anyway.'

Milligan frowned. 'Go on.'

'It's about Raymond.'

The frown deepened. 'What now?'

'I think he's cracking up.'

'He's a little tense I grant you and he has good reason to be. He's getting death threats — from his blasted dummy for Christ's sake. And on top of that he's the main suspect for a murder. He's allowed to be a bit wobbly.'

Warren's face darkened. 'He's more than a bit wobbly. You should have seen him last night. He lost it a couple of times on the stage. Dried completely. And afterwards, he was knocking back the booze in his dressing room like there was no tomorrow. I reckon that private detective — the guy with the eye-patch — had spooked him somewhat. He'd seen him before the show. Ray is getting really paranoid. If he gives in to his fears, it could ruin his career completely. You know how fickle the public are.'

'They make you; they break you.' Milligan glanced at the pictures around the room. Some, stars a few years ago, were now forgotten names.

'Yeah,' said Warren, following Milligan's

gaze. 'I popped round to his flat this morning because I was concerned about him. He opened the door looking like death — ideal casting for the *Phantom of the Opera*. He was still fully dressed and reeking of alcohol. He hadn't been to bed at all. Reckoned he had expected a call from the killer and had waited up for him. That is not a bit wobbly — that's nuts, mister.'

Milligan sighed heavily. 'And what am I supposed to do about it? It's a rhetorical question, Al. I know that as his manager he's my responsibility, but I've been here before with other acts. Some of them seem to have an inbuilt self-destruct button. Certainly Raymond's having a tough time, but a stronger more self-contained fellow could cope with it. But he . . . well, it looks like he's deliberately steering himself towards the rocks. If that's the case neither you, nor I, nor all the bleeding king's horses and all the king's men can stop him.'

'We've got to try.'

'Oh, sure, we've got to try and we will. I will and I'm sure you will but in the end . . . ' He left the rest of his thought unspoken.

Both men lapsed into silence for a moment.

'You don't think he actually killed old Arthur, do you?' Warren said at length.

Milligan narrowed his eyes and appeared to chew his lip for a moment before replying. 'No, I don't think so,' he said, shaking his head. 'But then again, I don't know for certain. It's my experience that all vents have a screw loose. It comes from making a living talking to yourself. They form a very strange relationship with that lump of wood they have on their knee. It makes having normal relationships difficult. I knew one vent who treated the dummy like his own son. He even set a place for him at the dinner table. It totally spooked his children. When he died he was buried with the doll in the coffin as he'd requested in his will.'

'Now that is weird.'

'They're all weird. I've seen some vents who have almost been taken over by their dolls. One fellow I was interested in signing insisted that his bloody dummy did all the negotiating. When you take on a vent act you take on the man himself and the dummy as well. Split personality. That's what they've got: living out the other side of their character through their doll. Half human — half dummy. I reckon with some of them it wouldn't take much to tip the balance and then the dummy becomes the dominant one. The one who controls the other. Maybe Raymond Carter fits into that category.'

The two men looked at each other for a moment, their faces stern masks, hiding their unspoken thoughts.

At length Milligan sighed and broke the spell. 'Look Al, I appreciate you coming round to let me know how things are. I'll pop round to the Palladium this afternoon before the matinee and check on our friend. We'll just have to keep monitoring the situation and hope that this crazy chap who keeps phoning him up loses interest or gets caught.'

'I'm with you on that,' said Warren, rising from the chair. 'I just thought you'd like to know how things were. We need to protect our interests as best as we can.'

'I don't suppose that you have any notion who might be behind these threats? Someone who's really got it in for Raymond?'

Warren looked as though he was about to come out with a glib one-liner but then at the last minute changed his mind and just shook his head. 'Raymond isn't the most popular guy on the planet, but I can't think of anyone who hates him enough to drive him batty.'

'And yet there is someone.'

Both men fell silent for a moment as they contemplated this truth.

'Anyway,' said Milligan breezily, snapping out of his reflective mood, 'as I said, I am rather busy, Al.' He began shepherding the writer towards the door and then he stopped abruptly and looked Warren straight in the eyes. 'You know that if everything goes horribly wrong for Ray, you'll be all right, don't you? There's dozens of comics would give their right arm to have you writing for them.'

'That's all I need: a one-armed comedian.' Al grinned weakly and left.

★ ★ ★

Raymond Carter sat on the sofa in his sitting room and gazed across the room at Charlie Dokes. Carter's face was pale and drawn with dark semi-circles under the eyes bearing witness to his lack of sleep. He held a mug of coffee in his hands. It was now nearly cold and he had barely touched it. He felt too weary to drink. In fact he felt too weary for almost anything.

'Things are starting to unravel, Charlie,' he said quietly.

'You're telling me,' the doll replied without moving its lips.

'No, I'm telling me, I suppose.'

'Never mind, old boy, you've still got your old Charlie. The star of the show. For the time being, that is. I reckon there are other vents out there who'd be more than happy to take on a lively prospect like me if you fail. You see it's you who are going down the plughole, old boy, not me. You see, Ray, my friend, I don't really need you. Charlie Dokes will survive, even if you don't. Now, if you want my advice — '

'No, I don't want your advice. Shut up! Shut up!' Carter cried wildly, his body shaking with anger.

'Temper, temper. That will never do. Remember, I'm the boss in this outfit and what I say goes.'

'Leave me alone,' bellowed Carter, ruffling his hair savagely as though trying to exorcise a demon from beneath his scalp. As he did so he spilt some coffee. He ignored the damp patch on his trousers and slumped back on the sofa and closed his eyes desperate for his tired body and aching brain to be overtaken by sleep.

21

With some effort, I cast thoughts of the delicious Maxine Summers from my mind and pondered about the mask that lodged snugly inside my ventilated overcoat. If it really was Raymond Carter who had ordered Maxine to make the mask and if it was Raymond Carter who had worn it to attack me last night, then I was not only dealing with a lunatic, but it could be that for the first time in my career as a detective, my client turned out to be the murderer. However, those two big 'ifs' meant I had to find out more before I could reach a definite conclusion. It was highly unlikely that Carter would buy a mask using his own name. I could have cleared up that little problem by asking Maxine to describe her client, the Raymond Carter who ordered the mask bringing with him a picture of Charlie Dokes, but I knew she would have refused. After all, I'd had to bully her just to get the name.

On leaving Maxine's shop I made my way to Benny's café. On the way I called in at a little shop in Croxford Court, just off the lower end of Charing Cross Road. The establishment called 'Danny's' sold second-hand clothes and for certain customers it was just a matter of handing over a suitable amount of cash — no clothes coupons were required. Danny was a diminutive, red-faced Irishman who'd been a successful jockey in a past life. I had done him a little favour once upon a time, oiling the wheels for his divorce by spying on his missus while she was fraternizing with a burly sailor. I knew he'd do me a good deal on a nice second-hand coat. And he did.

'You look the bee's knees in that, my boy,' he said, as I examined myself in the long mirror in his shop. It was nice — a thick, dark-brown herringbone overcoat which fitted perfectly. But it was priced at nine guineas. When I saw the tag, I cringed.

'Ouch,' I said.

'Oh, come now, Johnny. Don't give me the sob story. A successful chap like yourself can afford it. You won't find a finer coat in London for the money.'

I reckoned he was right about the price, but it was still more than I was happy to pay.

'How about seven quid and I'll tell everyone where I bought it.'

'Are you sure you've not kissed the Blarney stone yourself?' he laughed. 'Go on with you, you rascal. Call it seven pounds and ten shillin's and we got a deal.'

Five minutes later I was back out on the street in my new posh overcoat while my old ventilated version was languishing in the dustbin behind Danny's shop.

Saturday lunchtime was a quiet time for Benny. His regulars, the folk who worked in the offices and businesses nearby who filled the café during the week, were absent. When I entered there were only about half-a-dozen customers in the place and Benny was leaning on the counter staring into space, deep in thought. He greeted me with a smile.

'Johnny, how nice to see you,' he said.

'Well, I suppose it's always nice to see a customer.'

'Precisely.' His grin broadened. Then he gave me the once over. 'You come into some money? That's a nice bit of schmutter, my boy,' he said running his fingers along the lapel of my new coat.

'You like?'

'Very smart. You'll get a lady now.'

It was Benny's mission in life to see me married.

'I need a little help,' I said, changing the subject.

'Takings have not been so good this month.'

I shook my head. 'I don't need a loan; I need some medical treatment.'

That really caught his attention. I explained about my injuries, without giving the full details of how I received them. Although Benny was aware that in my line of work, the odd cut and blow to the head were occupational hazards, it did not stop him clucking round me like a mother hen and a very Jewish mother hen at that. He put his head round the kitchen door and asked Doris 'to keep an eye on things while I turn doctor for a while.'

Doris was happy to oblige and knew her boss well enough not to ask him to explain himself. Benny led me upstairs to his little flat and pulled a large first-aid box from the sideboard. I slipped off my jacket, rolled up my sleeve and removed my ham-fisted dressing to expose the wound.

On seeing it, Benny gave a sharp intake of breath. 'Ooh, that's a nasty gash,' he said. 'I'll need to clean it first.' He disappeared into his bathroom and returned with a damp cloth which he used to cleanse the wound before treating it with antiseptic cream and dressing it with a clean bandage.

'How did this all come about?' he asked, as he carried out his ministrations with great care.

'I was attacked.'

'That much I could have deduced. Who by and why?'

'You don't really want to know. In fact, I'm not really sure myself.'

'Some detective you are,' he observed, pulling the bandage tight, making me wince. 'There . . . all done. Florence Nightingale couldn't have made a better job of it.'

He was right. It was a superior piece of work all right.

'Now let's have a look at the other one.'

I slipped my trousers down far enough to expose the bandaged wound. Once the dressing was removed, the actual cut did not look as bad as it had the night before but it still throbbed like hell. Deftly and with skill, Benny repeated the procedure of cleansing, anointing with cream and bandaging and in less than five minutes I was ready to go out into the world again, albeit in a rather jerky fashion.

'What you need now is a hot cup of tea and one of my Eccles cakes.'

'Sounds good to me.'

Benny grinned. 'It's just what the doctor ordered.'

We went downstairs and I sat at one of the tables while Benny went off to bring me the tea and cake. While I indulged myself, Benny drew up a chair and chatted with me. He asked me about Peter and reprimanded me for not bringing him to see his 'Uncle Benny' for at 'least a couple of weeks'. And then, in a blatantly obvious fashion, he attempted to find more out about the knife wounds. I deflected his questions with one of my own about the café. 'How's business these days?' I asked casually.

It was the usual trigger for my old friend to moan about customers' manners, his uncertain profits and the high prices he paid for his supplies. I grinned through the performance having heard it all before, knowing full well that Benny's café was going from strength to strength; it was just that the old guy seemed to get some kick out of painting a bleaker picture. It somehow made him feel better.

'Much obliged for the snack,' I said at last, brushing away the errant flakes of the Eccles cake from front of my new coat, 'and for the medical treatment.'

'My bill will be in the post,' Benny grinned. 'You want another cup of tea?'

I shook my head. 'Thanks, but I've got things to do.'

Benny accompanied me to the door. 'Don't forget. I want to see that little scamp Peter. You bring him round here soon.'

I assured him that I would and left.

Now, I had a man to see about a case of adultery.

Percy Goodall lived in a small flat on Queen Anne Street, barely a stone's throw from Broadcasting House. I had taken a chance of catching him in. The chance paid off. I had hardly stopped knocking at the door before it was wrenched open and the man himself stood before me. He was tall, but with a pear-shaped body which bulged in the middle putting a great strain on the buttons of his waistcoat. He was possessed of rather soft feminine features which he had tried to disguise with a small moustache and goatee beard. I had never seen him before, but as soon as he spoke I recognized his voice from numerous radio programmes.

'Can I help you?' he asked, in a tone that was not exactly friendly.

I passed him my card and, as he perused it, I tried an old trick of mine which no doubt Danny would have attributed to my familiarity with the Blarney Stone. 'I'm helping the police with their enquiries into Arthur Keating's death,' I said firmly, with what I hoped was a note of official menace.

'Helping the police? I've already spoken to the police. There's nothing more to say.'

'Well, it's rather more to do with your relationship with Raymond Carter, sir. If I could come inside and have a few words . . . '

Goodall did not budge.

'It will only take a few minutes and then we can clear the matter up and you won't be bothered again.' I gave him a knowing look and added pointedly, 'It's in your best interests.'

At last this brought about some reaction. He looked a little unnerved now and with ill grace he showed me into a tiny sitting room which was very tidy and bleakly Spartan.

'What exactly is this all about?' he asked. He maintained his well-modulated tones, but I could tell from the awkward stance he adopted and his fluttering hands that he was nervous.

'Raymond Carter.'

'What about Raymond Carter?'

'I gather there is no love lost between the two of you.'

'And how do you gather that?'

'I know that he had a brief affair with your wife and then she left you.'

'So he did. And so she did,' Goodall observed bitterly. 'What has that got to do with you?'

'Raymond Carter is receiving death threats.'

'Is he now? Well, I am not surprised' He paused as though some amusing thought had struck him and his eyes sparkled with

amusement. 'Oh . . . I see. You think . . . '
Suddenly Goodall emitted a strange little
noise. It was more of a whinny than a
full-blown laugh. 'You think it's me. You think
I'm sending him death threats.' He whinnied
again, the hands flapping even more erratically now. He was obviously finding the idea
quite hilarious.

'And you're not?'

'Of course I'm not. I don't like the man; in
fact, I detest him, but if I was going to kill
him, I certainly wouldn't warn him about it
in advance. And if — if, mind you — I was
going to do it, I'd have done it some time
ago.'

'When your wife left you?'

Suddenly, Goodall seemed to relax, he
folded his tall frame into an armchair and
indicated I take the one opposite him.

'What angered me about Carter was his
betrayal of me as a fellow broadcaster. He
went behind my back and seduced my wife.
They were not the actions of a gentleman.
That's what I can't forgive him for. But it's
hardly a matter for murder is it? As for
Dorothy — my wife — leaving me, he
actually did me a favour. I was glad to get rid
of the silly cow. I must admit that I fell for her
beauty not her brains and then I discovered
that she didn't have any at all . . . brains that

is. Or morals for that matter. If it hadn't been Carter it would have been some other chap she'd have been bed-hopping with. I'm better off without her. So you see, there is no hard coal of burning hatred in my heart for Raymond Carter. As I say, I dislike the man. He's a bounder and a bloody cad but I wouldn't soil my hands by sending him death threats.' He glanced down at my card which he was still holding in his hand. 'So, Mr . . . Hawke, I hope that settles the matter.'

'Where is your wife now?'

I got the whinny of a laugh again. 'How should I know? Bedlam for all I care. She'll not be far from some poor devil's bed I'll be bound.' He found this thought very amusing and laughed again.

I realized that I was going to get no further relevant information from this chap, maybe a few more effeminate high-pitched giggles but little else. I rose from my chair and made my way to the door.

'So who do you think is behind these death threats then?' Goodall asked. 'Who is your main suspect?'

I shrugged. 'Your guess is as good as mine,' I said.

22

Maxine Summers consulted her watch. It was 3.15 and already dark outside. Business had been slow today — not that it was particularly good any day. Even at the best of times theatrical mask-making was very much a niche market, but before the war when her father was alive and in charge, the business had done quite well. It wasn't just the theatre world they supplied: the idle rich also came to them to purchase masks for their champagne parties and various fancy dress soirées. But since the outbreak of war, there had been less and less demand for their frivolous trade. Fun and extravagance were in short supply. When her father had died suddenly from a brain haemorrhage, Maxine had seriously considered shutting down the business but it was all she knew and so she kept it on in the hope that things would improve. However, now she was hardly making enough to live on. The order book had but a few entries — various masks for a couple of provincial pantomimes — and that was all. Some days not one customer came into the little shop. It was a lonely and depressing business, made more so by the absence of her beloved father. She missed him so much.

As she stood by the door staring out through the glass into the cold dark street outside, she felt as though she was looking at her future. She gave an involuntary shiver and wrapped her arms around herself.

And then out of the gloom she saw a figure approaching the shop, hurriedly, with a purpose. She stepped back as the figure entered, causing the bell to ring eerily in the empty premises. The customer was a tall man with his trilby hat pulled down over his face.

Maxine retreated behind the counter and smiled at him. 'Good afternoon, how may I help you?' she said brightly.

Slowly, the man lifted his head so that she could see his features. He had a pair of thick-lensed glasses and the lower half of his face was covered by a heavy beard. He looked rather like a comic version of a foreign spy or anarchist. His appearance made her smile. However, she had seen the fellow before. He was a customer. He had ordered a mask to be made. He grinned at her in a strange way as he noted her recognition.

'You remember me,' he said, in an unusual guttural fashion as though he was swallowing something at the same time as he was speaking.

She nodded. 'Yes, of course.'

'I ordered a mask from you. The one that looked like a ventriloquist's dummy. Charlie Dokes.' He produced a photograph from his overcoat pocket and held it up for her perusal. It was a picture of the ventriloquist's doll.

'I remember it very well. It was an unusual request,' she smiled. 'I do not get many customers who want masks to look like someone . . . something else so specifically.'

'Good. I just wonder if you've had anyone coming in here asking about the mask.'

For the second time that afternoon, Maxine felt herself shiver. There was an underlying menace in the way the man asked the question. There was no humour or even common courtesy in his tone. Nevertheless she found herself answering truthfully. 'Well, yes, as a matter of fact . . . ' she said.

'Was it a man with an eye-patch?' The voice was openly aggressive now, threatening.

She recalled the man with the eye-patch and his claim to be a detective, investigating an important case. She hadn't known whether to believe him or not at the time; she had been infuriated by his forceful manner and his arrogance. Now she was inclined to believe him. The man who stood before her was beginning to frighten her.

'I don't remember,' she found herself saying. Some instinct within her told her not to give too much away or it would place the one-eyed detective in danger.

Max's answer did not please the bearded man. He leaned over towards her and grabbed her arms, his fingers digging into her flesh. With a sudden movement he dragged her roughly towards him so that she was held over the counter. She gave a slight gasp of shock at this sudden act of violence.

'Don't give me that,' he growled. 'It was the man with the eye-patch wasn't it? You can hardly forget that, can you? A man with one eye.'

She felt his warm breath on her face. Now she really was frightened. She could see that this man had a reckless danger in his eyes which glared at her, maliciously, through the thick lenses of his spectacles. She also noticed that his beard was not real. It was fake hair that had been stuck on with spirit gum as they did in the theatre. His whole appearance was false — a disguise. He had something to hide. This discovery intensified her fear and she tried to pull away from him but his grip was strong and she couldn't move.

'Yes, yes,' she admitted, quietly.

'What did you tell him?'

'Nothing.' Maxine realized that if she had

told the truth, he may do her more harm.

'I don't believe you,' he snarled, tightening his grip on her arms.

'It's true,' she cried, tried to force back the tears that were moistening her eyes. 'I always keep customers' details private. It's the shop's policy.'

The bearded man stared at her for a while as though debating with himself whether to believe her or not.

'It is true,' she added in an earnest whisper.

'Did you describe me to him?'

'No, no. I swear. No. I just told him I couldn't give him the information that he wanted and then he went away.'

After a brief pause he released his hold of the girl. He gave her a tight smile as though to acknowledge that he was satisfied that she was telling him the truth. Maxine edged backwards, away from the counter, making sure she was out of his reach, although he didn't seem to notice. His mind seemed to be on other things.

'Now little lady, I was never here, right? You do not breathe a word of my visit to a soul. You got that?'

Maxine nodded again. She knew that could be her only response. She feared for her life otherwise.

'Believe me, if you squeal, I will hear about

it and I'll come back and then I won't be quite so pleasant. Talk and it will be the worse for you. Do you understand?'

'I understand.'

'Good girl.' He raised his hand to his hat in a farewell greeting and threw the girl a chilling smile before disappearing out into the November dusk.

23

After my interview with Percy Goodall, I made my way home. I wasn't quite sure whether I could cross the smooth Mr Announcer with the effeminate giggle off my list of suspects. I tended to think so. Although he had seemed relaxed, equitable even, about Carter's affair with his wife, maybe that giggle suggested that he had interests elsewhere and she had just been a convenient cover. My gossipmonger friend, Limelight Lionel, might be able to fill me in on the sexual proclivities of Mr P. Goodall.

Despite my wounds throbbing with less insistence, thanks no doubt to Benny's ministering, I still felt weary as I trudged my way up the stairs to my place. The lack of sleep in recent nights and the physical damage I had undergone were beginning to take their toll. My intention was to catch forty winks before going over to pick Peter up for our Saturday treat, a slap-up tea and a trip to the theatre. How I was going to cope with that, I didn't know. As I closed the door behind me I was already having difficulty preventing my eyelid from drooping. I didn't want to end up drifting off in the Palladium and snoring loudly in the stalls. I kicked off my shoes, undid my tie, lay on the couch and it wasn't very long before I was off to the land of Nod. Unfortunately, the forty winks doubled in number at least, and when I surfaced some-what groggily from my slumbers, the room was quite dark. Pulling on the blackout curtains, I switched on the lamp and glanced at my watch. It was coming up to four o'clock. I swore and reached for the telephone. It was Peter who answered, the weary tone in his voice informing me that he knew it was me — me with another excuse for being late. I had lost count of the occasions I had turned up hours after the appointed time or even not at all when pressures of work kept me away. I always felt bad about letting the boy down, but a fellow's got to make a living.

I imagined Peter at the other end of the line, hair neatly combed, shiny of face but glum of expression, in his new belted raincoat all ready for my arrival as he would have been for the best part of an hour.

'I've been delayed but I'll be with you in about thirty minutes, I promise,' I said with mock cheeriness.

'OK,' came the muted reply. He'd heard that promise before and it was one that had been broken several times. But not today, I vowed.

As I replaced the receiver, I felt rotten. I was fully aware how disappointed a child could feel when let down by an adult. They put such faith in our words. As an orphan myself, I knew better than most the pain that can be caused by the casual disregard that grown ups sometimes applied to promises. I remembered from my own childhood those supposed special treats that never materialized: that big dipper ride of slowly riding high with anticipation only to swoop down to the depths with disappointment. I promised myself that I would make it up to the lad by giving him a really special night.

With the speed of a frightened leopard, I gave myself a quick wash, knotted up one of my flashier ties and grabbed my new coat and was ready to rush out into the street and grab a taxi when the telephone rang.

I was about to ignore it. I didn't want to be delayed further but my professional detective conscience overruled such sloppy behaviour. As I lifted the receiver, I hoped that it was Peter just checking to see if I was about to leave.

It wasn't.

'Mr Hawke. Is that Mr John Hawke?'

I recognized the voice immediately. Who

could forget those soft, alluring Gallic tones? It was the lovely Maxine Summers.

'Yes, this is John Hawke. How can I help you Mademoiselle Summers.'

She gave a gentle gasp of surprise. 'You knew it was me?'

'Your accent . . . I recognized your voice.'

'Of course. Mr Hawke, I think I am in danger. That man has been back to the shop and . . . he threatened me.'

'That man? The one who ordered the mask? You mean Raymond Carter.'

'Yes. Him. Can you come to my place now? I . . . I don't feel safe.'

I looked at my watch and cursed silently. I couldn't break my promise to Peter and yet here was a damsel in distress and a pretty cute damsel at that. My conscience was about to indulge in a tug of war with itself but sometimes my brain manages to arrange things before I have had the time to sort them out myself. Suddenly I found myself saying; 'Yes, I'll get a cab and I'll be with you in about ten minutes, but then you'll have to come along with me. You see I'm due to pick up Peter, my twelve-year-old nephew, [Peter was always my 'nephew' to people who didn't know us — it saved a lot of explanations] and I'm already late. I promised to take him to tea in the West End and I can't disappoint him.

You must join us too so we can talk.'

There was a pause as though she was working out which was a greater threat: the mysterious and threatening customer, or spending time with me in a taxi. 'Very well,' she said eventually, making no attempt to disguise the note of reluctant resignation in her voice. I was, it seemed to me, only the slightly better choice between the two alternatives.

'Good. I'll be with you shortly,' I said, in a snappy businesslike tone and replaced the receiver.

It couldn't be *the* Raymond Carter who had returned to the mask shop to threaten Maxine, I pondered, as I sat back in the taxi rumbling through the murk that was London in the blackout where phantom buildings and ghostly pedestrians slid silently by. I reasoned that the real Carter wouldn't be that reckless or stupid enough. Surely? Unless, of course, he really had lost his marbles. I ruled that scenario out — for the moment. No, I told myself, it must be someone impersonating him. The same someone who had knifed me the night before and who had brought about the demise of my old overcoat. As I snuggled down in my new posh double-breasted replacement, I thought that I had at least one thing for which I could thank my assailant.

Maxine was waiting in the doorway of her

shop when the taxi pulled up. She emerged from the shadows when I alighted. She was wearing a white trench coat and a plain black headscarf and looked adorable. I raised my hat in greeting and opened the door of the cab for her. She threw me a nervous smile and got in without a word.

'You'd better tell me exactly what happened today?' I said, when the cab was in motion once more.

She turned to me and in the shadowy light, I could see from her strained features and nervous glances that she was really frightened. I squeezed her hand as a mark of encouragement but she drew it away. 'That man, the one you were interested in . . . well, he came into the shop this afternoon and he asked if anyone had been enquiring about the mask . . . the one you showed me. The . . . Charlie Dokes design.'

'You are sure it was the same fellow who ordered the mask in the first place.'

'Oh, yes.'

'Can you describe him for me?'

'He was tall and lean, but I think he wore a disguise.'

'What makes you say that?'

'When he came close to me I could see that his beard . . . it was false. It was fake hair stuck on like an actor on stage. And probably his big glasses with the thick lenses were there to hide his face. And he spoke in an odd fashion as though he had a frog in his throat.'

'To disguise his real voice. You say that he threatened you.'

'Yes, yes he did. He grabbed me and shook me. He looked very angry as though he couldn't control his feelings. He wanted to know if anyone had been asking about the mask. He really frightened me.'

'I'm sorry.'

'He knew about you.'

'Me?'

She nodded. 'He knew you'd been in the shop asking questions and he wanted to know what I had told you about him. I thought he was going to hit me, or do something worse.' She turned her face away from me as her eyes grew moist with emotion. With fear.

I took her limp hands in mine once more and squeezed gently. This time she did not pull away. 'Don't worry,' I said gently. 'You're safe now.' I knew I couldn't be absolutely sure of that but I hoped the idea would make her feel better.

'It just took me by surprise. I've never been threatened in such a way before.'

'I understand. What did you tell him?'

'Nothing. I said that I hadn't told you a

thing. I was frightened that he would really hurt me.'

I nodded sympathetically. 'That was brave and sensible.'

'He seemed to believe me. He said that if I kept quiet, I would be safe but if I told you anything it would be 'the worse' for me. Those were his words: 'The worse'.' The girl shivered as she spoke. The experience had really unnerved her.

'And yet you have disobeyed him.'

'He is a bad man, yes?'

'Yes, he is a bad man.' I could have added that he had already murdered one man and tried to kill me, but I didn't fancy having to placate an hysterical French girl in a moving taxi.

'I thought as much. In that case his words mean nothing. He could do me harm whether I speak to you or not. And you are a policeman, yes?'

'I am a detective. A good guy. I work with the police.'

'Then you will catch him.'

I could not help smile at the simplicity of her equation. I was the good guy therefore it followed as the night the day that I would catch the bad guy. Simple as that. In the movies that formula worked a treat but not always in real life, alas.

'Why are you smiling?' she asked, her own features softening.

'It's not often I get someone who has such faith in my powers.'

'You are not a good detective?'

'Quite good, I suppose,' I replied, with a mixture of pride and embarrassment. I really was smiling now and my amusement puzzled Maxine all the more.

'I do not understand the joke. This is serious.'

'There is no joke. And I know it's serious. And, to be honest, it has become a little more serious in the last ten minutes.'

'Why so?'

'Because you have told me. Because you are in my company. While Mr False Beard is on the loose, you'll need protection. Do you live with your parents? Friends?'

She shook her head. 'I live alone. I have a small flat above the shop.'

So, I thought, he'll know where to find you.

Briefly as I could I told her about the real Raymond Carter and the threats he had been receiving. I said I believed that the joker who had waltzed into her shop and ordered the mask was most likely the fellow who was behind the threats. It was clear that he was a nasty piece of work and he was unpredictable. I didn't frighten the girl further by telling her about Arthur Keating's murder. I reckoned Maxine was in danger now and she had to be protected and as such she couldn't go back to her place tonight.

At this point the taxi pulled up outside Orchid Villa, the home of the Horner sisters.

'I'm just going to pick up Peter . . . '

'Your nephew.'

'Yes. And then we'll go for something to eat and talk some more.'

★ ★ ★

Peter was waiting in the porch for me, but I popped inside to have a few words with Edith and Martha Horner, the spinster ladies who looked after my orphan friend for most of the time. They told me how excited he'd been at the prospect of seeing Charlie Dokes. If only they knew the truth!

Before getting into the taxi, I told Peter that there would be a lady with us this evening. He gave me a sly grin. 'Is she your girlfriend?' he said.

'No, no, nothing like that. She's just a friend. A new friend and she's in a bit of trouble.'

Peter's eyes bulged with excitement. 'Are some crooks after her? Trying to kill her? Is she one of your customers?'

I couldn't help but smile. Peter viewed my career as a detective in comic-book terms. I was the square-jawed crime-fighter always up against criminal masterminds who were determined to kill me, but I always managed to escape the cunning torture chamber or the burning building in time to see the baddies rounded up and imprisoned. No matter how I tried to disabuse him of this notion, he retained the fiction. Fate had deemed that we had shared a few dangerous moments together in the past which had strengthened this belief. He perceived my life as glamorous and exciting instead of what it was: mainly routine with some rather unpleasant interludes where I'm attacked with a knife and wounded in the arm and thigh.

'No,' I said wearily, 'some crooks are not after her. And I don't have customers, Peter. I have clients.'

'Is she your client then?'

'Not exactly. As I said, she's just a friend who I'm helping out.'

Peter looked a little disappointed at this explanation.

As I shepherded him towards the cab, I whispered, 'Now you be polite to the lady — her name is Maxine — and don't go asking her any awkward questions.'

'OK,' he said, without enthusiasm.

I bundled him into the taxi and carried out hurried introductions before instructing the driver to take us west. Maxine and Peter said hello to each other, while shaking hands in a formal manner.

'Are you coming to see Charlie Dokes with us at the Palladium tonight?' Peter asked.

'Er, no I don't think so.' At the mention of the name Maxine's eyes narrowed with apprehension and she cast me a worried glance.

I shook my head in an attempt to indicate to her there was nothing to worry about but I didn't really succeed. Maxine's frown remained in place. She sat back in the cab looking very uncomfortable. I didn't want to let the girl go home alone. At the moment she was vulnerable and possibly the target of an unpredictable killer. I needed to find her a safe gaff and for this I had an idea.

24

Larry Milligan stood at the back of the stalls of the Palladium and watched the second act finale of the Charlie Dokes Show. The audience was laughing merrily at the dummy's snide remarks and crisp one-liners and Raymond Carter seemed expertly in charge of the act, but Milligan, who had seen Carter perform countless times before, knew there was something missing. There was neither heart nor soul in the performance. He was just going through the routine like a well-trained robot. Although the audience didn't seem to notice, there were a few mistimed lines and Carter's eyes were as dead as those of his dummy.

Al Warren had been right: this man was beginning to crumble. Imperceptibly to his adoring public, maybe . . . but it was only a matter of time. He had placed his feet on the slippery slope downwards and no one but himself could prevent his descent. Milligan knew that if Carter continued like this, he'd be washed up within six months. It wouldn't take long for the punters to realize they weren't getting the full package. The faults would grow and the spark would die away completely.

Milligan lit a cigarette and deliberately let the smoke cloud up before his eyes masking his view of the stage. He didn't want to see any more. His steel-grey eyes narrowed and a slight sardonic smile touched his lips briefly.

★　★　★

'You shouldn't drink between shows,' Milligan said in a sharp tone, indicating that this was not an observation but an instruction.

It was fifteen minutes later and he was standing in Raymond Carter's dressing room gazing down at his client who was sitting in his vest and underpants at the make-up mirror with a bottle of gin in his hand.

Milligan lifted the bottle from Carter's limp grasp and placed it on the shelf above the mirror. 'After tonight's show . . . maybe.'

'I need something to help me get through — '

'Don't be pathetic. Use adrenalin like you used to,' snapped Milligan, pulling up a chair and sitting close to Carter. 'I watched you out there this afternoon. It was like an end-of-the-pier side show. There was no life, no warmth, no . . . nothing. You got away with it by the skin of your teeth.'

Carter shook his head fiercely as though he wanted to dislodge some thought, some violent memory from it and then he scrabbled in his trouser pocket and retrieved a sheet of paper which he passed to Milligan.

'I found this on my dressing room table when I got here this afternoon.'

Milligan unfolded the paper. There were words scrawled in red ink across the sheet: 'Tap, tap, tap. Death is about to come knocking.'

'He's been here . . . in this room. He's close to me. He could attack at any moment. Is it any wonder that I'm bloody well lacking life and warmth? I am bloody scared, that's why. Terrified.' His voice had risen to an hysterical pitch.

'Have you told the police?'

'I've not had time, have I? The show must go on, you know. And what good would it do to tell them anyway? They'd only say I'd written it myself, or just file it away to use as evidence after they'd found my dead body. They're no bloody good.'

'What about that detective of yours?'

'No results there either. I'd give him the push but I've got to have some lifeline.'

Milligan lifted the gin bottle off the shelf and handed it to Carter. 'I reckon you could do with a slug of this after all.'

Without a word, Carter grabbed the bottle and splashed a very generous measure into a tumbler on the table and swilled half of it down in one go.

'You realize that you are playing right into his hands, don't you?' said Milligan, leaning back on his chair and lighting up.

'Who?'

'The bastard who's taunting you with these messages.'

'And leaving a corpse on my doorstep, eh?'

'Yes. He's playing a game and he's got Raymond Carter on the losing side. He seems determined to destroy you but he's cunning enough to let you do it yourself. He'll get more pleasure from that than from just bumping you off. If you can be strong, you can foil him.'

'I wonder,' said Carter, glancing at Milligan over the rim of the glass, 'if you would be so confident in your analysis if this creep were doing these things to you?'

For that, Milligan had no reply.

Carter finished off his glass of gin, turned back to the mirror and began removing his make-up. 'It's the not knowing . . . the uncertainty of it all. I've no idea what to expect next. A call in the middle of the night. Another body. A personal attack.'

'If only we had some clue, some inkling

who's behind it all.'

Carter glared at his own complexion in the mirror and gave a twisted grin. 'It's obvious, isn't it? It's me, of course. I'm the guy behind it all,' he said sneeringly in his Charlie Dokes voice, his eyes fixing into a manic stare. 'It's me. I'm the killer!'

★ ★ ★

After Milligan left, Carter made a phone call to Evelyn.

'I just wanted to hear you . . . hear you speak soft words,' he said, and she could easily detect the emotion in his voice.

'Has something happened?' she asked.

'No, nothing. I'm just feeling rather low. Despite what I said this morning, all this . . . this mess is getting to me, I'm afraid. I'm trying to be strong but failing somewhat.'

'You can do it.'

'Perhaps . . . with your help. Look, sweetie, let's forget about going on the town after the show tonight. How about me coming round to your place when I'm done here with a bottle of Champers and you can soothe my furrowed brow?'

If Raymond could have seen Evelyn's face at that moment he would not have been comforted in the least. She wore a cold, grim mask, her forehead wrinkled in distaste. She did not like the way that things were going with her sugar daddy. She was prepared to sleep with the fellow in pursuit of her ends, but she certainly didn't want to take on the role of comforter and nurse Carter's shattered nerves as his life began to crumble. She was beginning to think that if this particular money boat were about to founder, it would be best to abandon ship now. If there was to be scandal and tragedy, she had to be sure none of it tainted her. However, at the moment, in lieu of no better excuse, she agreed to his suggestion.

'I'll look forward to it,' she said, with as much enthusiasm as she could muster.

Unaware of her emotional restraint, Carter smiled and cooed, 'Thank you, Evie.'

'See you later,' was her final, brief response before she put down the telephone.

Ray replaced the receiver in his dressing-room. He was still smiling.

Perhaps, he mused, he was fonder of Evie than he realized.

He was about to lie down on the sofa and catch an hour's sleep before getting ready for the next show when there was a sharp rap on the door and Al Warren entered.

'Hi,' he said cheerfully. 'I hope I'm not interrupting. Just came to see if you're OK.'

Despite himself Carter was genuinely

pleased to see Warren. His youth, enthusiasm and apparently ruffle-free persona were a tonic to him.

'I'm surviving,' he said, sitting on the edge of the sofa. 'Take a seat.'

Warren dragged across the bentwood chair by the make-up mirror so that it faced Carter, and draped his tall elegant frame on it. 'No further developments with the Keating investigation?'

'None that I've heard about. I want to pick your brains.'

'Sure. Go ahead. Shoot!'

'I'm not sure just how much you know of my predicament.'

Al shrugged. 'Most of it, I guess. I know you're getting death threats on the telephone from some crazy guy who impersonates Charlie ... and I know that Arthur Keating was murdered probably by the same crazy guy ... no doubt with a view to having the big police finger of guilt point at you. However, I reckon they're not buying it ...'

'For the time being. They're waiting for 'further developments'.'

'To see who you'll bump off next, eh?'

'Something like that.'

'And that's about it ... Oh, yes and you've got a one-eyed private detective on the case also.'

Carter nodded.

Al smiled. 'Couldn't you get one with two eyes? Or did he come cheaper? I thought it odd you took on a guy who can only see half of what's going on.'

Carter couldn't help but smile at this observation. 'He's OK. Although he doesn't seem to have dug up much so far.' Carter suddenly leaned forward touching Warren gently on the knee, his face pale and serious. 'As I said, I just wanted to pick your brain on this, Al. You're a bright, perceptive, creative chap with a vivid imagination, I wondered if you have any ideas or theories.'

Al raised his eyebrows in surprise. 'You want me to play Sherlock Holmes?'

'Just let me have your thoughts about things. If you have any, of course.'

Al seemed to chew his lip for a minute before he spoke again. 'Of course I have some notions. I care about you, Ray, and your career and I'd do anything to protect both, so I have already given this nasty business some thought. Sadly my conclusions are only common-sense ones. I reckon the guy — and I presume it's a guy — behind it all is not crazy, as I suggested, but very cunning. One line of thought is that he's someone who has a real issue with you. At some point, whether you know it or not, you have seriously upset him and rather than kill you straight away, I reckon he's out to destroy you slowly — chipping away at your sanity. Another possibility is that he's a fan, an unhinged fan, who, for some reason, has taken against you in a big way. It can happen. There was a case in the States a few years ago of a fellow who drove a B-movie actor to suicide.'

Carter shook his head. 'I had my script tampered with at the BBC. It has to be someone connected with the show.'

'These crazy fellows have their methods. It isn't an idea I'd reject out of hand. But one thing is certain, Ray, this man wants to see you suffer — almost to the point where you'd welcome a quick bullet to the brain.'

Carter hugged himself and shivered involuntarily. 'You really . . . think that?'

Al nodded. 'Don't you? And it seems to me his plan is working. You are seriously rattled. And the more you let him get to you, the more successful he becomes.'

'Well, I know, but it's difficult . . .'

Al flashed a wry grin. 'I can appreciate that. It's always easier to hand out advice than take it, but if you could maintain a calm equilibrium and not let the threats get to you, then you'll frustrate the bastard and then he may well make a slip.'

It was the same message that Milligan had

espoused. Ignore the bastard and everything will be OK.

'Thanks for your honesty, Al. I much appreciate your words. We'll see what we can do, eh Charlie?' Carter threw a glance over to the doll in the corner.

'Yes, siree,' came the squeaky response.

'Look,' said Al seriously, 'I'm here for you. If there is anything I can do to help — at any time of day or night, you come a-running. You understand?'

'I understand,' said Carter.

'You go out there tonight and give them a bloody good show. Weave the old Carter magic. That'll give you a lift.'

Carter flashed a brief smile at Warren as he waved goodbye.

Left alone in the dressing room, he turned and looked at himself in the mirror. He looked tired and old.

'Are you sure you know where you left it, eh, Ray old boy?' asked Charlie from the corner. 'The old Carter magic. Are you sure you can get it back?'

25

As we dined that evening at Bradley's, a nice little restaurant on Eastcastle Street, near Oxford Circus, I had to adopt the role of social tight-rope walker maintaining a steady and even balance between my two companions: Peter and Maxine. I was aware that I had to keep both happy and relaxed, never letting either of them feel that they were being neglected or ignored. After chatting with Peter about his school work and his latest comics, I switched tack and asked Maxine how a French girl had landed up living in London.

'My father was English,' she told me. 'He met my mother on a business trip just before the First War and stayed over in France and married her. They started up the theatrical mask and costume business and were quite successful, but when my mother died, we came back to England. I was just twelve at the time. That was ten years ago.'

Peter seemed as enchanted by Maxine as I was. She had a sweet innocent air, but her eyes indicated a sharp mind and a strong personality. While we ate, she seemed relaxed and there were no signs of the nervous tensions she was obviously feeling.

Peter couldn't resist the temptation.

'Are you one of Johnny's cust — clients?' he asked, between gulps of food.

Maxine smiled. 'I'm not sure.'

'I told you, Peter,' I said, 'Maxine is just a friend. I'm helping her with a little bit of trouble.'

Peter looked unconvinced. I knew that he was bright enough to recognize flannel and waffle when he heard it. And so he ploughed on, 'What sort of trouble?' he asked eagerly.

'A man has threatened me,' said Maxine simply, before I could intervene. She appeared quite unperturbed at the idea of letting Peter know her problem.

'And Johnny's going to get him, eh?'

'Something like that,' I said quickly, trying to bring this particular train of conversation into a siding. 'Now why don't you wipe your chin before that gravy drips on to your shirt.'

Just before the pudding arrived, Peter nipped to the lavatory giving me a chance to broach the subject of our mysterious Raymond Carter impersonator. 'I know you told me that he wore a false beard and had on thick glasses, can you think of any other distinguishing features that might help to identify the man?'

Maxine's face clouded and her feline eyes misted a little as she thought back to the encounter in her shop with the man.

'There was something, I think, which could help,' she said after a while.

'Yes?'

'I remember that he wore his wrist watch the wrong way round.' She twisted her own arm to reveal the flat of her hand. 'The dial was on the back of his wrist.'

I nodded to indicate that I understood. 'You didn't happen to notice the make of the watch?'

'No. It was silver with a black strap, that's all.'

'Good girl. That's a start. You see, I am convinced that the man who threatened you and who has been doing the same to the real Raymond Carter is close to him — a colleague or even a friend. It's probably someone I've met. Those clues are invaluable.'

A smile flickered for a moment on her pale features but was gone again in a trice. 'I feel like I have stepped out of real life into . . . into a film or a novel. It all seems so unreal. Are you sure that I can't go home tonight?'

'It would be very unwise. I may be being over-cautious, but Mr Nasty knows where you live and if he takes it into his head that you are a threat to preserving his anonymity . . . which of course you are . . . then he may well come calling again. And this time he won't be so polite.'

Max shivered. 'You really think he would do me harm?'

She knew I did and was only expressing her own fears. I gave her a brief nod as I spied Peter weaving his way though the restaurant towards our table.

'Where am I to go? I cannot really afford a hotel.'

'I have a friend who will put you up for a few days,' I said quickly. 'I will take you there later tonight.'

'What about my things? My clothes . . . '

I hadn't thought about that. 'After the theatre, we'll go back to your place so you can pick up the essentials.'

By now Peter had returned to his seat, his face glowing with curiosity. 'Is Maxine coming to the Palladium with us?'

'Yes, she is.'

'Oh, goody,' grinned Peter excitedly. 'Do you like Charlie Dokes as well?'

This question rather nonplussed Maxine and she faltered in answering.

'She's not as big a fan as you,' I said, ruffling Peter's hair.

'I've got all his comics and I listen to his

radio show every week.'

'You must be very excited at actually seeing him on the stage,' Maxine said.

'I am. I am,' Peter beamed.

Before we left the restaurant, I called up Benny from the phone cubicle in reception and explained my dilemma. With mock reluctance, he agreed to provide lodgings for Maxine.

'This isn't a hotel for your girlfriends,' he jibed, tongue in cheek.

'She is not a girlfriend. If she were a girlfriend, I wouldn't be bringing her round to your place to spend the night, would I?'

'How do I know? You're like God, Johnny, you work in mysterious ways.'

I chuckled. 'I'll see you later,' I said as I replaced the receiver. Benny loved to moan, but he was as reliable as daybreak.

★　★　★

It did not surprise me that there were no tickets waiting for me at the Palladium box office. Raymond Carter had forgotten to reserve them. It was to be expected, I supposed, with all that he had on his mind but it grieved me to have to fork out the money for three seats in the stalls when I could have had two of them for free. I saw that Maxine and Peter were comfortably seated with a programme and a bag of sweets in the theatre and excused myself. It was twenty minutes before curtain up and I wanted to nip backstage to see my client and check up on things. Without explaining my mission, I left my two charges before they could ask any awkward questions.

Making it seem like a matter of life and death, I flashed my card and persuaded one of the usherettes to show me backstage. Reluctantly she complied and as I was now reasonably familiar with the geography of the building; within minutes I was approaching the star dressing room. As I did so, I saw a tall young man in a smart tweed overcoat just leaving. It was Al Warren. He caught sight of me and nodded briefly. 'I hope you've got some good news for him,' he said tersely. With these words he slapped his trilby to his head and squeezed past me.

I stared after him for a while, wondering what I had done to deserve such brusqueness. But then perhaps I did know.

Carter was applying his stage make-up when I eventually entered his dressing room.

'Ah, Mr Hawke, I've just remembered. I was supposed to get some tickets for you, wasn't I?'

'Well, yes, you were, but that doesn't

263

matter now, I managed to get my own. I just popped around to see how you were and if you've had any further contact with our mystery man.'

'I'm OK, I suppose. I found this in my dressing room today.'

He handed me a piece of paper with the words, 'Tap, tap tap. Death is about to come knocking,' scribbled in red ink. It looked like the same handwriting as that on the script.

'Not a familiar hand, I suppose.'

Carter shook his head. 'Just another little nail in my side. It almost makes me wish the fellow would have a go at me. At least then I'd know who the devil he was.'

Not necessarily, I thought, remembering my own attack by the killer in the Charlie Dokes mask; but I kept those thoughts to myself.

'Have you made any progress?' Carter asked, almost casually as though he knew my answer already.

I didn't quite know what to say to this. I certainly couldn't wave some kind of detective magic wand and state that the danger was over. That's what Carter really wanted. Although I was accumulating various disparate scraps of information and therefore in one sense making progress, I still had nothing that would give me a definite lead. I

264

had no intention of telling Carter about the killer's attack on me or his threats to Maxine. The more cards I held to my chest, the greater the chance I had of exposing the demon. However, in reality, I knew that at present, I was still standing on the sidelines watching the shadows. I reckoned that to my endangered client I must have seemed to be either incompetent or impotent — or both.

'We'll both have to be patient,' I said quietly, almost ashamed to let this platitudinous morsel pass my lips.

'Easy for you to do. Less so for me. Waiting for my executioner to strike.'

I was dried up now. I could manufacture no further comment and so I turned to leave. Then a thought struck me. 'I'll be in touch tomorrow. I assume I'll be able to contact you at home.'

Carter nodded. 'I have no plans to go anywhere.'

I hoped that would be the case.

I returned to the auditorium, which was now almost full and buzzing with noise from the relaxed and expectant audience eager to escape their day-to-day worries in the magical garish greasepaint world beyond the footlights. Peter and Max were in deep animated conversation when I reached them and it seemed they had hardly missed me. Peter grinned as I took my seat and offered me one of his wine gums.

The lights dimmed and then the large orchestra began to play. It was a dramatic arrangement of the tune that was used to introduce the Okey Dokes radio show. At this the audience gave a spontaneous burst of applause which increased when Raymond Carter walked on to the stage carrying Charlie. It was a strange experience for me to see this man, here bathed in creamy spotlight, glamorous and self-contained as he strode to the microphone, the man I had seen hunched up and dispirited in his dressing room not ten minutes earlier, the man whom I suspected was falling apart because of the death threats he was receiving. Certainly there was no hint of weakness or uncertainty in his performance now. It was slick, confident and, I have to admit, funny.

In essence this spot was a brief taster giving the audience an assurance that indeed Raymond Carter and Charlie were in the show. Charlie made some disparaging remarks about certain people on the front row, cracked a few schoolboy howler type gags and then they were off as the curtain pulled back to reveal a string of chorus girls who shimmied to the front of the stage for the opening number.

We didn't see Carter and Charlie again for another forty-five minutes. We were presented with some clever jugglers, a fire-eater, a rather serious and stodgy baritone who completed his act with a strangulated version of *Old Man River* and twin sisters who tap-danced so fast it was a wonder their feet remained attached to their ankles. As this varied array of entertainment paraded before our eyes, I kept glancing at Peter. He seemed mesmerized by the gay spectacle, his hand hovering in a frozen pose over the bag of wine gums. Even when the baritone was struggling for the high notes his attention never wavered.

But it was when Charlie Dokes returned just before the finale of the first act that the little mite's face really brightened. He grinned, chuckled and guffawed at all the gags, squirming in his seat with joy. Max, too, seemed thoroughly entranced with the man and his dummy and I have to admit I chuckled at the jokes which were a clever and witty combination of the naïve and the sophisticated.

Then the lights came up for the interval while the auditorium was still ringing with the applause.

'It's great, Johnny,' said Peter, his face split from ear to ear with a wide grin.

'Really. I thought it was a bit dull,' I said mischievously.

Max giggled. 'Don't be awful, Johnny. It's wonderful. A real tonic.'

'If you say so,' I beamed. 'Now, who'd like an ice cream?'

The second half was very much a re-run of the first half — we even had to endure more strangulated musical proclamations from the baritone. The climax of the show was a spectacular comic sketch with Carter and Charlie supposedly on holiday on a house-boat. Every time one of the many portholes was opened, water gushed through dousing Carter in the face but miraculously missing his voluble doll. During a storm sequence, the whole set trembled as though being buffeted by the waves, sending Carter spinning from one side of the houseboat to the other. This clever blend of slapstick and the comic patter (from Charlie) delighted the audience, prompting them into spontaneous applause in between their bursts of raucous laughter. Peter could hardly contain himself with joy, wriggling in his seat with fits of giggles and rocking backwards and forwards with glee, along with the other children in the audience, every time the water poured through a porthole to drench the unfortunate ventriloquist.

Before we knew it, it was finale time when all the performers returned to the stage and walked down to the footlights to take a bow. The audience were so relaxed and merry now, everyone clapped and cheered generously; even the podgy baritone garnered a few cheers. But the tidal wave of applause and adulation was reserved for the final act. Raymond Carter came on now dressed in a smart dinner suit carrying Charlie Dokes who was similarly attired. As they stood on the edge of the stage acknowledging the audience's warm reaction, Charlie's spangled bow tie revolved like a glittery windmill.

The cast retreated, took a final bow and then the curtains swished together. The show was over. I gazed down at Peter. His face was flushed and shining.

'That was the best ever,' he said, grabbing my hand. 'Thank you for bringing me.'

'You're most welcome,' I grinned.

'Now I know what I want to do when I grow up. I want to be a ventriloquist.'

'Mmm,' I said, 'I thought you wanted to be a detective.'

His face grew serious for a moment. 'Oh, I do. Perhaps . . . perhaps I could do both.'

'Perhaps you could. But for the moment, let's get you home to bed, eh?'

Under different circumstances I might well

have taken Peter around to Carter's dressing-room to meet his hero, but I was unsure with the ventriloquist's current mental state how we would be received and I didn't want the lad to be disillusioned. Also I didn't want Carter to see Maxine and I had no intention of leaving her alone in the foyer while we visited the star of the show. So Max, Peter and I joined the swarm of people filing out of the theatre, spilling on to the cold dark streets of blackout London.

'Come on,' I said, dragging them up towards Oxford Street, leaving the throng of theatregoers behind. 'We'll get a cab much easier up here.'

And sure enough we did.

We hadn't travelled very far before Peter fell asleep, his head resting in the crook of my arm. I nudged Max and indicated our sleeping partner.

She smiled sweetly. 'He has had such a good time. Oh, how I wish we never lost the innocent pleasures of childhood.'

'But you enjoyed the show also?' I ventured.

'Yes. Oh yes, I did. It was very clever and funny at times. But seeing that doll, its face, I couldn't forget the mask that I made just like it and the man, that terrible man who frightened me.'

I grimaced in the shadows. 'I'm sorry,' I said. 'I didn't think how it would affect you. What an idiot I am.'

She stroked my hand, her eyes shining brightly. 'Don't worry. I still had a good time. I knew I was safe with you.'

I tingled a little at this pronouncement.

When the cab pulled up outside the Horner household, reluctantly I brought the snoozing Peter back into the land of the living. I held his hand and escorted my sleepy young friend to the door. Martha took him inside. 'Did you have a good time?' she asked.

'It was wonderful,' mumbled Peter, stifling a yawn.

She grinned and gave me a knowing nod. 'Do you want to come in for a cup of tea, John?'

I shook my head. 'Thank you, but I've got a cab waiting. I've still a little business to see to.'

'Very well. I'll get this little imp washed and ready for bed before he falls asleep in the hall.'

We shook hands and parted. 'I'll be in touch,' I said, as the door began to close and headed back to the cab, which was chugging noisily on the roadside.

Our next port of call was Max's flat above Masks Unlimited for her to pick up some of her things to see her through her stay in her new lodgings.

When the cab pulled up outside the shop, Max squeezed my hand. 'Please come inside with me, Johnny.'

'Of course,' I said gently, and instructed the driver to wait once again.

'Sure, mate,' he said, lighting up a cigarette, thinking, no doubt, of the juicy fare he was going to extract from me.

Like the shop premises below, Max's flat was tiny. It was in fact one room. There was a single bed in the far corner while one alcove was curtained off as a wardrobe and the other as the kitchen area with a small sink, a draining board and a gas ring. There was a folding table, two chairs, and an armchair. Somewhere beyond was a small bathroom. While Max busied herself collecting a few clothes and toiletries, I stood by the door. Well, for two people to step inside the room would have crowded it.

'There,' she said at last, clutching a small suitcase, 'I think that will do.' She was breathless and her face shimmered with a fine gloss of perspiration. When I didn't respond, her eyes widened in a quizzical stare. I didn't reply because I was captivated by her — this pretty young woman with the broad smile and bright alluring eyes. She looked so vulnerable while at the same time quite beautiful that I had an over-whelming desire to take her in my arms and kiss her. Not one of those platonic pecks but a real full-blown Hollywood movie kiss. I resisted the temptation to make a fool of myself with a little throat-clearing noise and a garbled, 'Right, if you're ready, let's be off.'

She grabbed my arm and we left. On the short journey over to Benny's, I told her a little about the fellow, warning her that he would no doubt assume that she was my girlfriend. 'When Benny sees me with any girl, he sees that as a clear indication that wedding bells are in the offing.'

Max giggled. 'He sounds like my father. He so wanted me to be married. Especially towards the end when he knew he was dying. He wanted to feel that I had someone to look after me — to protect me. But you cannot manufacture these things. They just happen naturally.'

I nodded in what I hope looked like a wise and knowing manner.

'But tell me, Johnny, do you not have a girlfriend?'

'Who'd have me?' I asked. 'A scruffy one-eyed bloke?'

She didn't reply, but turned her head away and gazed out of the taxi window at the darkened streets of the city.

★ ★ ★

As I expected, Benny made a fuss of Max, preparing her a hot drink and plying her with some biscuits, before showing her the spare room.

'She's a lovely girl,' he whispered in my ear, as Max unpacked her small case. 'You could do a lot worse.'

'I know,' I said, suddenly discovering that I had run out of flippant replies. 'I know.'

26

Raymond Carter felt strangely relaxed as he parked the car not far from the building where Evelyn Munro lived. He'd had a very successful show tonight. All the gags had worked and the Saturday-night audience had been an enthusiastic one. He had tried hard to recapture the old 'Carter magic' as Al had referred to it and good old Doctor Theatre, that strange phenomena which robs the brain of all worries and imbues one with confidence and energy when one steps out in front of the footlights, had worked overtime for him this evening. He'd left the theatre quite exhilarated and twenty minutes later he was still in the same intoxicated state. Certainly the prospect of a few glasses of champagne and a night in bed with a shapely and desirable young woman did much to maintain his sense of bonhomie. For a time all thoughts of dead bodies on the doorstep and threatening telephone calls had been banished from his mind.

Carter pulled the case containing Charlie out of the boot. Despite the fact that Evie hated the dummy coming into her home, he wasn't going to leave the little fellow in the car overnight. Charlie was too precious. He needed to keep him close.

Carter sauntered towards the block of flats breathing in the cold night air and then allowing it to float out on a fine grey breathy cloud. Rather than take the lift, he walked up the two flights to Evie's flat. He found the door slightly ajar and from inside he could hear the jaunty tones of a dance band playing on the radio. He dropped Charlie's case in the hallway and then he wandered into the sitting room, slipped off his coat and scarf and flung them down on one of the armchairs. The room was empty, but he was expected: the champagne was nestling in an ice bucket and two glasses gleamed in readiness at its side.

'Darling, where are you?' he called, hoisting out the champagne and attacking the cork with practised aplomb. There was a sharp pop as it flopped on to the carpet and the champagne bubbled forth.

'You'd better hurry up, or I'll drink all the bubbly myself.'

He poured out two glasses and took a sip from his own while he listened for a response.

There was none.

Evelyn was no doubt in the bedroom making last-minute adjustments to her make-up. He knew that she was a stickler for looking just right.

He waited another minute, sipping champagne and tapping his foot in time to the music. Then with some purpose he strode towards the bedroom.

'Come on, old girl,' he called somewhat impatiently, opening the door. 'I'm sure you look perfect.'

He had been right. Evelyn was in the bedroom. But she was not attending to her make-up. Instead, she was lying on her back on the bed, her eyes wide open staring sightlessly at the ceiling. Her mouth was also open, agape in a silent scream.

It seemed like some weird trick of the light. The shadows and the soft lighting had conjoined to create this sadistic and bizarre effect. Surely Evelyn was just having a nap. She'd probably had a few cocktails while waiting for him to arrive and they had made her drowsy. She had just dropped off to sleep. Certainly her awkward pose on the bed — her legs splayed apart, one arm limply hanging over the edge — suggested that sleep had taken her unawares. He would give her a little shake and then she would rouse herself. Rouse herself and give him a little kiss.

But it was not sleep that had taken her unawares; it was death.

At first Raymond Carter couldn't quite believe what he was seeing. It was a surreal mirage. The lights and his imagination playing games.

Surely.

For God's sake. Surely.

He edged his way a little closer to the bed, staring with horror at that beautiful face frozen in panic, the eyes mirroring the shock and fear she must have experienced when she knew. When she knew that she was going to die.

And still the dance band played on. It was a foxtrot now, Carter noted inconsequentially, his body beginning to shake with dread.

Leaning over her body now, he saw the bruising at her throat. Dark red weals were forming around her smooth, tender neck. She had been strangled. She had been murdered.

Carter's stomach suddenly heaved and he staggered backwards as bile rushed into his mouth. He tried to force it back but some of it dribbled down his chin and on to his shirt front. He ran to the bathroom and was sick into the lavatory bowl, groaning and moaning, his body racked with shudders as the contents of his stomach gushed past his lips. When he'd finished, he sank to his knees and began sobbing. His body shook like a man with palsy. If asked why he was weeping, he would have found it difficult to explain. Was it for the loss of his beautiful girlfriend, a sweet thing cut down in her youth? Was it for himself and the further misery and despair this second brutal murder would bring to his door? Or was it because he felt so helpless and lost? It was probably all these things and more. For Raymond Carter, rationality had fled and gut feelings were in charge.

He lay on the bathroom floor some ten minutes before he felt able to move again. Slowly he pulled himself to his feet and swilled his face in the basin. His drained and bleary features gazed back at him from the bathroom mirror. He noted that the over-riding emotion stamped there was fear.

He gave a swift glance towards the door — the door leading back into the bedroom. Dare he go back in there? Dare he go back and see the dead body again?

He had to.

Like a somnambulist, he made his way back.

She was still there. Exactly as he'd left her. She hadn't miraculously roused herself to pour a glass of champagne. No, Evelyn was still sprawled on the bed, with her mouth held in that frozen scream.

Evelyn was still dead.

And then the telephone rang.

The fierce insistent ring pierced Carter's senses, constricting his heart and squeezing his bladder.

He knew that he shouldn't answer it.

He knew that he just had to.

Like a fluttering dove, his hand hovered over the telephone as its case vibrated with ferocious persistence. Gently he scooped up the receiver and slowly brought it close to his ear.

He heard an obscene giggle and then the familiar Charlie Dokes voice. 'Howdy chum. How are you doing? Did you like my little surprise?'

Carter searched his mind in vain for something to say, a response to this monster on the other end of the telephone, but he failed.

'You should have been there, Ray old boy. My, my, was she surprised when I put my hands around her neck. At first she thought I was fooling. Well, as you know, I'm that kind of fellow. But then . . . when I tightened my grip, she soon stopped smiling. I pressed a little harder and you know what, she soon stopped breathing as well.'

'You're crazy,' stammered Carter. 'Bloody crazy.'

'You know what, Raymond, I reckon that's what the police are going to say to you when they find out what you've done.'

'What I've — '

'Murdered your girlfriend. Strangling the poor little thing until there was no air left in her pretty little body. That's not a nice thing to do.'

It was about this time that Carter's brain stopped functioning in any kind of coherent fashion. It couldn't cope any more with what was happening to him. The dead body and the concept that his own doll was accusing him of murder was too much for him. Certain thought processes in his brain began to shut down — to help him escape from reality. Just before the dizziness affected his balance, he was quite aware that the doll man on the phone was right. The police would believe that he had murdered Evie. This time there would be no doubt in their minds.

Slamming the receiver down, he managed to stagger to an armchair before the grey mists of unconsciousness enshrouded him. He collapsed inelegantly in a deep faint.

The shutdown was brief. Within five minutes he was slowly groping his way back to consciousness once again. The dance band was still playing over the radio. The syrupy strains of *Moonlight Serenade* wafted through the flat adding an unnerving veneer of unreality. He was living his own nightmare.

At last Carter was able to pull himself to his feet and make his way to the drinks cabinet and pour himself a large gin, which he downed in two gulps. The alcohol burned the back of his throat and made his eyes water. Somehow he found the discomfort rather pleasing.

What the hell was he to do now? he asked himself, trying desperately to quell the sense of panic that was mushrooming inside him. It seemed to Carter that his life was in ruins. This was the end of the road. He would be accused of Evie's murder. Arrested. His radio show would be cancelled. His career as a family entertainer was down the sewer. He might even go to the gallows for a crime he didn't commit. He had a vision of himself dangling at the end of a rope, his body twisting in spasms.

He was a dead man.

He moaned out loud in his pain.

Then suddenly he knew what he had to do. He knew with amazing clarity what his only option was.

He had to escape. To run away. To go into hiding.

He couldn't allow himself to be arrested. To go meekly into a dank cell — maybe never to leave it. He had to flee London. Hightail it to the provinces. Scotland maybe. He could lose himself there. He had some money back at his flat. That would keep him afloat for a while. At least it would buy him some time.

A strange, tight smile crossed his tortured features. It wasn't much of a plan, he thought, but it was a plan of sorts. It was something that he could do. He picked up his coat and quickly shrugged himself into it and then hung his scarf loosely round his neck. He had to get away, he kept telling himself. A sense of urgency now gripped him. He scanned the flat for any signs of his presence. The champagne glass. He washed it at the sink and put it in one of the cupboards.

He moved to the hall, instinctively picking up the case containing Charlie Dokes. He wasn't going to leave him behind. Charlie came with him wherever he went. And anyway, he needed a friend now more than ever he had done in his life before.

He paused before the outer door and took a deep breath before opening it.

His breath emerged as a strangled croak for there on the threshold stood a man. He was little more than a menacing silhouette, the light from the corridor framing him with a pale yellow aura. The man's features were in deep shadow but Carter believed that he knew him.

The shock of finding someone on the

doorstep caused Carter to retreat into the hallway. The man did not move but now Carter could see that he held a gun in his hand with the barrel pointing directly at his heart. The crazy thought struck him that perhaps he was still in his faint and this was some wild dream and he'd regain consciousness any time now.

'Don't shoot me,' he found himself saying. 'Please,' he added desperately.

The silhouette chuckled. 'How you doing, Ray old boy?' he said, the voice belonging to Charlie Dokes.

'What do you want with me? Is it money . . . ?'

'It's revenge, old boy. Simple as that. Good old-fashioned revenge.'

'I don't understand. I've never done you any harm . . . '

The man chuckled again. 'Turn around, Raymond. Turn around so you've got your back to me.'

'Why, what are you going to do?'

'Just do as you are told, Raymond. Don't be a naughty boy,' the Charlie Dokes voice sneered at him from the gloom.

'Please . . . please don't shoot me,' he said again.

'Do as you're told, Raymond.' The voice now had an impatient dangerous edge to it.

284

Reluctantly Raymond Carter turned slowly and awkwardly, still clutching the case containing his dummy.

There was a sudden movement behind him and he felt a fierce blow to the back of the head. Pain, like an electric current seared through his body and his vision dimmed. He had only time to utter a muffled gasp of pain before he crumpled to the floor into a deep pool of darkness.

27

Max and I were having a picnic. We were sitting on a riverbank with a hamper groaning with food and she was feeding me a piece of chicken and giggling. Bees buzzed in the background, ducks played on the river and the sunlight warmed my face. I couldn't remember feeling happier in my whole life. I dabbed my lips on a napkin and leaned over to kiss her. She responded readily, her arms encircling me. In the distance I could hear church bells ringing. They seemed to be chiming in rhythm with the beat of my heart. The more we kissed, the louder the bells sounded. They became unnaturally loud, the booming calls filling the air around me with deafening tones.

I shook my head desperately to rid myself of the noise which began to thunder in my head. Suddenly the skies clouded, as though someone had turned off the sun, and a blackness invaded the land. I was left in a dark clammy void with just the ringing in my ears. I opened my mouth to cry out and in doing so I woke myself up. The riverbank, the food and Max had disappeared and I was in my dreary bedroom amid a heap of rumpled sheets with the telephone ringing its head off on the bedside table. I glanced at my watch. It was nearly eleven o'clock. But then, I reminded myself, it was Sunday, supposedly the day of rest. However this thought was swiftly accompanied by the one about there being no rest for the wicked.

My dream wrecker was David Llewellyn.

'I thought you'd like to know the latest, boyo, especially as it looks like your client has done a bunk.'

'Carter.'

'That's the fellow. I'm at his girlfriend's flat right now. Evelyn Munro. She's been murdered.'

My heart sank and I flopped back against the pillows. 'Murdered. And you think Carter did it?'

'Correct. Yes, I do think Carter did it. As I say he's done a bunk — scarpered. There's no trace of him. If that's not the action of a guilty man, I don't know what is.'

I thought that it was also the action of a frightened man, but I kept that thought to myself.

'How was she killed?'

'Same as Keating. Strangled. Look I'm going to be here for a while at the flat. If you want to pop over and have a look around for yourself, come and join me.'

I noted the address and said I'd be there in half an hour.

Twenty minutes later, I was in Tottenham Court Road hailing a cab, my mind awhirl with ragged thoughts about the case. It looked very much like it was about to crumble to dust. Certainly, from the little I knew it seemed that Raymond Carter appeared as guilty as hell. However, I had learned long ago never to take the apparently obvious as gospel but in this instance it looked as though it was. I hoped I'd learn more to prove otherwise when I got to Evelyn Munro's flat, but I wasn't sanguine. I gazed glumly from the cab window at the empty Sunday streets of the damaged capital. It was a ghost city with just a few grey wraiths flitting through its dusty thoroughfares. It looked like some gigantic film set waiting for the extras to arrive. Some of the shops had already put up their rather sad and tawdry Christmas decorations. Somehow they depressed me even more.

There was an emaciated, sallow-faced constable on duty outside the flat when I arrived. He was hardly a threat to anyone wishing to gain entry illegally. A few hearty puffs in his direction and he'd collapse. I reckoned he'd come off worst in a scrap with a skeleton.

I told him who I was and that Inspector Llewellyn was expecting me.

He nodded sternly and allowed me to enter. I found David in the sitting room talking to Sergeant Sunderland.

'Morning, Johnny. Not a good one for you is it?'

I tipped my hat to the back of my head and sighed. 'Seems not.'

David cocked an eye at his assistant. 'Make a brew, Sergeant, will you? Nice and strong, with two sugars for both of us, eh.'

Sunderland did as he was told without a word, although I could tell that he didn't appreciate being treated like a skivvy and especially having to make tea for a 'non-professional'. I'd encountered him before. He was a decent copper with a bright mind and lively sense of humour which was not always fully appreciated or utilized by David.

'Give me the story then,' I said, plonking myself down on a chair and offering my friend a cigarette. There was a brief pause while we both lit up, encircling our heads in smoke.

'She was discovered by the milkman,' David said at length. 'He came early this morning, found the door open and the radio blaring. He thought it was odd and so he investigated. He found the lass in the bedroom, sprawled on the bed, dead as a doornail. Red marks around her neck.'

'Any sign of a struggle?'

'None. Come and have a look see.'

David led me into the bedroom. It was a simple, yet stylish room with cream décor. On one of the bedside tables there was a framed photograph of Evelyn. She was dressed in a dark, low-cut evening gown, leaning seductively against a wall. She was smiling.

'The lady in question has been taken away, of course, but the rest is just as we found it.'

They found it tidy. There were no overturned chairs, no rumpled rugs, no drawers hanging out of the dressing-table and no smashed ornaments. No sense of violence at all. The eiderdown was rumpled a little; that was all.

'It was a swift, neat and tidy job,' said David.

'And carried out by someone she knew. Someone she was happy to be in the bedroom with.'

'Exactly. And who is that likely to be? Her boyfriend, of course: Mr Raymond Carter.'

'She might have had more than one boyfriend.'

David threw me a glance heavy with cynicism.

'OK,' I said, 'supposing it was Carter who

did this. Why would he do it?'

'You tell me; he's your client.'

'I can't think of a reason. Unless he's lost his mind. Otherwise it would be professional and personal suicide — like cutting his own throat.'

'Perhaps she rejected him. Told him to sling his hook. He was a bit old for her wasn't he? Perhaps she fancied some younger meat.'

'But is he going to kill her for that? And are you saying that he murdered Keating too? Why would a man at the top of his profession in the entertainment world suddenly turn killer and in doing so throw away all he's worked for for years? It doesn't make sense.'

Sergeant Sunderland entered carrying two mugs of tea.

'Thank you,' I said taking one from him.

He nodded stoically.

The tea, my first of the day, tasted good.

'If he's not our guilty party,' continued David, 'why has he gone missing?'

'Probably to escape being arrested. Anyway, is there any evidence that he was even at this flat last night?'

'Yes,' said Sunderland piping up. 'There is. His car was found parked just a street away from here.'

'Sorry, boyo, but it all looks rather black for Mr Carter.'

'Maybe, but, tell me, why is his car still there? If he's done a bunk, made a bid to escape the police, why didn't he take his car with him? Makes for a much quicker getaway, wouldn't you say?'

David gave me a look which told me that he hadn't thought of that one.

'The number plate is easily identifiable,' said Sunderland.

'Nevertheless, he'd have had a good few hours' start . . .'

David shook his head. 'I'm sorry, Johnny, you're fighting a losing battle here. Until we get any evidence to the contrary we are regarding Raymond Carter as a murderer on the run and the Press will be informed shortly, asking the public to be on the lookout for him.'

Strangely, I didn't feel as depressed about this news as I expected. In my conversation with David I had actually convinced myself of my own arguments. Unless Raymond Carter had suddenly had some kind of brainstorm and taken a trip down Insanity Lane — which I doubted — there was no sensible reason to bump off Evelyn Munro or Arthur Keating. And then there was the fellow who threatened Max in Masks Unlimited. I reckoned he was the key to this mystery. However, while my strong conviction that my client was innocent of these murders was, to some extent, encouraging to me, I still had to contend with the bleak and depressing knowledge that I had no definite notion who the real killer was.

Brains needed to be cudgelled in a big way.

I swilled down the last of my tea. 'Thanks for letting me look around. Please keep me informed of any developments, eh.'

'And you do the same,' said David with a knowing nod.

'Of course,' I replied, squashing the thin pang of guilt with a smile. I really ought to tell David about the mask and the man calling himself Raymond Carter who threatened Max, but some instinct told me that it wasn't time yet, that I needed to clasp that little piece of information to my bosom for the time being.

I waved goodbye and made my way out of the flat. However, as I neared the door something caught my eye down by the skirting-board in the narrow hallway leading to the outer door. A dark, smeary mark. I knelt down to examine it. It was blood. Fresh blood. It was dry now but it was covering the fine film of dust running along the skirting-board which had been there a while. And there were some tiny spots of blood on the carpet also.

What did this mean?

Well, it meant there was another form of violence that took place in the flat last night apart from the strangling. Violence which had caused a small spillage of blood. So, this matter was not as clear cut as my dear friend Detective Inspector David Llewellyn of Scotland Yard believed.

With a smug smile, I left the flat and the gaunt bobby guarding it.

28

Consciousness returned very slowly and erratically to him. He waxed and waned, sensing that he was emerging from the thick fog of sleep only to slip back into its embrace within seconds. In those brief semi-waking moments he became aware of little except the darkness around him and the severe pain at the back of his head as though someone had stuck a large axe there and left it deeply embedded in his skull. As his mind struggled to comprehend what had happened to him, where he was and even who he was, the effort exhausted him and he drifted off once more into artificial sleep. Eventually these intervals of wakefulness grew longer as time passed until he managed to remain conscious for a few minutes. It was during this time that he was able to establish a few simple facts concerning his situation.

He realized that his hands and feet were bound and some foul, sticky, tape-like material was stretched across his mouth, which impaired his breathing and prevented him from making any clear sound or loud utterance. A cry for help was futile. It emerged as a muffled whimper. He was lying on a hard, damp wooden floor and, unless he'd gone blind, he was in total darkness. He was cold and his body ached, especially the back of his head which throbbed mercilessly. There was also a strange noise, an unusual whooshing sound coming from somewhere out there in the black void. Or was it in his brain? He couldn't be sure. How on earth had he got here, wherever here was?

Before he could answer that one, he floated away from the world once again. It was some time later before his mind and body thought it safe to bring him back to the surface again. Now he was aware of his desperate need to urinate. The pressure on his bladder was great and competed with his thudding headache for precedence. He attempted to move but his body was still too weak and his bonds were too secure and restrictive. He tried to call out but the best that he could produce was a faint croak which was completely muffled by the tape over his mouth.

After an agonizing time, he could wait no longer and he grimaced as the warm urine trickled out down his leg, dampening his trousers. He moaned at the indignity of it and the pure hopelessness of his situation. He lay in the darkness wishing he were dead.

'I suppose you've heard,' Edward Simmons' face was gloomy and gaunt as he strode past Larry Milligan.

'Indeed, I have,' said Milligan, shutting his front door and showing Simmons into his living room. 'The police have been here most of the afternoon. I was just about to ring you.'

It was Sunday evening and the news had seeped out about Evelyn Munro's murder and the fact that the police were searching for the famous radio star Raymond Carter in connection with the crime.

'What a mess,' cried the radio producer, running both hands through his hair. 'The star of the show is a murderer on the run. We like publicity at the BBC — but not like this. You realize it's the end of 'Okey Dokes'.'

'Of course I do. For you it's just a radio show; there'll be another along in any minute. For me, I've lost my most important client. Whatever happens now, he'll never headline again — except in prison concerts.'

'Yes. I'm sorry. That bastard has left us both in the dung. I've been speaking to my masters at Broadcasting House today. They're cancelling the series forthwith along with my contract. They'll be putting repeats of ITMA in the slot for the rest of this season. There's nothing I can do about it. I just came round here to moan and let off steam.'

'I reckon we could both do with a drink. How about a gin and tonic?'

'Make mine a triple at least.'

While Milligan saw to the drinks, Simmons paced up and down. 'I just didn't see this coming,' he muttered almost to himself. 'I'd have never suspected Carter of murderous tendencies. Never thought the bastard had enough passion in him. I'd always got him down for a cold fish.'

'They're sometimes the worst kind,' said Milligan, passing Simmons his drink. 'I always thought there was more to Carter than met the eye. Something darker, more sinister beneath that charmless veneer. I reckon in the end we are both better off without him.'

'I must say you're taking all this in a much calmer fashion than me.'

'Maybe. I'm a bit of a swan.'

'What?'

'All calm on the surface and churning like billy-oh underneath.'

'Oh, I see. Well, I'm a producer. I'm quite used to blowing my top. I reckon I'll be suicidal tomorrow.'

'Why wait twenty-four hours?' Milligan gave a wry grin and raised his glass as in a toast. 'Here's to Charlie Dokes and his homicidal handler. May they rot in hell.'

'I'll second that.'

Both men drank and then fell into silence, each quietly contemplating their lot. Whatever contemplations circulated in their minds, neither gave a thought to the dead girl, Evelyn Munro, brutally strangled in her own flat. Her death did not impinge on either of their consciences. Both men had other concerns.

'Have you spoken to Al?' asked Simmons after a time, pushing his errant glasses back on to the bridge of his nose.

Milligan shook his head. 'Not yet. But he'll be all right. There'll be crowds of comedians clamouring for his services. Those in the know are fully aware that he was, in a sense, the star of the Charlie Dokes circus. Without Al's material, Carter was just a fairly efficient vent. They're ten a penny.'

'So it's just you and me in the dustbin, eh?'

Milligan wanted to say that it was only Simmons who was the sole occupant of that particular receptacle. He had other clients who earned him sufficient commission to keep him comfortable. Now there was a vacancy, as it were, in the prime spot; he'd just have to go out and get himself another name. He'd done it before. While these thoughts were at the forefront of his mind, he kept them to himself. Instead of saying anything, he just nodded.

'And then there's the cast. They'll have to be told,' Simmons mused, swirling the ice around in his glass, causing a little whirlpool.

'The much decimated cast, eh? Two dead and two on the run.'

'Two on the run?'

Milligan forced a grin. 'Carter and Charlie.'

Simmons cast him an odd glance. In a strange way, it seemed that Milligan was finding the situation amusing. Well, perhaps that was the best face to put on things. It was less extreme than his own amateur ranting performance.

'Fancy a top up?' Milligan raised his empty glass as a prompt.

'Better not,' said Simmons, turning his wrist to glance at his watch. 'I've got somewhere else to go.' He gave Milligan a swift enigmatic smile.

After Simmons had gone, Milligan wandered over to his desk and withdrew a photograph from the drawer. It was of a pretty young woman whom he and Simmons had studiously avoided mentioning. She'd never be a big star now, he mused objectively. He carried the picture to the fireplace, tore it in half and threw it on the flames.

Some time later, in another room, elsewhere, just beyond the darkness in which the trussed-up figure of Raymond Carter lay, drifting in and out of consciousness, a man was crying. Silent, gentle tears. Tears that had been saved up for such a long time. Tears of pain. Of regret. And of satisfaction. He made no attempt to stem them or wipe them away with his sleeve. He let them flow, as through his blurred vision he gazed down on an old photograph. It was cracked and faded now, the sepia tint gradually disappearing. It was a photograph he had kept close to him for years. It was the photograph that had given him the strength and determination and it was the photograph that had helped to keep the fire of his anger aflame.

Suddenly, despite the tears he grinned. And why shouldn't he? What he had desired, what he had planned for had come to pass. There were just a few more days, maybe less, and it would be over. But he mustn't rush things. It would be as he had planned. A few more days. And then the revenge would be complete. Raymond Carter would be destroyed.

* * *

The telephone rang in the hall. Edith Horner put down her knitting and went to answer it. The caller was John Hawke.

'Hello, John. Do you want to talk to Peter?'

'Not just now. I need to have a word with you . . .'

'Of course. Is there something wrong?'

'Nothing to get concerned about really . . . You know we went to see Charlie Dokes at the Palladium last night.'

Edith chuckled. 'Do I? Peter has been full of it all day. His school pal Andrew's round here now; they're supposed to be working on a little Christmas play for school, but all Peter's done is chatter about the show.'

'That's part of the difficulty. The ventriloquist . . . Raymond Carter is now a murder suspect and has disappeared. The police think he's on the run.'

'Good heavens. How awful.'

'It may well be on the six o'clock news and it certainly will be in the newspapers tomorrow.'

'He seemed such a nice man when I've heard him on the radio.'

'Nice isn't quite how I'd describe him, but I do believe he's innocent. He's my client and I'm working on the case.'

'I see. Does Peter know this?'

'No, he doesn't, and I don't want him to.

Not for the present anyway. The main thing is, will you please try to keep him from finding out about Carter's disappearance and the fact that he's wanted for murder? Just for a few days if possible. It will really upset Peter.'

'Oh, yes it will. I know that. Well, we'll do our best, of course. Peter doesn't really listen to the news on the wireless and I'll make sure we keep the paper hidden. But, of course, when he goes to school tomorrow his friends are likely to know and pass on the information.'

'Possibly. As soon as he does find out, please get in touch and I'll come over and have a talk with him.'

'Why don't you do that now? Wouldn't that be for the best?'

'No, not really. I don't want to pre-empt the issue. I'm hoping that the theatrical memories of last night will fade a little before ugly reality hits the lad in the face.'

'I understand. We'll do what we can, John.'

'I know you will. Thanks.'

'Goodnight John . . . and take care.'

★ ★ ★

There was a movement in the darkness, a thin shaft of dim amber light streaked across the chamber where Raymond Carter was lying. A door had been opened. He tried once again to cry out for help but all that emerged was an inarticulate murmur. He wriggled desperately, trying to hoist himself up into a sitting position. As he did so the rope binding his wrists bit maliciously into his flesh causing him to wince.

A shape appeared in the bright margin of illumination and then the door swung to, plunging the chamber into darkness once more. He could feel the presence of the intruder — his captor no doubt — and hear his heavy, excited breathing. He moved closer to Carter. What the hell now, he asked himself? Whatever it was, it would be unpleasant. Possibly fatal. At this thought, he felt his heartbeat falter and an icy numbness steal into his body.

There was a click and a small finger of light appeared. A torch. At first it was shone directly into Carter's eyes blinding him and then the beam swung around and focused on a small face. A small, brightly painted and shiny face. The face of Charlie Dokes.

'Hi there, Raymond,' he said. 'How ya doin'?' The mouth clapped open and shut viciously.

Raymond Carter screamed.

29

The neo-classical white stone façade of Somerset House shone brilliantly in the sharp early morning sunshine. This imposing building sits on the south side of the Strand overlooking the River Thames, just east of Waterloo Bridge. The overnight frost still patterned the stone steps as I made my way towards the north wing, the repository for all births deaths and marriages since . . . well, a long time ago. I'm no historian.

Its sister, the south wing, had been hit by bombs in 1940 and it would take more than all the king's horses and all the king's men to put this lovely structure back together again. The blind, boarded windows, the damaged stonework and rough scaffolding were a blight on this architectural beauty in the heart of London.

However, it was, I hoped, going to reveal to me some information which I reckoned would be vital for the case.

It was Monday morning and I was so early, I was their first customer. A bright ginger-haired, middle-aged woman with wire-rimmed glasses and a friendly efficient manner saw to my needs. And in less than an hour I was progressing down the steps towards the Embankment again with the information I came for, the frost now having surrendered to the gentle coaxing warmth of the late November sun.

I was a little wiser. I had followed the trail of a marriage, a birth and a death. And this, I hoped would lead me to Greta Fielding. I had an address and finding her could unlock a few of the secret compartments in the Raymond Carter mystery. All I had to pray for was that she hadn't moved house or remarried in twenty years. It was a lot to pray for but I'd been a good boy and you never know, someone up there might be listening. I would have to wait and see.

I made my way up to Piccadilly and popped into the Kardomah for a cup of tea and a cigarette while I played around with the couple of theories that I had constructed out of the bits and pieces of information I had gleaned since this investigation began. Then I attempted to glue them together with some intuition and detective-type hunches. Slowly the mist was clearing and I was beginning to make sense of it. I now felt that the Hawke built theory held water, but it still had to be tested.

The clientele of the Kardomah was mainly

306

made up of business-suited gentlemen in pinstriped trousers who nursed their bowler hats on their knees while they read the financial pages of the *Times*; at other tables were affluent middle-class women who had nothing better to do on a Monday morning than to come up to Town for tea and cake and a little bit of light shopping. They all gave the impression that they were totally oblivious of the war and its various deprivations, sacrifices and inconveniences. They seemed to demonstrate no awareness that their casual and indolent way of life which they were so determined to preserve was actually in great peril of being destroyed forever. The women were all smartly attired in neat and apparently expensive outfits. There was no sense of make do and mend here. It was still 1938 in those cocooned minds. In a strange way, I hoped they were right in their 'if we ignore it, it will go away' attitude. I possessed neither the blinkered courage nor stubborn foolishness to follow that particular route.

I was glad to leave the café and get out into the fresh air again. It was better to face reality head on and cope with it as best you could than live in a delusional version of the past. Anyway, I told myself, it was now time for me to grasp my particular nettle. I checked the address again and hopped on a bus to

Islington. As I settled down on the dusty seat, I pulled out the newspaper I'd bought to read *en route*. Raymond Carter had made the front page — as had Charlie Dokes. A grainy photograph showing the incongruous pairing of murder suspect and his wooden doll was placed beneath the headline DOLLY KILLER AT LARGE. The story was thin, however, some of it dreamed up by a journalist in the absence of hard facts. Apparently, Raymond Carter of 'radio's Okey Dokes fame' had killed his girlfriend after a passionate row in the early hours of Sunday morning and then had gone on the run from the police taking his 'precious dolly' with him. Well, now the whole world knew and the whole world would judge Carter as guilty. Whoever had been threatening to kill him needn't bother now. Raymond Carter was dead anyway.

Henry Street was a narrow thoroughfare not a stone's throw from The Old King's Head on the Essex Road. It was crammed with tall terraced houses that, like the good old city, had seen better days. Peeling paintwork, cracked panes and sagging gutters were the order of the day. There were a couple of youngsters playing hopscotch and an old codger sitting on the steps of one house smoking a pipe and staring plaintively into the middle distance.

It didn't take me long to find the number I wanted. As I knocked hard on the door, the old pipe smoker glanced in my direction with unabashed curiosity. He kept his eyes trained on me until the door opened. A thin rake of a man in a dingy ill-knitted pullover and thick cord trousers stood on the threshold, a copy of the *Daily Mirror* in his hand and a roll up cigarette dangling by a hair's-breadth from his mouth.

'Yeah?' he said, a mixture of suspicion and aggression radiating from his weasel eyes.

'I'm wanting a word with Greta Fielding.'

The man said nothing but continued to stare at me. I could not determine what he was thinking, if he was indeed thinking at all.

'Greta Fielding,' I said again as a kind of *aide-mémoire*.

The man sucked on his roll up.

'Who are you?'

I knew if I mentioned anything about me being a detective or someone involved in an investigation, I would have the door slammed in my face.

'Just an old friend of the family . . . ' I said, somewhat lamely.

The man narrowed his eyes. 'Greta Fielding, you say.'

'Yes.'

'Never heard of her.' He began to close the

door when there came a woman's voice from the inner recesses of the house.

'Who is it, Frank?'

'Some geezer looking for a Greta Fielding.'

'Greta,' said the woman, who now appeared at the side of the man, peering out at me as I though I was some mysterious exhibit in a museum. 'You looking for Greta Fielding?'

I nodded. 'This was the address I was given.'

The woman, dressed in a pinafore and flowery turban, clasping a faded tea towel in her hands, smiled indulgently.

'Lord bless you, she hasn't lived here for years. At least ten I should guess.'

My heart sank.

'Isn't that right, Frank?'

'Don't ask me. I never heard of her.'

She flapped the tea towel against his arm in gentle remonstrance. ''Course you have. She rented the top floor when we first moved in. You remember. Peroxide hair. A bit tarty but a very kind soul.'

Frank gave an indignant shrug. He had lost all interest in this interchange and without a word turned his back and retreated into the house.

The woman gave an indulgent smile. 'He's always in a bad mood, Mondays,' she said as some form of explanation.

'Have you any idea where Greta Fielding is living now?'

'Well, she's still local. She moved out to look after her sister who was bad with her chest. But I think she's dead now. The sister, I mean. Greta's still knocking about but I'm not sure of her address. We didn't really keep in touch after she moved out. In '33 I think it was. Wait a minute though; I know how you probably can find her.' Her eyes flashed with inspiration. 'Of course. She goes for a snifter at the King's most lunchtimes. That's The Old Kings Head not far from here.'

'I know it.'

'Well, I reckon you'll catch her in the saloon bar around half past twelve or so. She likes her drink, does Greta. Is she in any kind of trouble?'

'No, nothing like that. I just want to have a chat with her.'

★   ★   ★

If Hollywood wanted to create a replica of a typical English pub on the back lot at MGM or Warner Brothers or some other large film studio, they would most likely come up with something looking like The Old Kings Head on the Essex Road in Islington. With its

311

substantial façade, dominating the corner on which it stands, and its high ceilings, tarred with cigarette fumes, drinking booths separated by warm mahogany partitions inset with smoky glass etched with curlicue designs, the large curving bar with the bright shiny brass foot rest running along the bottom and a tinkling joanna in the corner being played by some old codger whose foaming pint is resting and rattling on the top as he thumps out a tune, The Old King's Head is a cliché of a cliché. By the time I wandered in around 12.15, it was already doing a brisk business and the air was developing a fine mist of cigarette smoke. I reckoned that in about an hour or so the bar might well be obscured by fag fog.

I bought myself a half of bitter from a cheery barmaid, her face fresh and shiny, adorned with a vivid scarlet smear of lipstick. As she was passing me my wet change, I offered to buy her a drink.

'Oh, ta,' she said brightly. 'I don't mind if I do. I could really fancy a port and lemon.'

I smiled and handed over some more money and watched her pour herself a generous measure of port with just a splash of lemon.

'I'm looking for an old friend of mine,' I said, gaining her attention again. 'I gather she's a regular here. Greta Fielding.'

The girl pursed her lips and shrugged her shoulders. 'Doesn't ring a bell, dear. Don't often get to know the customers' names.'

'She'll be a lady in her sixties. I believe she likes a drop of gin.'

'Oh, if she's an old 'un, she'll most likely be in the snug. It's quieter in there. Most of the old 'uns find it too noisy in here. Ta for the drink.'

With that she bustled off to serve elsewhere.

Taking my glass of bitter, I wandered round into the snug. By comparison with the main bar, it was sepulchral in here. The lighting was dimmer and there was no brash hum of conversation.

Most of the tables were occupied — groups of men in flat caps with mufflers and grey faces indulging in muttered conversations and the odd elderly married couple staring blankly into space, each nursing their drink as though it were a fragile object. There was one solitary drinker, a woman with a pale aquiline face and a clutch of frizzy grey hair. She was sipping a large gin while reading a newspaper. I reckoned Johnny had found his lady.

I went to the bar and bought another big gin and took it over to her table.

'Please have a drink on me, Greta,' I said in

as friendly a fashion I could muster without seeming creepy.

The lady looked up at me in surprise and then her eyes narrowed with suspicion.

'What's this for? I don't know you.'

Still retaining my smile, I pulled up a chair and sat by her. 'I hoped we could have a little chat.'

'Who are you?'

I passed her one of my cards.

She read it, her face growing sterner all the while. 'A private investigator. What the devil do you want with me?'

'Just a chat, that's all. There's nothing to worry you.'

'A chat? What about?'

'Raymond Carter.'

Her eyes widened and a knowing smile touched her lips. 'Oh, you're trying to trace the bastard, are you?' She gestured to the newspaper.

I nodded.

'Good luck to you. I hope you find him dead.'

'I understand your feelings.'

'I doubt it.'

'I know that he deserted your daughter and her baby and that as a result she committed suicide.'

She stared at me for some moments, her

face an expressionless mask and then slowly she pulled the glass of gin I had bought her to her side. 'What do you want to know, Mr Investigator?'

'What happened to the child? It was a boy, wasn't it?'

Greta Fielding nodded, her eyes moistening slightly.

'It was a boy, yes. Little Freddie. A little angel.'

'What happened?' I prompted gently.

'After Sally . . . died. I tried to look after him for a while but in the end I had to give him up, didn't I? I was an out-of-work widow with a dead daughter. I couldn't cope with the mite. I had to put him up for adoption. I had to . . . let him go. My little grandson.' She was crying now, the tears streaking down her face making little tracks through her face powder. 'I can tell you something, Mr Investigator, if I had my time over again, I wouldn't do it. I'd rather cut off my arm instead. I've lived with that regret, that guilt for the rest of my life.'

'Do you know who adopted Freddie?'

She shook her head. 'No. The agency, the adoption agency, dealt with all that. It was a place recommended by a friend. I reckon they was a bit shady. Well, I know they were but I was in a bit of a spot and I really had no option. Beggars can't be choosers, y'know. I signed the forms and just handed over the baby and they gave me twenty pounds. Blood money, eh? I heard there was an American couple sniffing around for a kid. Maybe they got him and took him off to Texas or wherever. I just don't know. Oh, if I could turn back the clock . . . ' She rooted in her coat pocket for a while before extracting a large handkerchief and then proceeded to blow her nose.

'So you have no idea where he is now?'

She gave me a weary smile. 'I don't and it's not for the want of trying. Don't waste your time, mister. He's been swallowed up. There's no reaching him. The adoption agency has disappeared. There are no records anywhere. Little Freddie has become the invisible man.'

'How old would he be now? In his mid-twenties, I guess.'

'Yes. He's got a birthday coming up next February. February the tenth. What I'd give to be able to plant a birthday kiss on his cheek.' To prevent another bout of tears, she took a large gulp of gin.

'Does his father know anything about Freddie or his whereabouts?'

Greta gave a snort of derision. 'Does he hell. He wanted to know nothing about the baby as soon as he found out that Sally was pregnant. He thought it would interfere with his career and his bloody philandering. What kind of man is that? When they were schooling first rate bastards, Raymond Carter was top of the class.' Her finger jabbed the newspaper before her. 'And it seems he's still at it. I see he's murdered his latest girlfriend. Well I hope you catch him and he dangles at the end of a rope. That's what he deserves. It'll be good riddance to bad rubbish.' Her eyes had brightened now and an angry flush had reddened her cheeks. I gazed at her, the shape of her face, the turn of her nose and the attractive hazel colouring of her eyes and got the tingle: the Hawke tingle when I've made some sort of breakthrough. Yes I had seen those features before. Quite recently. But they were on a man.

30

'It's true, I tell you. It's true.' Andrew Booth's eyes nearly popped out of his head as he blurted out the story that he'd heard on the wireless that morning. 'Raymond Carter has strangled a woman. To death!'

With enthusiasm, he gripped Peter by the throat and in demonstration pretended to strangle him. Much to Andrew's chagrin, Peter did not respond to this dramatic re-enactment; instead he stood limply as Andrew's fingers circled his neck.

The two boys were standing in the school playground at morning playtime, surrounded by a seething tide of boisterous schoolboys who took no notice of this apparently murderous attack on one of their fellows, their attentions focused on other raucous activities.

'Come on,' said Andrew, in frustration, attempting to shake his friend into action. 'Scream or something.'

'Just get off,' responded Peter sullenly, pulling away.

Andrew obeyed. 'What's up?'

'Are you sure about this? Or are you making it up?' Peter's face was dark with concern.

'What, about Raymond Carter and Charlie Dokes?' Andrew giggled. '''Cos Charlie's gone on the run too, y'know.' Andrew did an arthritic impersonation of a ventriloquist's doll on the run.

'It's not funny, Andy.'

'''Course I'm telling the truth. I wouldn't make such stuff up, would I?'

Peter nodded. He knew that to be true. 'I liked Raymond Carter and Charlie,' he said simply, trying to explain his dismay. 'I've got all their comics. I saw him on Saturday night. At the Palladium.'

'Yes, you told me.'

'I thought he was a nice man. Funny . . . and . . . nice.'

'Well, according to the man on the wireless he strangled his girlfriend, that woman who's on his radio show.'

'What? Evelyn Munro?'

Andrew shrugged. 'Don't know her name.'

A wave of misery swept over Peter. In his short life he had been let down so often by people whom he had liked and respected. Here again was another shallow deceiver who had misled him. Although he had never met the man Raymond Carter, and had only seen him once from a distance on a brightly coloured stage, he had warmed to him and his cheeky pal Charlie through the radio shows and the comics. Raymond and Charlie had become part of his world, part of his imaginary family. In essence he had become one of Peter's heroes. Now he had turned out to be someone else, someone who couldn't be trusted. A bad man. A murderer.

Andrew could see from Peter's glum expression that he had taken his news rather more to heart than he had expected. He placed a consoling hand on his friend's shoulder. 'Never mind,' he said with forced cheeriness, 'when the police catch him perhaps they'll let him do his radio show from the jail.'

'I don't think I want to hear him ever again,' said Peter grimly.

Suddenly the air was rent with three sharp bursts on a whistle: the signal that it was the end of playtime. A plump, stern-looking woman in grey tweeds and wearing her grey hair in a severe bun stood menacingly on the steps of the school. The sound of the whistle and her presence silenced the boys immediately. All frenzied activity came to an abrupt halt, the youngsters frozen in action by the Pavlovian whistle. Without another word, Peter and Andrew slowly and mechanically joined the throng of boys filing reluctantly back into the school.

Raymond Carter had no idea how long he had been lying in the dark. He had gone past hunger and discomfort. His mind was now drifting towards delirium. He now began to wonder if what he was experiencing was real after all. Was it actually happening? His life before this sable night of incarceration had dominated him was vague and difficult to conjure up. The old Raymond was a mere foggy fragmented memory. His new life was clearer. He recollected that he had been visited in this prison by his old friend Charlie Dokes who had spoken very kindly to him. It had been good to see Charlie again. His one true friend.

Perhaps he was dead? Perhaps this dark chamber was some kind of waiting room where you were held until They decided where you go. Up in the lift to Heaven or down in a bucket to Hell. Carter giggled at this concept. Or perhaps he was mad. That thought had occurred to him also. But, he reasoned, if he were mad would he wonder whether he was mad or not? Surely madmen do not doubt their sanity. Or do they?

His attention was diverted from this conundrum by a sudden noise. It was the door opening and again a pale sliver of yellow

321

light stretched across the floor as someone entered and then it disappeared as the door was closed.

There was the click of the torch and once more Charlie Dokes's grinning face appeared as if by magic floating in the darkness.

'Hello Raymond, old boy. How are you?' The red lips moved noisily, hypnotically with the words.

Raymond smiled. 'Hello, Charlie,' he muttered behind the tape.

'I've come to say goodbye, Raymond. My work is over. The job is done. You'll not be seeing me again.'

Raymond shivered with emotion. This can't be real. Can't be true, Surely Charlie wasn't going to desert him. Not his old friend Charlie. 'No,' he wailed, and tears welled in his eyes and began to roll down his cheeks. 'Don't go. Don't leave me,' he cried desperately, the words muffled by the tape.

'How touching. Parting is such sweet sorrow, eh pal. But now I have to go. You see, I've served my purpose. There is no need for me any more. It's time for me to take my final curtain call. Bye bye.'

The torch clicked off and the face of Charlie Dokes vanished.

Raymond Carter squirmed in despair and emitted an inarticulate moan.

From the darkness, came the eerie voice of the dummy. 'Now cracks a corrupt heart. Goodnight, sweet prince. And flights of Angels sing thee to thy rest.'

★   ★   ★

Constable Ernest Barker walked along the side of the Thames by Chiswick basin, indulging in a crafty smoke. There was nobody about and it was that in-between time of day when it was neither day nor dusk. But the clouds had gathered and the light had begun to fade and it was sufficiently dim enough to conceal the glowing fag inside his gloved hands between puffs. He stopped for a moment and stared out at the great expanse of the grey seething water. No matter what Hitler is doing to us or will do in the future, thought PC Barker, in a rare moment of contemplation, he'll never stop the constant surge of Old Father Thames as it makes its determined way down to the sea. He smiled to himself in satisfaction at this piece of homespun philosophy.

Then he saw it. The thing in the river. At first he thought his eyes might be deceiving him. He leaned forward and peered hard, focusing on the strange object that was floating in the water. Flinging his fag away, he hurried down to the water's edge to get a better view. Crikey, he thought, it can't be . . . But it was. He wasn't wrong. It was . . . a body. A small body, lying face down, shifting rhythmically with the swell of the current.

'Oh, my God,' he whispered, as the body drifted closer to the shore. 'It's the body of a child.'

He glanced around him for help. Moments earlier he had been pleased there was no one about, but now he could do with somebody to assist him. He had to get that . . . that child out of the water, sharpish. But as his eyes scanned his surroundings, he realized that he truly was alone in this venture. He spied a small rowing-boat fifty yards ahead tied to a wooden pier. Again he gazed around only to establish for certain that he was the solitary figure on the watery landscape. Well, there was no other alternative. He certainly didn't come from a seafaring family and his only experience was the paddleboats in Regent's Park lake but . . .

He clambered aboard the little craft that bobbed with unnerving instability as he did so and then struggled for some moments to retrieve the oars from the canvas wrapping in the bottom and place them in the rowlocks. While he did all this, he was aware that the sky was now darkening at a faster rate. He swore in frustration and then cast the little vessel out on to the swell of the big river.

It took him about a minute to establish some kind of rhythm with the oars and then he tried to point the recalcitrant vessel in the right direction — towards the shape floating in the river some way behind him. He used the word 'shape' in his mind, avoiding the term 'body' although in his heart of hearts he knew that was what it was.

As he pulled manfully on the oars, the boat drew nearer and nearer until it was almost floating alongside the 'shape'. PC Barker drew in his oars and leaned forward over the edge, reaching out towards it. He saw now that it was a little thing, not man-sized at all. His heart sank as he realized that it was, as he suspected, the body of a small child. A young boy.

Gradually, the boat edged closer until he was able to grab hold of one of the arms which were floating outstretched. As he did so, he gave a yelp of surprise and dropped it back in the water. There appeared to be nothing in the sleeve as though . . . as though it were empty.

Gingerly, he reached out again and grabbed the arm and hauled the thing aboard. It was as light as a feather. It fell, a sodden mess in the bottom of the boat.

Barker gazed down at it and his jaw dropped open in shock and surprise. The thing he had retrieved from the river was not a child. It was not a living thing of any description. It was a doll. A dummy dressed in a brightly striped blazer and brown slacks. The shiny immobile face stared up at him with a grisly rictal grin. Then he noticed that planted in the centre of its chest was the handle of a knife.

31

Leaving The Old King's Head, I made my way back to my office, my mind buzzing. After my talk with Greta Fielding I was now certain who my man was — the fellow who had been threatening Raymond Carter and who had murdered Arthur Keating and Evelyn Munro. Despite my detective work bearing fat juicy fruit, strangely I experienced no sense of elation or relief at reaching this conclusion. I just felt rather weary. It was a sad and depressing business and I knew there could be no happy ending for anyone. I was dealing with damaged lives and probably an unhinged mind. However, it was my duty to try and rescue Raymond Carter, if it was not too late.

On reaching Hawke Towers, I made myself a strong black coffee to clear my head. Then I made two phone calls. The first gave me the necessary information I required to make my next move. I scribbled down the address I needed and then rang Max at her shop. I knew she would be there during the daylight hours. It was a joy to hear her voice again. The gentle, soothing Gallic tones were like a tonic to my ragged soul. She told me that she was fine and it had been good that she had opened up the shop today after all because she had just received a large order for a set of Pierrot masks for some theatrical extravaganza due to open at one of the big London theatres in the spring. I was very happy for her. I also told her that I believed she was no longer in danger. Without going into any details, I let her know that I thought the case was coming to a conclusion.

'That is good news, Johnny. But please take care,' she said quietly, so quietly it was difficult to hear her voice above the hiss on the line.

'I will and when it's all over I'll take you out for a celebratory meal. Just the two of us this time.'

'I will look forward to that.'

I was still smiling after I'd put the receiver down. But the smile did not linger. I had work to do and, as usual, I had no idea what the outcome would be. Reluctantly I retrieved my revolver from the locked drawer of my desk. I didn't like guns and didn't feel comfortable carrying one. I knew that they cancelled things out in a final way. There was no going back after the trigger was pulled. In my book life wasn't cheap; and it wasn't my job to be a dispassionate avenging executioner. I liked to discover the truth without the need for violence, but I knew that I'd be a fool to set out on this expedition without some kind of solid protection. I did want to come back after all. I slipped the gun into my coat pocket and then retrieved the small torch from the kitchen.

'Right, boy,' I said to myself, 'time for Johnny Hawke to ride to the rescue.'

I was just about to switch the light off and leave when my office door creaked open to reveal a small shape in the doorway. It was Peter.

'Hello, Johnny,' he said wistfully.

'What on earth are you doing here?' I cried, ushering him in and closing the door. He stood before me, a plaintive little creature in his grey belted gabardine and school cap almost pulled over one eye. With his scuffed shoes and wrinkled socks, one around his ankle and the other pulled up to the knee, he looked like the archetypal schoolboy of the cartoonist's imagination. A sort of forlorn Just William.

'I needed to talk to you,' he said with a sniff, his eyes beginning to water.

Now of all times.

His face looked as cold and miserable as one of Benny's stale buns. 'What's the matter, old chap?'

'It's . . . Raymond and Charlie, Charlie

Dokes. I thought you could tell me the truth. I'd heard that he . . . Raymond was a murderer. That he'd killed Miss Munro off his radio show. I know you're on a case for him, I thought you'd know all about it. He didn't do it, did he?' Peter recited this almost like an automaton as though he had been rehearsing the speech. When he finished, his body seem to deflate.

'Let me get you a cup of tea and a biscuit. And then we'll see what I can tell you.'

Without a word, he followed me through into the section I grandly called my living-quarters. I lit the gas fire and placed my shivering pal in a chair in front of it while I brewed him a pot of tea. I managed to find a couple of fairly edible digestive biscuits to accompany it.

Once he was slurping the brew I sat opposite him. Where to start? 'I can see you're upset at the idea of someone as funny and nice as Mr Carter actually killing someone. Well, I can tell you that I'm fairly certain that he didn't.'

Peter gazed at me over the brim of the mug, his features brightening for a moment. 'Then why did he run away?'

I smiled and gave a little shrug. 'Well, I don't know everything, Peter. But I think that he has gone into hiding so that the real murderer doesn't find him. And now it's my job to discover where he is before the real killer does.'

Peter's eyes widened in excitement. 'Who is the real killer?'

'We don't know yet.'

'But you are on the case?'

I nodded. 'Oh, yes.'

'So Raymond is an innocent man.' He leaned forward eagerly, desperate for the confirmation that his hero Raymond Carter was not stained with sin.

'He's not a murderer, but he is perhaps not as nice a man as you might think from his radio show and seeing him on stage. That's just a performance.'

Peter gave me a puzzled look.

I ran the back of my hand gently down his cheek and smiled sympathetically. 'Life is not so simple as good men and bad men, Pete, old boy,' I said, remembering my own youthful *naïveté* and the harsh awakening as gradually the veils were lifted to reveal the truth about mankind. 'We all have a bit of both in us — some good and some not so good. You will admit that you are a bit naughty sometimes and maybe a bit selfish.'

He nodded reluctantly.

'Well, I reckon so am I. And indeed all grown ups are to some extent, but of course it's more serious then. Most folk are only slightly naughty or selfish or cruel, but a small number of people let this side of their character take charge.'

'Like Harryboy Jenkins.' Peter shuddered as he mentioned the name of the man who had kidnapped him and nearly killed him some time before. I think I had allowed the name, the character and the incident seep out of my memory like sand in an egg-timer. But just the mention of this demon brought it all back, crisp and vivid.

'Yes,' I said at length, testing myself to say that name again, 'like Harryboy Jenkins.'

'But Raymond Carter isn't like Harryboy, is he?'

'No, no, he's not a killer but he has done some bad things in the past.'

'What has he done?'

'I'll tell you some other time.'

'I want to know now.'

'Maybe you do, but I say no. If you want to be treated like a grown up you have to get used to people saying no and meaning it. And you need to be more considerate of others . . . '

'What do you mean?'

'Have you seen the time? It's after four. You should be home now. Edith and Martha will be worrying about where you are. You've come here because you wanted to find something out and you've not given them a thought. You've not bothered to consider the worry you're causing them.'

Peter's face clouded with concern. 'I didn't think.'

'That, my young sir, is a pretty weak excuse. I want you to telephone them now and put their minds at rest. Apologize for being thoughtless, explain where you are and say that I'm putting you in a taxi in five minutes to take you home.'

'Aah, can't I stay a bit longer?'

I gave him a look, furrowed brows and staring eyes. 'Phone,' I said sharply. 'You're delaying me; I have urgent business to attend to.'

With slumped shoulders and a face puckered with dismay, Peter trudged to the telephone and dialled the number. It was Edith who answered. In humble tones he explained his wayward actions and apologized, adding that he'd be home shortly. I indicated that I wanted a word.

'Thank goodness,' said Edith. 'We were really getting concerned.'

'He's a bit upset about the Raymond Carter business, but that's no real excuse. Anyway, I'm popping him in a taxi now and he should be with you in fifteen minutes. I suggest you give him his supper and send him straight to bed.' I knew that they wouldn't. They'd welcome him with open arms like the prodigal son and make such a fuss of him, but at least Peter had heard my view on the matter. He had to be discouraged from just pleasing himself on a whim. I wasn't very good at discipline — or hadn't been in the past, but I was beginning to realize that always being soft with the boy was not only bad for him but I was failing to live up to my responsibilities. He was no kin of mine, but I regarded him as a son or much younger brother. There was a bond between us and as I was the older and, therefore, supposedly more sensible and responsible, I needed to act like a caring and mindful guardian.

'Right,' I said as I replaced the receiver, 'let's get you into a taxi.' I paused only to snatch up the piece of paper with the important address before escorting the mute Peter to the door.

32

Raymond Carter was dragged from the dark realm of surreal dreams by a fierce cold sensation which thrust him into breathtaking consciousness. In his now fragile mind it was like travelling in a lift from the basement to ground level at supersonic speed and being dumped with great force on the floor outside the lift. He blinked feverishly only to discover that he was still in his dark prison and that he was still bound and gagged. The sharp freezing sensation came again. It was cold water, which was being splashed in his face. The shock of it made him gasp and attempt to coil up into a foetal position but his limbs, tired, stiff and bruised failed to function properly. The icy water came again, dousing his head. For a split second he had a flashback. He was on the stage of the Palladium in the houseboat sketch. Charlie was giggling heartily as another porthole opened, allowing water to gush all over him. The audience roared with pleasure. The moment faded and reality reasserted itself.

'Wakey, wakey,' said a voice in the darkness.

It was a voice he knew.

He felt a hand touch his face and then the tape that covered his mouth was ripped away with some violence. His sharp bleating cry echoed in the blackness. It was a mixture of shock, pain and fear. Then he gasped for air. At last he could breathe properly once more.

His tormentor spoke again. 'Is that better, Dad?'

'What?' Raymond found his voice harsh, croaky and faint as though his vocal chords had forgotten how to function.

'I said is that better?'

'You said 'Dad'.' Carter really had to concentrate with all his energy to turn his blurry thoughts into words.

'Yes, so I did. Dad.'

'Why . . . ?'

'Why did I call you Dad? The answer is simple. Because I'm your son.'

★ ★ ★

The taxi had only just turned the corner, obliterating the waving figure of Johnny Hawke from view before Peter began to moan noisily and clutch his stomach in a melodramatic fashion. The driver glanced in his mirror to catch a view of his young passenger who seemed to be rolling about on

336

the back seat in some discomfort. He frowned. 'You all right, son?' he called.

'No,' groaned the boy. 'I think I'm going to be sick.'

The driver braked heavily. 'Not in my cab, you're not,' he muttered, pulling the vehicle up to the kerb. It had happened once before. A respectable-looking gentleman who, it turned out, was as pickled as a gherkin, vomited liberally in the back of his cab. It had taken him hours to clean up the mess and the smell had lingered for weeks, sometimes being the cause of a number of passengers curtailing their journey. If this little blighter was going to be sick, he was going to do it in the gutter.

The driver jumped out of the cab and wrenched the passenger door open.

'Come on, son, let's have you out in the fresh air. There's a drain over there. You can be sick down that.'

Peter obeyed without a word, his face contorted with discomfort. Once he was on the pavement and away from his precious cab, the driver heaved a sigh of relief. The boy walked gingerly to the drain and then did something quite surprising. He raised himself up from the semi-crouching pose and began to run. Down the street he fled without a glance back towards the deserted chauffeur.

'Oi!' shouted the taxi driver, but the boy was now too far away to hear him. He scratched his head. 'What the bleedin' hell was that all about? Little blighter,' he muttered to himself. He'd had many a punter try to scarper without paying the fare but not after they'd only been driven less than half a mile. Still, he thought, philosophically, he wasn't sick in my cab. I can be thankful for that.

By the time the cabbie drove off again in the search for regular fare-paying passengers, Peter was many streets away, lurking in a shop doorway, catching his breath. For comfort he rubbed the coins in his pocket that Johnny had given him to pay for the taxi ride. He would certainly use them to pay for a ride, but the journey would take him to another destination other than home. He murmured the address to himself — the one he had observed on the pad by the telephone in Johnny's office — just to make sure he remembered it. He had forced it into his memory like a religious mantra. He knew it was important. He knew it was connected with the Raymond Carter case. He knew that it was to this address that Johnny was now making his way. He knew that he had to go there too.

He learned very quickly that no cab driver

was going to stop to pick up a schoolboy in short trousers no matter how desperately he tried to flag one down. He had no idea where Chiswick Reach was so he couldn't go by tube or bus. He really had to get a cab. Then he had the spark of an idea. If he found a hotel where cabs dropped passengers off, he could try and hire one there. He could show the driver his shiny coins to prove that he had the wherewithal to pay his fare. Surely, if he did that no self-respecting cabbie would deny him his ride? With this plan in mind, he made his way to Tottenham Court Road and on to Store Street. It was here he discovered what looked from a distance like a small, smart hotel. On approaching it, he saw that it was indeed small but the rather shabby entrance declared that it wasn't particularly smart. Nevertheless, it was here that Peter thought that he would try his luck. After a five-minute wait, a cab drew up and two large giggling ladies emerged carrying shopping bags. Their faces were flushed and shiny with paint. They paid their fare and jostled merrily into the hotel. In an instant, Peter was up at the driver's window. He tapped gently and the grizzled cabbie wound it down.

'Can you take me to Chiswick Reach?' asked Peter, in his most grown-up manner.

'Why, d'you fancy a swim?' The cabbie

chortled at his own joke.

'I . . . er . . . I want to get home for tea.'

The cabbie frowned. 'Well, you're a long way from home and I reckon it's a little past your teatime.'

Peter nodded vigorously. 'It is. I need to get home before my mother worries too much.' He held up the coins. 'I can pay.'

'Can you now?' The cabbie squinted at the coins. 'Well, then I reckon I can take you. Hop in lad. Chiswick Reach it is.'

Peter settled back in the cab as it lurched forward into the darkness, a bevy of flitting butterflies played in his stomach. He felt a strange mixture of worried concern and suppressed excitement. He knew that he was disobeying Johnny's instructions, which didn't please him, but he thrilled in anticipation of doing his own detective work. He permitted himself a grim little smile. Peter Blake was on the case.

33

'Now then Dad, how about a little drink, eh?'

'Oh, yes, please.' At the mention of a drink Raymond Carter instinctively ran his sandpaper tongue along his cracked lips. He was still bewildered and confused as to why this disembodied voice speaking to him from the blackness referred to him as 'Dad', but his thirst overrode such concerns for the moment. His mind conjured up an image of a large gushing fountain of cool clear water. Its gurgling spray sparkling like diamonds caught by the rays of sunlight. He saw himself lying beneath it, the water showering on him like liquid needles. He could almost taste the ice-cold freshness as the liquid trickled down his parched throat.

Suddenly he found the neck of a bottle rammed aggressively against his teeth and gums. The vision vanished in an instant and he cried out in shock as some of the liquid spilled down his chin.

'Come on, Dad, drink up.'

Eagerly, he sucked hard on the neck of the bottle and the contents gushed into his mouth. He spluttered and cried out in disgust. It burnt his throat and caused his eyes to moisten. It was gin. It wasn't cool, thirst-quenching water. It was warm gin.

'Thought you'd like a cocktail,' said the voice, retracting the bottle and casting it aside. Carter heard it clatter and thud as it fell to the floor somewhere out there in the darkness.

'Now, Dad, I think it's time for the finale, don't you? This entertaining cabaret has gone on too long, hasn't it? It's time for the last act and then we can bring down the curtain once and for all.'

That voice. That voice, he knew it. If only his brain would allow him to remember it. But Carter's brain wouldn't. It had ceased to function normally. He now could barely remember his own name, let alone that of a purring disembodied voice. And why 'Dad'? He wasn't anyone's father . . . was he?

The torch clicked on again, but instead of Charlie Dokes's shiny features springing out from the dark as on previous occasions, it was a real man's face. Long, young and with an aquiline nose on which was perched a large pair of tortoiseshell spectacles. The features were stoical, but for a brief moment they relaxed into a smile.

Recognition came to Carter. It was . . . It was Al. This face before him. Yes, it was Al

Warren. What on earth is Al doing here? Here . . . in the darkness. With me. Then the thought struck him, struck him so hard that he thought his heart would burst as it pounded within his breast. A kind of truth exposed itself to Carter rather like a self-assembling jigsaw. It was Al who was doing all this to him. It was Al who had tied him up and kept him prisoner. It was Al who had clubbed him. It was Al . . . He pushed harder at the thoughts. Yes . . . it was Al then who . . . who had killed her. Killed the girl. What was her name? But yes, he had killed her. An image of her dead body splayed on the bed, the red-lipped mouth agape in that silent scream, flashed into his ravaged mind, and he emitted a gagging cry of pain.

'You . . . killed her,' he croaked.

'Evie?' said Al evenly. 'Yes, I suppose I did.'

Evie, that was her name mused Carter. Yes, Evie. Evelyn. And Al had killed her.

'Why?'

'All part of the plan, Poppa. All part of the grand design. It's still not clear to you yet, is it? You see, I'm your little Freddie all growed up.'

'Freddie?' Carter shook his head in bewilderment.

'You should remember the name if not the face. I can understand why you don't recognize me. After all I was only a few weeks old when you left. Just a bawling, mewling scrap of humanity. But you do remember when you left me, don't you? And my mother.'

'Sally.' From nowhere it came. The name that had not crossed his lips in a lifetime. And it came to him along with the dread memories from out of the past. He forced his mind to find a clearing in the fog, to focus on what the voice was saying and its implications. As he did so, a frightening possibility occurred to him. 'Sally was your mother?' For a brief moment her face floated before him and then faded into the gloom.

'And you . . . my father,' said Al Warren, simply.

Tears welled up in Carter's eyes and his body shuddered with emotion but he had no idea why. Blind unfathomed feelings engulfed him like it does with a young child whose senses are only roughly formed with logic playing no part in pain or pleasure.

'I was the last inconvenient straw,' the strangely illuminated face was saying. 'You had grown tired of my mother and then when she was careless enough to fall pregnant with me, you wanted out. A kid and a wife was too much baggage for Raymond Carter, eh? They got in the way of your career and your womanizing.' The voice now had a sharp, angry edge to it and the eyes flashed fiercely in the harsh torchlight. 'I suppose you had the decency to wait until I was born before you did the dirty. Perhaps you were hoping she'd have a miscarriage. Heaven knows you knocked her about enough. But sadly for you there was no miscarriage. Your wife — my mother — had a healthy and a very smart cookie. Me. So you upped sticks and left. You deserted us. You simply cut us out of your life. Left my mother to fend for herself.' Warren's voice cracked and he paused to inhale and bring his emotions under control. After a moment, he continued, his voice stronger, his anger greater.

'And my mother who, God help her, loved you couldn't bear it. Despite all you'd done to her, she still loved you. You left her with no alternative. So she killed herself.'

'Sally,' said Carter hoarsely, as the frail fragment of memory returned to him. He remembered now. It was so long ago. Another life. It seemed as though it had all happened to another person. Another Raymond Carter. Not him.

'Sally,' repeated the face tenderly. 'My mother.'

'Freddie.'

'Yes, baby Freddie. That's me. Orphan

Freddie. Because you refused to have anything to do with me, I was auctioned off to an American couple who smuggled me into the States. It was there I grew up and it was there I became Al Warren. When I eventually found out that I'd been adopted, I was determined to find my real parents. To discover the truth. And I did. I didn't have to dig too deep. And when I knew the truth, I was determined that you would pay. You were responsible for my mother's death and you would pay. And so I came after you.'

'Are you going to kill me?'

Suddenly Al Warren laughed and the torchlight left his face for a few moments.

'Kill you? Oh, that would be too easy. Too quick, old boy. I've waited a long time for this. I'm not going to end things with a sudden moment of frenzied passion. I've had too many of those over the years. They're not all they're cracked up to be. No, this has got to be a slow process. I'm a scriptwriter, remember and I've scripted this scenario down to the last comma and full stop. I took you from being a third-rate music-hall act to being a national star. We did it. Me and Charlie Dokes. My scripts made you famous. You never knew it, but you were my dummy. I was playing you and what a great pleasure it gave me. It was all done for a purpose, you

346

see. To build you up so that I could knock you down. The greater the height: the greater the fall.'

Carter screwed up his face with concentration. 'You planned all that . . . just to kill me.'

'Just to have my revenge, Daddy dear. And it is true what they say: revenge is sweet. Very tasty indeed.'

'Please . . . it was all a long time ago. It . . . was a mistake. I didn't know your mother would take her own life. She was always a little . . . melodramatic.'

'Like me, I guess. This is all a bit melodramatic, isn't it?'

'Don't do it. I beg you. Don't kill me.'

'I'm not going to kill you. I wouldn't soil my hands.' Warren paused for effect and then grinned. 'I'm just going to damage you.'

The torch went out and there the sound of movement in the darkness and then suddenly a bright yellow light flooded the area. In bewildered fascination, Carter stared upwards and saw the naked light bulb dangling above him, its filament glowing fiercely.

Warren towered over him, grinning. In his right hand he held something that was bright and shiny. Carter focused on it. It was a knife.

34

The address I had been given was in a sense another piece of evidence that fitted in nicely with my theory concerning the identity of the murderer. A houseboat on the river at Chiswick. A houseboat on the river. I was reminded of the final sketch in the Palladium show which had been set on a houseboat, the sketch in which Raymond Carter was regularly drenched with water, to the great amusement of the audience. There was an element of indignity for the star in that scenario and it had struck me at the time that the writer of the sketch must have a cruel sense of humour to subject Carter to being deluged on stage every night. The writer of the sketch was, of course, Al Warren.

From the very start of this investigation, I had been of the strong opinion that Carter's tormentor had to be someone concerned with the Okey Dokes radio show. There was the warning message on the script and the culprit obviously was in possession of so much inside information. It could easily have been the announcer Percy Goodall finally exacting his revenge for Carter's adulterous fling with his wife; or Edward Simmons the producer of the show and obviously far from being a fan of the ventriloquist; or Larry Milligan, his long suffering agent, who had struck me as a very cold fish indeed. But the key to the case was motive and theirs, if they really had one, did not seem strong enough, certainly not strong enough to lead them from intense dislike to actual murder.

My digging into Carter's past had brought its rewards. The conversation I'd had with Greta Fielding and Cyril Sarony had filled in many pieces of this difficult jigsaw. Thanks to Greta I now knew what happened to Carter's son whom she had abandoned twenty-five years ago. I was seeing the picture which was forming before my eyes with greater clarity and I was convinced that Greta was correct in thinking that maybe the boy had been adopted by an American couple. Mr and Mrs Yankee would have whipped him off to the States and brought him up there. This scenario not only focused the beam of suspicion on one particular fellow in my chosen crew of suspects, but it also allowed me to construct an all important, albeit makeshift, motive. The old Hawke brain with its dubious convolutions suggested to me that it was possible, probable even, that the twenty-five year old Al Warren with the trans-Atlantic accent was my man. And yet it didn't make sense. Warren had been Carter's saviour. It was Warren's scripts and advice that were the bedrock of the ventriloquist's success. And there seemed real affection between the two men. Why would Warren do that if he hated Carter? As I mulled these thoughts over in my mind during the taxi ride to Chiswick, I came to realize that perhaps I hadn't yet got to the bottom of the case. There were still some important pieces missing. I hoped that my trip to Warren's houseboat would bring further clarification, but I was aware that it would not necessarily bring closure.

The bloodstain I'd found in Evelyn Munro's flat suggested to me that Carter had been attacked by her murderer and captured by him or dumped somewhere. The river was always a reliable repository for a dead body. I shivered at this thought. I didn't want to think of my client as a corpse. I hoped that he was still alive. Somewhere.

If Warren was the murderer, then he knew the whereabouts of Raymond Carter. Whether the ventriloquist was alive or dead was a question I could not answer and one I didn't really want to think about.

I paid off the taxi and walked down on to the towpath that ran along by the side of the river. It was dark now and there was only a faintly perceptible shift in the depth of blackness between the sky and the land. A faint moon, enveloped in cloud, provided some illumination. Gradually, as my eyes became acclimatized to the starless night, I could just about make out the vague contours of the horizon across the river. I was able to determine the vague shape of the gantry of a crane, like a skeletal finger pointing up to the heavens.

On my side of the river, I could see a flotilla — if that's the word — of houseboats moored along this stretch of the Thames. I was looking for one called *Mermaid III*. Slowly I made my way from houseboat to houseboat, flashing my torch surreptitiously along the side looking for a name plate, looking, no doubt, like a rather arrogant burglar. I came across *The Golden Hind*, *Water Repos*, *Ratty's Bolthole* and other watery nomenclatures. But there was no *Mermaid III*. Not even *Mermaids I* and *II*.

I was about to give up hope as I approached the final vessel in the line when the narrow beam of my torch caught out the faded lettering on the side. There it was: *Mermaid III*. It had to be the last one of course. It was shrouded in darkness, but in these days of the blackout that meant nothing. It certainly did not prove that there was 'no one home'.

Clutching the revolver in my coat pocket, I crossed the little gangplank and boarded *Mermaid III*. I moved down the side of the vessel and crouched by one of the long narrow windows and listened. At first I thought there was no sound at all, but I was mistaken. It had been masked by the sharp breeze rippling some tarpaulin on deck and the lapping of the water, but, as I strained my ears until I could feel the wax shift, I felt certain I could catch the faint strains of music, jolly jazz-type music. It may have been the radio or the gramophone but it was certainly coming from inside the houseboat. So, someone was in residence and surely that someone was Al Warren.

I was about to raise myself up into a standing position when I felt something cold and hard prod into the back of my neck.

'I knew sooner or later someone would come prowling round here,' said a voice, 'and I reckon I'd have put money on it being you, Mr Hawke.'

I didn't move. I was fairly sure that the cold metal object pressed hard against my medulla oblongata, one of my favourite organs, was a gun.

'Good evening, Mr Warren.'

'Not for you, I fear. However, let us continue this conversation in the warm. Stand up slowly and we'll go inside. As they say on the movies, 'No funny business now or I'll blow your head off'.'

I thought it better to remain silent. A response might be regarded as funny business.

Warren prodded me forward along the deck and towards the cabin door.

'I have a little device rigged up so that anyone crossing the gangplank sets off a buzzer inside to alert me of unwelcome visitors. Comes in handy. Certainly did tonight.'

We passed through a galley kitchen into a long well-furnished room, softly but dimly illuminated by a series of oil lamps. Now Warren moved in front of me for the first time. He seemed relaxed and assured as though all this meant nothing to him.

'Take a seat, Mr Hawke.' He indicated an armchair with the barrel of his gun.

I did as I was told. There was something unnerving about Warren's relaxed, almost charming manner. There seemed to be no anger or resentment in his demeanour. Such behaviour was scary; especially in a man toting a gun.

My captor took a seat opposite me, one in which he had been sitting before if the glass of whisky and the ashtray bore accurate witness. As he sat back, I observed that he wore a large silver watch with a black strap, the face of which was on the inside of his right wrist — just as Max had described her attacker.

'Now then, to what do I owe the pleasure of your visit?'

'I want to know what you've done with Raymond Carter.'

Warren smiled and for a moment stared into the distance beyond me. 'He need not concern us any more.'

'You've killed him?'

He raised his eyebrows in a mischievous glance. 'You're the detective. You tell me. You've done very well to get this far, Mr Hawke, but I'm afraid this is as far as you go. Whatever we say to each other now, in the end I'll have to kill you.'

'Like Arthur Keating and Evelyn Munro.'

'Not quite like Arthur Keating and Evelyn Munro. I don't relish the thought of strangling you. I think a bullet through the heart will have to suffice on this occasion.'

'All this has been done in the name of revenge.'

'Sounds rather melodramatic like that but . . . yes, you're right. You've worked it out then?'

'Some of it. I know that you are Raymond Carter's son, the one he abandoned twenty-five years ago and you have come back into his life to kill him.'

'Not to kill him. To destroy him. Yes old Ray is my dad — the man who dumped me and my mother. She committed suicide as a result. Did you know that?'

I nodded.

'Of course you did. You're a clever fellow. Raymond Carter orphaned me at a stroke and I was shipped off to America with a cruel set of bastards called Warren. They changed my name from Freddie to Al and they tried to change me. They wanted a model, obedient, subservient all-American kid with no personality of his own. They made my life hell. They didn't want a child, they wanted a whipping boy. Whenever I didn't conform to their notion of what a good little son should be — they beat me. They left scars — mental scars — that have never healed. And it was all Raymond's fault. I didn't blame them. I blamed him!

'Luckily I had a high-school teacher who saw my potential as a writer and encouraged me. For fun I'd write him little sketches and jokes and they would make him laugh. He'd say that what I wrote was better than the stuff on the radio. That was my seed and it soon grew. I left home as soon as I could and hiked it to New York in search of a life as a radio writer. I managed to get a job as an office boy at a radio station. I became friendly with one of the writers and before long I was supplying him with gags and then routines and then . . . well, you're bright, you can guess the rest. When I'd established myself as a comedy writer at the ripe old age of twenty one, I came to England to seek further fame and fortune . . . and my father.'

'To make him pay?'

Warren smiled. 'In a way. I needed to make him suffer and — very importantly — I wanted to witness that suffering first hand. Just killing him wouldn't assuage the pain . . . and the hurt that had built up inside me all those years. Never for one moment did I forget who I was and what he had done to me and my mother. That hatred grew like some kind of canker within me. It burns here still.'

He tapped his chest and the smile faded for a moment before returning broader than before.

'I eventually found him touring third-rate music halls with the same tired act he'd been doing for years,' he said, continuing his tale. 'He was a has-been and a failure. Where was the pleasure in just killing such a deadbeat? It would almost have been an act of kindness. So I set about building him up. He was a decent vent but his material stank. Well, funny lines are my department so it seemed quite fortuitous. I befriended him, wormed my way into his confidence, nurtured him and helped to make him a star. You know, Mr Hawke, there were times when I was sad knowing that it had to end the way I planned. I wished that I could forgive him. I wished that I could love him. There were times when he'd do something for me or say something kind and for a brief moment my resolve would waver. But then I'd remember. I'd remember the real Raymond Carter and what he had done. The scars are too deep to erase with sweet words and gestures.'

'You didn't think that you were destroying your life as well?'

'That is of no consequence. My mission was all. Avenging my mother and me. It was all I've considered important for most of my life. I couldn't abandon it. Nothing else matters.'

'Well, it seems that you have succeeded in destroying his career.'

Warren nodded with satisfaction. 'It does, doesn't it? And Charlie Dokes was an excellent associate in the process. Once the radio show was a smash I knew that it was time to start the demolition process of the smug Mr Raymond Carter. I wanted to see him crumble, to gibber and bleat. To lose all sense of reality.'

'But in doing so, you killed two innocent bystanders.'

'Not really so innocent. Washed-up dead-beat Arthur Keating who staggered from one performance to another for the sole purpose of supporting his need for alcohol. He was drinking himself to an early grave — I just provided assisted passage. I was doing him a favour, bringing his wretched existence to a close.'

This wasn't rhetoric. He really believed what he was saying. There was a kind of feverish zeal flashing brightly in Warren's eyes. All the while he was talking I kept a steady gaze on the revolver pointing in my direction. I knew that if I made any uncertain movement he would pull the trigger.

'And Evie, the career tramp, who'd sleep with anyone to further her career. She'd have seduced Charlie Dokes and serviced a wooden pecker if she'd thought it would have been beneficial for her. Darling little Evie. Y'know she really couldn't choose between me and Raymond. Couldn't quite make up her mind which of us would be most useful to her and her dreams of stardom. It gave me

358

great pleasure to bed the same girl as my errant father without him knowing. Very great pleasure indeed.'

By now Warren was almost talking to himself, indulging in a self-congratulatory monologue. In the dim light his eyes stared wildly and perspiration trickled down his brow. I reckoned it was time to bring him back to reality.

'You don't think you're going to get away with this do you?' I observed ironically.

Warren gave me a sympathetic look. 'Of course not, Mr Hawke. I was aware of that fact from the beginning. A man may kill a stranger and get away with it as you put it, but to murder those known to you, close to you, will eventually lead to exposure. I knew that from the start. All that ever mattered to me was that I achieve my ambition. To destroy the man who was responsible for the death of my mother and who abandoned me.'

'What have you done with Carter?'

This question prompted a fit of unsteady laughter from my captor. His whole frame shook with a mad kind of unrestricted glee. For a split second, I thought of making a move on him; either rushing forward and grabbing his gun or pulling out mine and taking a shot. But all the while he laughed, his pistol remained steady and trained on my heart.

Suddenly, almost as though a switch had been pressed, the laughter stopped and Warren's features froze in a mask of hate. 'What have I done with Carter?' he chewed my words back at me. 'What have I done with him? I have crushed him. I have reduced him to a gibbering idiot who will never function as a rational human being again. That, Mr Hawke, is a thousand times better than killing the bastard. As a mark of my very satisfying feat, I have a personal keepsake from my father to remind me of what I have achieved.' His left hand twitched slightly. 'Would you like to see it?'

I didn't reply. My attention for the moment was on the gun still aimed at me in what seemed a very unsteady and angry grasp. It veered a little as Warren reached into one of the side pockets of his jacket.

'Would . . . you . . . like to . . . have a look . . . ?' he said, producing a small shiny object from his pocket. It glistened red in the dim lighting. Proudly, he held the object out on the palm of his hand for me to see. It looked like a small piece of raw meat, slimy with red blood. It glistened unpleasantly in the dim lighting.

I stared at it in puzzlement at first and then

360

with a growing sense of horror as I began to realize what the thing was.

Warren read my thoughts and confirmed my stomach-churning suspicions.

'Yes, Mr Hawke, it's my father's tongue.'

35

Peter pulled the collar of his raincoat up around his chin, partly to keep the sharp evening breeze from his face and partly because it replicated the way detectives in his comics behaved when involved in covert investigations. He thrilled at the idea that he was actually on a case, following clues, trailing Johnny to unravel the mystery surrounding Raymond Carter's disappearance.

It was really dark down by the river. It was only the moonlight reflecting on water that provided any real illumination and then wispy clouds trailed across the surface of the moon dimming the light even more. He cursed himself for not having brought a torch. A good detective should always be prepared. He made a mental note to acquire one with next week's pocket money. He stared at the long line of barges along this section of the waterway with dismay, each one a large black amorphous creature defying identification. How on earth was he going to be able to find *Mermaid III* amongst this lot? He'd read about houseboats in one of his annuals but he had never seen one until now. The idea of actually living on the water appealed to him. He thought it would be exciting. When he was grown up and a fully fledged detective like Johnny, perhaps he'd get one for himself.

He dragged his mind from the wish-fulfilment future to the task in hand.

He crouched down by the side of the first barge and slithered along the ground looking for the name of the vessel. Eventually he came to a plaque with fancy lettering that spelt out *Mary Ann*. One down, he thought. Lots more to go. He carried out this painful process all down the line of barges, his knees getting muddier, he shoes more scuffed and his patience being stretched to its limit.

Eventually he reached his goal: *Mermaid III*, the last barge in the line. He grinned as he stood upright at last and rubbed his aching knees, displacing the tiny particles of grit that were lodged there. Then came the question to which he'd given no thought. What did he do now? Having successfully arrived at the address he'd memorized from Johnny's pad, what was he going to do about it? He looked around for some sort of answer. The darkness of the night pressed in on him. He was alone, isolated on the inky landscape. There was no sign of Johnny and, indeed, there was no sign of life from *Mermaid III* or anywhere else for that matter. It was a dead world.

Well, he knew what he ought to do. Be a good boy and go home before he got himself into further trouble. But that is not what a successful detective would do — and he aimed to be a good detective. He needed to investigate further. That meant trespassing. Breaking the law. Johnny would not be at all pleased with him doing that. Well, Peter reckoned, Johnny wouldn't be happy to discover that he'd not gone home either. He was in for a roasting anyway so he may as well be hanged for a sheep as for a lamb — it was a phrase he had heard the grown ups mutter when they were about to take a risk, but he had never understood it. For a brief moment Peter felt a small pang of guilt, but he quickly quelled it. He had come this far so it would be stupid just to give in now. He had some serious sleuthing to do.

He looked around to assure himself that he was not being watched, and then very much in the manner of Errol Flynn's Captain Blood, he leapt from the bank on to the deck of the houseboat, ignoring the sedentary gangplank. He landed quietly but he tottered off balance and in panic clasped the side rail tightly. The last thing he wanted was to fall backwards and land in the river.

He waited a few moments to get his breath

back and calm his nerves before taking further action. Like all the other vessels it was shrouded in darkness. He stood for a moment on the little deck area and strained his ears in an attempt to detect any sound from within. All he heard was the eerie moan of the wind whipping across the great river and the gentle slap of the water on the side of the boat.

Crouching down, Peter felt his way, slowly and gingerly, round the front of the main hulk of the houseboat to the river side so that he could not be observed from the tow path should anyone pass. A thin cloud that had been veiling the moon for some minutes slipped past into the dark blue. It was as though someone had switched on a low wattage bulb. The boats and the river were now bathed in a soft creamy light and Peter could see things much more clearly. He observed that there were three low rectangular windows at his knee height along the side of the boat. He observed that there was a thin sliver of light escaping down the side of the third window along. He made his way towards it on his hands and knees. His luck was in: the curtain had wrinkled, exposing a small gap of about an inch which revealed a portion of the interior. This allowed Peter to see inside. Pressing his face close to the glass and twisting his head awkwardly, he peered into the dimly lighted room. He saw a man he did not recognize. He was youngish and wore large glasses. The man was sitting in an armchair, leaning forward, talking to someone in an animated manner. But what gave the boy's heart a jolt was the fact that his hand held a revolver and it was pointing at the person he was talking to — someone who was out of Peter's range of vision.

'Crikey,' he muttered to himself, as he felt his stomach flip over. After he had absorbed this piece of frightening information, he shifted his position, twisting his body in a desperate attempt to view the room from the other perspective and in particular to catch sight of the person the killer was threatening with his gun; but all he could see were the victim's feet. It was a man. At least he could determine that, but that information wasn't much use.

Suddenly it became clear that 'the victim' had begun talking. He couldn't hear the words but the voice had a different tone and the feet which had been still now began moving. And then the man leaned forward as though addressing his captor with a kind of earnest passion. The man wore a hat so that Peter could still not see his face. But he recognized the hat. There was no mistaking that battered trilby.

It was Johnny's.

Peter gave a gasp of horror and recoiled in shock.

Then it struck him. Of course it was Johnny. He had come here to arrest this man, or discover some vital piece of evidence. But he had been caught.

Trapped by the murderer!

And now this man was going to kill Johnny.

Peter's stomach lurched once more. Instinctively he rose to his feet, his body shuddering with fear. His hand flew to his mouth and he found himself biting on his knuckles to stifle a cry. Blindly, he staggered backwards, his foot slipping on the wet deck.

As he did so, he heard something on the cold night air that caused his heart to constrict with anguish, causing him to lose his balance.

It was a shot.

Loud and clear.

Peter gave a bleating cry of horror and lost his footing completely. He felt a rush of night air and before he knew it, he had fallen from the deck of the houseboat and was hurtling towards the cold embrace of the seething river. As he hit the icy water, which shook all the breath out of him, Peter's overriding thoughts were that Johnny was dead and that he couldn't swim.

36

I gazed with a strange mixture of fascination and horror at the grisly chunk of human flesh which Al Warren held out on his left hand: Raymond Carter's tongue.

'I'd like to see him do a vent act now,' he beamed, his eyes feverish behind his owl-like lenses. 'Or try to chat up the ladies.' The grin turned into a chuckle.

For some moments I couldn't keep my eyes off the gruesome severed tongue while the contents of my stomach thrashed and boiled inside me. With a Herculean effort I managed to quell my guts. Now, I told myself, was not the time to be sick.

Eventually, I found my voice. 'Where is he?' I asked again, gently, trying to keep any trace of emotion from my voice.

'He's around. You'll see him later, no doubt. I hope the world sees him later, too. That would be the icing on my particular cake.'

I shifted my position and leaned forward in my chair. As I did so I slipped my hand surreptitiously into my overcoat pocket. It sought out the revolver nestling inside. I could, I believed, if necessary, fire it from there and wound Warren. But, if I did so, it was more than likely he would blast me too. Besides I didn't want to use the gun if I could help it. I don't like shooting people and I didn't want to damage my nice new overcoat.

'Look, hasn't this thing gone as far as it should?' I said with some passion. 'Isn't it time to give yourself up? Killing me will only give you a little more time.'

Warren beamed at me as though I was a silly little child. 'I'm afraid I lied to you, Mr Hawke. I've no intention of killing you if I can at all help it. As far as I am able to make out you are a good man who is trying to do his job. Killing you would take the focus away from the real motive of my revenge. As I indicated, Evie and that drunken oaf were pawns in my game, essential to the end result. You are not. You are not even *in* the game.'

'Then you'll give yourself up,' I said eagerly with some relief, releasing the grip on the revolver in my pocket.

But Warren shook his head. 'No, I shall not give myself up or be caught. I have no wish to be a living fun fair attraction in the courts and then on the gallows. Again it will take the attention away from the real monster in this grisly scenario: Raymond Carter. He will be the one to live on with the pain of life and become his own sideshow. Meanwhile, I will just . . . slip away.'

With great speed he placed the barrel of his revolver into his mouth and pulled the trigger.

There was a brief muffled crack and Warren's body jerked violently. The gun fell to the floor and he slumped gently backwards in the chair while the wall of the cabin behind him was sprayed with fine spots of blood. Blood also pulsed from the wound at the back of his head, running down the back of the chair. Mouth agape with a vivid scarlet trickle meandering down his chin, Warren gazed sightlessly at the ceiling.

I had never seen a man kill himself before. Whether it was the sheer shock of such a desperate action or simply the horror of the scene, I don't know but I found my whole body shaking with unrecognizable emotion. Now, I thought, it is time to be sick and before I knew what was happening, I was leaning over the chair and ejecting the contents of my stomach on to the floor, my throat burning as I spewed out the vomit. I hung in this undignified position for some moments until I felt certain that I had completed this unpleasant evacuation pro-cess. As I pulled myself upright once more, wiping my mouth with a handkerchief, a sound came to my ears in the fierce silence of the cabin. It was high-pitched and near at hand, but at first it was difficult to identify the actual sound and its location. I rose to my feet, avoiding a glance in the direction of my dead companion, and strained my ears. The sound came again. It was a cry. A human cry. A high-pitched shriek. It was from outside the boat. A cry for help as though . . .

As swift as my legs could carry me, I raced up on deck. The voice was now bright and clear and came from the darkness of the river. I could hear it quite clearly now and what it was saying.

'Help,' it cried. 'Help! I can't swim.'

I pulled out my torch and flashed the beam over the seething waters.

'Where are you?' I yelled.

'I'm here,' came the reply. A tiny frightened voice emerging out of the gloom.

My body stiffened with fearful apprehension. It was a voice I knew.

'Peter!' I bellowed, sweeping my torch in the direction I had heard his cry. 'Keep shouting. Keep shouting!'

But this time there was no response. And then the beam of the torch picked out something in the darkness. It was Peter's cap. At first I thought it was just floating on the surface but then as the waves shifted, I realized that Peter was still wearing it. He had slipped under the water.

With a cry of anger, I flung off my overcoat and dived over the side of the barge. My heart thudded against my chest as though it might explode with the shock of my immersion into the icy river. Thankfully my sense of self-preservation took over and as I rose to the surface, I began to swim furiously. I gasped desperately for air as I tried to move forward to where I had seen Peter. Without the benefit of my torch it was like playing a game of watery blind man's buff.

Since that terrible night, I have gone over these moments time and time again in my mind and I am still amazed at how I reacted to the situation. It was an automatic, an instinctive response. It was as if no thought patterns were involved. Never once did I pause to consider how surreal, bizarre and nightmarish this scenario was: I had just witnessed a murderer blow his brains out and moments later I was floundering about in the Arctic waters of the River Thames in the dark trying to rescue a drowning boy, my Peter. The question of how he'd got there never crossed my mind.

'Peter,' I yelled again, praying desperately for a response, but my words were swept away by the night wind leaving me with only silence. I thrashed about desperately, reaching out, hoping to find my boy.

'Oh, God,' I moaned, as the overpowering belief that I had lost him took hold of me.

'Peter!' I bellowed once more, my voice harsh with desperate passion.

Nothing.

Just the wind and the slapping of the water.

For some aching moment, time seemed to stand still, allowing the implications of my tragedy to burrow into my brain.

And then I heard something. A little cough, a splutter — just ahead of me to the right. Frantically, I swam in the direction of the noise. I heard it again. It was nearer now. I was almost on top of it. Suddenly, my hand touched something solid. My heart leapt. It was the inert body of Peter. He was floating like debris on the water. I managed to lift him up so that his head was above the surface, but his eyes remained closed and his features still. I had no real notion whether he was just unconscious or dead.

Swimming backwards with Peter floating on my chest, I made for the bank. There was a little jetty at water level running between the two house boats. I aimed for this and then with some difficultly I hauled Peter's sodden body on to the wooden planking. A lifeless water-logged twelve-year-old is quite a weight.

Now, Hawke, I told myself, cudgel your bloody brains and remember your drill from your days in the force. How to resuscitate a drowned rat! I laid Peter face down with his head lying over the edge of the jetty and massaged his back in a desperate attempt to get rid of some of the water from his lungs in order that he could breathe.

'Come on, Peter,' I cried in his ear, thrusting down on his tiny limp frame. 'You can do it. If Tiger Blake can do it, so can you!' Gradually water began to trickle from his mouth and the boy's eyelids started to flutter. I pumped even harder. If the patient survived, he would have bruises for weeks, I thought inconsequentially.

At last my efforts were rewarded with a brief choking cough. And then Peter's eyes flickered open momentarily. That was the breakthrough I'd been hoping for. I knew that if he had remained unconscious, no matter how much water I managed to pump from his body he would be a goner. Now I had to maintain that consciousness. I shook him vigorously and sat him upright. His eyes opened and focused on my face.

'Johnny,' he said in a ghost of whisper.

'That's me,' I said, smiling.

Now I had to get him somewhere warm so that the cold didn't overpower him. Half carrying and half-dragging my very wet boy, I managed to climb my way up a rickety staircase to the towpath and return to Warren's houseboat. I laid Peter down by the stove, which still provided a small amount of heat. I went in search of the bedroom and found it easily as it was merely a small area curtained off from the rest of the main room by a flowery curtain. It contained two bunk beds and a washbasin. From one of the beds I retrieved a sheet and an eiderdown. I draped the eiderdown around Peter who hugged it to his damp body gratefully. Meanwhile I flung the sheet over Warren's gruesome corpse, which lay still staring in amazement at the ceiling. I grimaced as the apparition disappeared behind the folds of the dingy covering.

In the galley kitchen I found some brandy. Diluting it slightly I gave a glass to Peter who was shivering now in a feverish way.

'Drink that slowly,' I ordered, 'and make sure you stay awake. Do you understand?'

He nodded.

'Drink this . . . and stay awake,' I repeated.

He put the glass to his lips and drank a little. He pulled a face of disgust as he tasted the brandy.

'It's like medicine,' he moaned.

'Exactly. It will make you better. Come on.

Have some more.'

He took another sip, but his disapprobation did not diminish.

'Good boy.' I said smoothing back his damp hair.

Now it was time for official business. Using the telephone on the houseboat, in quick succession I rang for an ambulance and interrupted David Llewellyn's evening peace yet again.

★ ★ ★

The ambulance arrived first. While I'd waited I kept talking to Peter, giving him simple quiz questions just to keep his brain active and his body awake. However, I could see that the fever was taking hold of him.

I explained the situation to the ambulance men and they gave him a quick examination.

'Well, all things considered, he seems in reasonable condition,' said the older of the two men who seemed to be in charge. 'I reckon he's got a little hypothermia and he's still got some water sloshing about in him but these young 'uns are toughies. A night under surveillance and some medication should see him well on the way to recovery.'

I smiled in gratitude.

'Where are you taking him?'

'Chiswick Lodge. It's only five minutes away from here.'

I gave Peter a hug. 'I'll see you in the morning, cowboy.'

He just beamed back at me dreamily and no doubt a little inebriatedly also. He had drunk all the brandy.

After the medical chaps had taken my damp friend with them, it was my turn to have a go with the brandy. But there was no watering it down for me. I think I deserved a little alcoholic ease after the night I'd had and I needed some Dutch courage also to peer behind that sheet once more at the remains of Al Warren.

I was just draining my glass when David Llewellyn and Sergeant Sunderland arrived with two strapping constables.

'Where is he then?' asked David gruffly.

I pulled back the sheet, unmasking the dead man. All four men blanched at the sight.

'Saved the hangman a job, then, did he?' said David.

I nodded. 'As I said on the phone, he turned the gun on himself.'

'He got a screw loose then?'

'Had a screw loose? Well, I suppose he had but there was method in his madness.'

'You'd better tell me.'

And I did. I told him how Raymond Carter

had abandoned his wife and his baby son twenty-five years ago; how she had committed suicide as a result and how the boy had grown up in America with a cruel couple who adopted him.

'It was in his formative years that the desire, the need for Warren to take revenge on his father for his mother's death and his own plight was fostered. It grew until it controlled his every thought and action. It became his obsession.'

David gave a low whistle of surprise. 'Blimey. What goes on in the heads of some men, eh? But why didn't he just kill him? Just put a bullet through his brain like he did to himself at the end?'

'That would have been too easy. He didn't want to end Carter's life . . . just destroy it.'

'You're beginning to lose me now, boyo.'

'He wanted the man whom he had hated all his life to suffer the indignity of failure, loss, and degradation. To have all that he had achieved, fame, money, security all taken from him.'

'So, you don't think Mr Carter is lying in a ditch somewhere. You think he's still living and breathing.'

'Living and breathing — but not talking.'

'Why do you say that?'

I leaned over and placed my hand into Al

Warren's jacket pocket and retrieved the jagged piece of flesh that had once belonged to Raymond Carter. I held it out on the palm of my hand for inspection by David and his men.

'What on earth's that thing?' my friend asked.

'It *was* . . . Raymond Carter's tongue. Warren cut it out.'

David groaned. 'My God, he had more than one screw loose. He had the whole bloody tool box adrift.'

I slipped the tongue back in Warren's pocket without comment.

'So where is Carter now, d'you think?' asked David.

All thoughts of Raymond Carter's where-abouts had been pushed from my mind, all thanks to my watery adventure and concerns about Peter, until now. I stood up quickly. 'I believe there's every likelihood that he's here on this boat,' I said.

David narrowed his eyes. I could tell from his expression that he was highly sceptical of my suggestion, but I also knew that he was canny enough a policeman not to reject any possible scenario out of hand if it had the slightest of possibilities of bearing fruit.

'Very well,' he said decisively. 'Let's test your theory. Let's search the place.'

37

We did find Raymond Carter on the boat. It is one of the moments in my life which will stay burnt on my memory as long as I walk this planet. How I wish I could eradicate the vision of it and the associated memories which rise from it. It is like some particularly unpleasant vignette from Dante's *Inferno*.

Behind the galley kitchen, towards the rear of the boat we discovered a secret door which led initially to a kind of antechamber which in turn led to what would seem to be a storeroom or junk room, the equivalent of a dusty old attic where all unwanted items were deposited.

All unwanted items.

It was in here that we discovered Raymond Carter.

Or what remained of him.

David and I had ventured into the antechamber, which had no electric light that we could see, so David pulled out his regulation police torch with a strong steady beam and flooded the chamber with a fierce white light. Mine was still out on the deck nestling, I hoped, in the pocket of my overcoat where I had dropped it before diving into the river.

As we stood quietly watching the beam of David's torch pick out the dimensions of the chamber and details of its scant contents, we heard a noise emanating from the room beyond. At first it seemed like an animal noise, mice or more likely rats but as we listened more carefully, it seemed to me unlike any noise I'd ever heard before.

Tentatively we opened the door and David shone his torch into the further chamber.

Very quickly, the beam picked out a figure sitting on a chair — later inspection revealed that he was firmly secured to it, tied both hands and feet with a tight cord around the chest. Carter was wearing heavy stage make-up, plastered on, no doubt by his demented captor. The thick pancake was coated with a mixture of flaking grains of powder and sweat. The eyes, wild and flickering, had been ringed with a black line and the cheeks had been violently rouged to represent bizarre shining apple cheeks. Lines had been drawn on his brow, down from his nose and at the side of his mouth towards his chin. The effect was vivid and grotesque. In the harsh glare of the torchlight he resembled a doll. In fact, he looked like a kind of Dorian Gray version of Charlie Dokes.

Carter's lips were bright red but the colour

was smeared all round his mouth. I was unsure whether it was greasepaint or blood from his severed tongue. At first Carter seemed to be gibbering quietly to himself but when he became aware of the bright torch's beam, his body jerked to attention and the eyes widened with what seemed a wild kind of pleasure. The eyelids flicked mechanically, while the mouth broadened into a surreal smile and the head twitched from side to side as though it were being operated by an unseen hand. And then it began to speak or to make sounds. It was a croaking formless noise that emanated from this tongue-less mouth but it sounded to my ears like the inarticulate bleatings of Charlie Dokes.

We stared for some time at this horrendous apparition before us, shocked into inaction. We were held in horror, pity and pain by the slobbering madman who had twisted his body as far as he could while gyrating his grotesque head. Raymond Carter had, through despair and fear, slipped into madness and thus mutated into a damaged version of his own creation.

★ ★ ★

It was just half an hour before closing time that same evening when, weary and sick at heart, David and I shuffled into The Guardsman pub near Scotland Yard. It had been a hell of a night. David had supervised the removal of Warren's corpse to the police morgue and Carter to the police hospital. It was clear to both of us, that if the fellow lived, as was likely, he would spend the rest of his days in an insane asylum.

I'd gone back to the Yard and given my lengthy and detailed statement concerning this tragic affair and then telephoned the hospital to find out how Peter was faring. A very kindly voiced night sister assured me that 'the little mite was doing fine' and that I could visit him in the morning. That cheered me somewhat, but I was still plagued by two fierce images that flashed with unpleasant regularity into my mind. There was Warren calmly placing the gun in his mouth — I could still hear the barrel clicking against his teeth — and then calmly blowing his brains out. I heard the sharp, muffled report and saw again the fine shower of red blood spray the walls. The second vision, though less violent, was the more disturbing: Raymond Carter's grotesquely made-up face caught in the beam of David's torch just like a theatre spotlight and the mouth clamping up and down like a ventriloquist's doll while inarticulate squeals and grunts emanated from it. It was the stuff of nightmares and it made my blood run cold.

David ordered the drinks and offered me a cigarette. We both lit up and obscured our faces in wisps of grey smoke.

'This has been a rum one and no mistake,' he said at length when the drinks arrived.

I nodded. 'It's strange but I can't help feeling sorry for both of them.'

'Nonsense. Warren was obviously a bit barmy and it turns out that Carter was a heartless sod.'

'True. But did they deserve their fates?'

'Oh, don't go down that route, old boy. I'm a policeman. It's my job to catch the buggers. You'll need to speak to priests and professors if you want to take the moralizing path. It was messy and unpleasant but it's cleared up now and we can move on to the next bit of nastiness. Don't let it hang around here.' He tapped his forehead. 'That way madness lies.'

I forced a grin. 'I guess you're right.'

'Too true, I am.' He raised his pint. 'Another couple of these and a good night's sleep and it'll just be a memory in the morning.'

I wasn't convinced, but I said nothing.

As it turned out David decided to go after he had drained his first pint. 'I'm not really in the mood, actually. I'll get home to the little woman. She's having a bit of a rough time at the moment with me being called out all hours.'

He hopped off his stool and patted me on the back. 'You did a good job, boyo. Just think on that and let the rest slip into the dustbin, eh?'

'Sure,' I said, as convincingly as I could. I watched him depart, his raincoat flapping behind him, causing eddies in the thick tobacco fug.

I knew that David was right. But he was Mr Uncomplicated Llewellyn with a loving wife at home to cushion the slings and arrows of his profession. I'd got a dingy empty flat and a small half-empty bottle of Johnnie Walker.

Then a thought struck me.

The phone rang for a very long time and I was just on the verge of replacing the receiver when it was answered.

'Hello,' said a quiet voice. It was hesitant and apprehensive.

'Max, it's me, Johnny.'

'Oh, Johnny.' The relief was tangible down the line. 'How are you?'

'It's over, Max. The whole thing's over.'

'Oh, Johnny, that's wonderful.'

'Max, I was wondering . . . '

'Yes?'

'I really don't feel like being on my own tonight. I sort of wondered if . . . ' At this point I ran out of steam or courage or nerve or something and just let the half-spoken sentence dangle in the air.

Max giggled. 'Of course,' she said. 'Come round, right away. We can have tea and toast. You can tell me all about it and I can soothe your fevered brow.'

I grinned. 'Thank you. That's wonderful. I can't remember a time when my fevered brow was in such need of soothing.'

38

That same night in a scruffy bar near Euston Station, a man sat by himself at a corner table nursing a bottle of Guinness. His face was in shadow, but any keen observer could see that he was crying. Tears gently rolled down his cheeks, hanging briefly on his chin before dropping down on to his shabby overcoat.

The man was Gilbert Manville. But strangely these tears were those of happiness, a state so foreign to him that when it had surprised him, the only reaction he could muster was to cry. And he had been crying on and off for two or three hours. It simply was that he couldn't believe his luck. He patted his coat to check that his wallet, his bulging wallet, was still there and still as plump.

Earlier that day he had been called in by the BBC to be told that the Charlie Dokes show had been cancelled and so his services were no longer required for this programme; but then he had been offered a featured part on 'All at Sea with the Navy' a new forces programme due to air on Sunday nights and a supporting role in a detective serial. These jobs would effectively double his income.

With this good news in mind, how could he not risk a fiver on a horse called Navy Boy with odds of 25 to 1? Miraculously — miraculously to Manville — it had won and he had been able to fill his wallet with crisp notes to the tune of £125. A fortune.

Father Christmas had come early for Manville. And, more importantly, Margaret could stay at the sanatorium. He'd rung her immediately and they had both cried over the phone.

He took a final slug from the Guinness and decided to go home. He had a busy day tomorrow. He was going to tidy up his flat.

39

Two weeks later. Saturday. The scene is Regent's Park. There are three figures on the landscape: a man, a woman and a young boy who is racing ahead of the grown ups as he flies his new kite — an early Christmas present. For all the world this trio looks like a family on a day out in the park.

The man is me, Johnny Hawke, happy and contented, a rare state for this one-eyed cynic; the boy is Peter, fully recovered from his encounter with the River Thames and full of beans once more; and the girl is Max, who is squeezing my hand with affection as we watch the animated antics of our energetic friend. From time to time she pulls me close to her and gives me an affectionate kiss on the cheek.

As I say: for all the world this trio looks like a family without a care in the world on a day out in the park.

We do hope that you have enjoyed reading this large print book.

Did you know that all of our titles are available for purchase?

We publish a wide range of high quality large print books including:
Romances, Mysteries, Classics
General Fiction
Non Fiction and Westerns

Special interest titles available in large print are:
The Little Oxford Dictionary
Music Book
Song Book
Hymn Book
Service Book

Also available from us courtesy of Oxford University Press:
Young Readers' Dictionary
(large print edition)
Young Readers' Thesaurus
(large print edition)

For further information or a free brochure, please contact us at:
Ulverscroft Large Print Books Ltd.,
The Green, Bradgate Road, Anstey,
Leicester, LE7 7FU, England.
Tel: (00 44) 0116 236 4325
Fax: (00 44) 0116 234 0205